# BEFORE THE FIRE

**Sarah Butler** is the author of *Ten Things I've Learnt About Love*, which was published in fifteen languages. She runs a consultancy which develops literature and arts projects that explore and question our relationship to place. Sarah has been writer in residence on the Central Line, the Greenwich Peninsula, and at Great Ormond Street Hospital, and has taught creative writing for the British Council in Kuala Lumpur. She lives in Manchester.

*Also by Sarah Butler*

TEN THINGS I'VE LEARNT ABOUT LOVE

*Sarah Butler*

# BEFORE THE FIRE

PICADOR

First published 2015 by Picador

First published in paperback 2016 by Picador
an imprint of Pan Macmillan
20 New Wharf Road, London N1 9RR
Associated companies throughout the world
www.panmacmillan.com

ISBN 978-1-4472-2253-8

Printed and bound by CPI Group (UK) Ltd, Croydon, CR0 4YY

Visit www.picador.com to read more about all our books
and to buy them. You will also find features, author interviews and
news of any author events, and you can sign up for e-newsletters
so that you're always first to hear about our new releases.

*For Matt*

9th August 2011

On the corner of Market Street and Spring Gardens, a boy who is almost, but not quite, a man flicks a plastic lighter until it yields a small yellow flame. His hood is pulled up around his face and a JD Sports bag slices a diagonal across his back. Behind him, people stand and watch, their phones raised to catch his movements, the buzz of burglar alarms and police sirens echoing across the city. The shop window is already broken. He steps over smashed glass to reach his hand in through the security bars, to the plastic dummy. She has a blank white face: no eyes, no nose, no mouth. But she has breasts, and hip bones – visible beneath her scarlet summer dress. He holds his lighter against a fold of material.

Then he turns away and crosses Market Street; stops by a shuttered-up shop, adjusts his hood, squares his shoulders, and looks back. Nothing but the smallest of flames, which seems to cling to the security bars, suspended between floor and ceiling. It is hardly big enough to notice. The people who watched him stand at the window with his lighter wait, nodding as if in agreement. The rest: the scared, the excited, the curious, the high, just walk past.

Soon enough the fire flares upwards – a skinny flame, gathering orange around its edges. Now some of the passers-by slow and turn their heads, though few break their stride. Something drops, molten gold, to the ground and another flame starts, as if from nowhere, to the right of the first, which is roaring now, reaching for the ceiling. The second is trying to catch up. Its audience has grown. Staring. Filming. Hypnotised. Black smoke gathers behind what is left of the window. The two flames join, and together they are unstoppable.

And now, as the crowd holds its breath, as a teenage couple kiss, as another alarm starts to wail, the fire grows. It stretches backwards and sideways, billowing behind the shuttered doors. It rushes forwards, its flames arcing from the window, pouring smoke up the brickwork, shattering what is left of the glass. It reaches for the onlookers and they shrink away, their movements short and panicked. Some turn and run. A man stumbles over a bike. A woman half trips and then rights herself. The couple, though, carry on kissing, their faces lit gold by the flames.

June 2011

# 1

It wasn't much of a noise, but it woke him. He was a light sleeper these days, the same as his mum. Stick stared at the greyed-out shapes of his room – the thin blue curtains, the map tacked to the wall, the wardrobe with its dodgy catch – and listened. There. Again. The brush of slippers across carpet; a faint but precise *click*, *click*, *click*. He turned onto his front, pressed his face into the pillow and put a hand over each ear. But it didn't help.

Stick pulled on yesterday's T-shirt as he crossed the landing and walked downstairs, tracing the wallpaper's raised pattern with his fingertips. The house was early-morning still, the street light bleeding yellow through the glass-paned front door.

She was on her hands and knees, reaching behind the sofa.

'They're off, Mum,' Stick said.

She carried on scrabbling, her bum stuck up in the air, the top half of her body wedged between the sofa and the wall. Stick pressed his teeth together until his whole face hurt.

'Mum?' He raised his voice, and this time she pulled herself upright and sat back on her heels.

'I'm nearly done here,' she said, as though he'd been there all along. 'You go on back to bed, love.' He could see her eyes fixed on the TV and knew she was thinking about the tangle of wires behind it.

'Did you listen to the CD?' he said.

She looked at him blankly.

He'd been eight the first time he'd come downstairs and found her checking the plug sockets, circling the edges of each room like a ghost. Instead of answering his questions she'd just looked at him with the same vacant stare she wore now.

'The whales,' Stick said. He'd raided the ice-cream carton on top of his wardrobe to buy it. Guaranteed relaxation, it promised. Soothe away anxiety, experience true tranquillity, sleep easy.

She smiled, still blank.

'I'll finish up here,' he said. 'You go and listen to it.'

She rubbed her fingers over her lips, her forehead creased in a frown. He wanted to kneel down in front of her, put his hands on her shoulders and shake her. Stop being mental, he wanted to shout. How am I supposed to leave when you're being mental? Instead, he reached out his hand and she took it and pulled herself to standing. She was wearing oversized slippers shaped like rabbits – pink noses, whiskers, fluffy white ears. Her legs looked too white, too thin, between the slippers and the bottom of her dressing gown. He'd got that from her as well – scrawny and pale.

'You'll—?' Her fingers fussed at the frayed blue belt around her waist.

'I'll check all of them. Will you put the CD on? I'll come in in ten minutes and turn it off.' He should have stayed in bed. It's like leaving a baby to cry – Mac had said, like Mac knew anything about babies – you've got to let her sort it out herself. But Stick had tried that and things had just got worse.

'Please?' he said.

She hesitated, swaying a little, as if she was standing on a boat, not the thin grey living-room carpet. Stick took her arm and led her towards the stairs. He watched her walk slow, zombie steps up to the landing, and when she turned he said, 'I'm on it, Mum, it's fine.' He made his voice sound light and unbothered, but he could feel the heaviness in his stomach, like he'd swallowed a bucketful of concrete.

He wanted to sit on the sofa and close his eyes for ten minutes, but she'd take one look at him and know, and the whole thing would start again. So instead he prowled around the house, checking every plug socket. Off. Off. Off. Off.

When he pushed her bedroom door open, she was sat on the edge of the bed facing the window. The room was silent.

'Will you give it a go, Mum?'

She didn't move.

Stick rubbed at his eyes. 'Mum?'

'You should be sleeping.'

'I'll put it on.'

'You've got big things ahead. Big night tomorrow. Big day on Saturday. And then—' Her voice petered out.

Stick reached under the chest of drawers and sensed his mum flinch as he switched on the socket. The CD player flashed *HELLO* in green digital text. Stick slotted the disc into the machine and watched the display start to count off the seconds. It took seventeen before he heard the faint brush of waves on a beach.

'Lie down, Mum,' he said. 'Come on.'

She stayed where she was. A flute or recorder or something started playing – soft, breathy notes.

'Mum?' Stick picked up the CD box; there was a picture of the sea at night on the cover – the moon like a car headlight over the waves.

'Is Mac a good driver, then?' his mum said.

Stick flicked the case open, closed it, flicked it open again. 'He passed first time. I told you.'

'But is he careful?'

He liked to rev the engine until it screamed; liked to make the brakes squeal by slamming them on hard and late. 'Mum, come on. It's four in the morning.'

'I was thinking about you out there.' She turned to him, her eyes bright. 'I couldn't sleep for thinking about it, Kieran.'

'Listen to the CD.' Pan pipes, that was the breathy noise. Like the men who played on Market Street at the weekend, wearing multicoloured blankets and feather headdresses. Pan pipes, and splashing waves, and a low regular sound like a heartbeat. It was probably just some guy in a recording studio in Hulme with a bucket of water and a keyboard.

'Did you check the sockets?' she said.

Stick put his hands over the weight in his stomach. 'Yes. All of them.'

'And the one in Sophie's room?'

Ten years. It had been ten fucking years since it was Sophie's room. But he swallowed and said, 'Behind the wardrobe. Yes.' He listed each socket, and when he'd finished she lowered herself down onto the bed, pulling the thin summer duvet over her.

'It's all right this, isn't it?' Stick said. 'Relaxing.'

'You will—'

'I'll turn it off. I'll wait a bit and then turn it off.'

She lay there for a while and Stick stood, shifting his weight from one foot to the other, watching the clock on the CD player and listening to the heartbeat and the waves.

'I'm sorry, love,' his mum said, her voice a whisper.

'It's all right.'

'It's just—'

Stick stared at the green numbers counting off the seconds. 'I know.'

She turned onto her side and drew a long breath in through her nose. Stick edged his way around her bed to the window, lifted the curtain just enough to get a view. The street lights gave out a soupy yellow glow. Patchwork tarmac. Two rows of skinny dark-brick houses the same as theirs. The kid next door's battered plastic tractor lying on its side. A red Ford Fiesta – V-reg, 120,000 miles, £250. Shit-bucket, Mac had said, laughing. It's a total shit-bucket and it's going to get us to Malaga. Won't get us home again but who gives a fuck about coming back?

'Is it still there?'

Stick turned. His mum was lying with her hands clasped up by her neck, her eyes open. 'No one's going to nick it, are they?' he said.

'It is safe? To drive? You've checked the brakes and the oil and everything?'

Stick balled a handful of curtain into his fist.

'You could ask your dad to look at it, couldn't you? He was always good with cars,' she said.

Stick glanced back outside. He counted five lit windows in the tower block at the end of the road. He tried to imagine what a street in Spain would look like but could only think of Manchester – buses heaving along Rochdale Road; Piccadilly Gardens in the rain; Mac on the back of Ricky's scooter, razzing down Monsall Street.

'Kieran?'

'It's all fine.'

'And you've got breakdown cover? I don't want you stuck in the middle of nowhere with a bust-up car. It doesn't look great, Kieran. I thought that when you brought it home. It doesn't look very reliable.'

We're not made of cash, Mac had said, and Stick had nodded along. Less money on the car, more money for beer and fags and weed. They had not got breakdown cover.

'Listen to the whales, Mum.'

She lay quiet a while, then, 'Which ones are the whales?'

'Try and go to sleep.'

'Do you think it's that low noise? The *dumpf, dumpf* one? I wouldn't have thought a whale sounded like that. Sounds like a baby's heart.' She paused. 'Or a machine or something.'

'You're on early shift tomorrow. You'll be knackered,' he said.

'I bet you'll be swimming in the sea.'

He'd never swum in the sea. Been in the grotty swimming pool down Miles Platting, but that was it – cricking his neck to keep his face out of the water, spitting every time it touched his lips.

'Are there sharks there?' she said.

Stick dropped the curtain back into place. 'I'm going to bed.' He made his way towards the door, his shins brushing against the mattress, stopped the CD and bent down to click off the plug socket.

'Kieran? Are you angry, love?'

He had his hand on the door; he was almost out. 'Sleep well, Mum.'

'You're a good boy, Kieran.'

'Night.' He opened the door, had his foot on the strip of metal between her carpet and the one on the landing.

'Are you seeing your dad tomorrow?'

Stick let out a breath. 'Yes.'

'So you can ask him about the car.'

'Night, Mum.'

'Has he given you some money?'

Stick squeezed his fingers around the door handle. He felt like his heart had pushed its way up towards his neck.

'For the trip,' his mum went on. 'I mean they spend enough on those girls, it's not like they can't afford—'

'Fuck's sake, Mum.' Stick closed the door harder than he'd meant to and went back to his room. He lay on the bed, staring at the map on his wall. Manchester to Malaga, he told himself. Manchester to Malaga. Come Saturday, they'd be on the road.


The next morning she'd left for work before he woke up. A cold cup of tea on the floor by his bed. A bowl and spoon on the table downstairs and all the cereal boxes left out. Which was her way of saying sorry.

Stick cooked the last of the bacon. He wedged the rashers between two slices of buttered bread and ate standing at the kitchen window, looking out at the back yard where a rectangle of sun folded itself around the side of the shed and the too-big daisies drooped in the heat. It had been hot the whole week, Manchester gripped by the sudden promise of summer. It's not like you need to go all the way to Spain, his mum had said, pretending it was a joke. It's like the Med here for once; even you might put a pair of shorts on.

Babs curled herself around his ankles, purring.

'I'm not feeding you.' His voice sounded thin. He had another go, lowering his chin and trying to boom the way Mac did. 'I'm not feeding you.'

She looked up at him, her eyes wide, and purred some more. He squatted and ran his hands over her head and along her back, furrowing his fingers through her long fur.

'It's up to you now, Babs,' he said. 'You're going to have to look after her, OK?' He could feel the cat's skull beneath his hand, hard and fragile at the same time. 'Make sure she listens to that CD before she goes to bed.' Babs narrowed her eyes and pushed her head against his palm. 'And don't let her go throwing herself at Dad,' he said. 'And don't die. Just because you're old, don't fucking die.' Babs tensed, her ears pricked to some noise outside. She slunk into the hallway and Stick listened for the slap-rattle of the cat flap closing behind her.

He dragged the ironing board out from under the stairs, filled the iron with water and lifted his jeans and blue shirt from the washing basket. He was all for just shoving their bags in the car and driving off. But Mac had insisted. *This is big*, he'd said. *We can't leave without a party.*

The iron hissed as Stick pushed it across his jeans, the denim warm beneath his palms. Mac wanted everyone to dress up, but he could fuck off. Stick hated dressing up. Sophie used to love it. He didn't remember all that much about her, but he remembered that. She'll be an actress, his mum used to say. You just wait, we'll be sitting here watching her on telly in ten years' time. And his dad would frown and say, not if he had anything to do with it – bunch of sharks, telly people. She was always putting on shows. Stick would try to slip out of the room, but his mum would catch his arm and glare at him, and when he opened his mouth to say how stupid the whole thing was she'd raise a hand and say, be nice.

Stick draped his jeans over the end of the ironing board and started on the shirt. Collar first, then sleeves. Everyone would be there to see them off, buy them a drink, pat them on the back and make jokes about Spanish birds and not forgetting where home was. Stick nosed the iron around the buttons the way his mum had shown him, and felt a tug of excitement beneath his ribcage.

14

Upstairs, he heaved his sports bag onto the bed. He was packed already: clothes, trainers, sunglasses, toothpaste, condoms, passport, money. The map was still on the wall opposite the window, fold lines running left to right, top to bottom. They'd bought it from WH Smith's in town, spread it out on the table downstairs and drawn on their route with a yellow highlighter: Manchester to Malaga. Mac had wanted to cut it into smaller sheets. You can't open that up in a car, he'd said, stretching his arms as wide as they'd go. But Stick liked the size of it: the fancy in-and-out of the coastlines; all the roads – orange, green, yellow, blue – like electric wires connecting places up. The sun had faded the highlighter a bit, but he pretty much knew the route off by heart anyway: *Manchester — Birmingham — Dover — Calais — Tours — Bordeaux — Bilbao — Madrid — Malaga*. And then a load of unpronounceable places along the way: *Nordausques — St Omer — Aire-sur-la-Lys — St-Hilaire-Cottes — Lillers*. He could close his eyes and trace the route in his head, reciting the place names as he went, like some kind of spell, like the kind of thing his nan might do now she was with Alan, with incense and crystals, feathers and drums.

Stick took hold of the bottom left-hand corner of the map and pulled it away from the wall. Too fast, a rip across the sea. For a moment, he almost carried on, tearing the whole thing from bottom to top, but he stopped himself and carefully prised the paper from the lumps of Blu-Tack. It refused to fold up the way it was supposed to and he ended up with a fat rectangle that wouldn't stay closed. He shoved it into the top of the bag, pulled the zip shut and sat down on the bed. The wall looked bare, a faint patch of damp he'd forgotten about, the blobs of Blu-Tack still marking out the shape of the map. We're leaving, he told himself. We're really actually properly leaving.

# 2

'I've got an hour,' Stick said, as soon as his dad opened the door.

'An hour?' His dad tugged his shirt down over his stomach. 'I've taken the afternoon off.'

'Got to go to Mac's. Sort stuff.' Stick fixed his gaze on the thick cream carpet, the neatly paired shoes lined up along the hall.

'I was thinking we'd go for lunch. There's a tapas place in town – get you in practice.' Stick's dad gave a little laugh. 'Have a glass of vino, even.' He paused. 'I'll not be seeing you for a while, will I? I thought it would be nice.'

'We've got stuff to sort out, for tomorrow.'

His dad rubbed at the side of his nose. 'Well, you'd better come in then. I think there's a pizza in the freezer. Do you want pizza?'

Stick shrugged and stepped inside. The house had its usual weird smell, like a mix of air freshener and paint.

'Drink?' his dad asked.

Stick followed him past the crowd of family photographs into the kitchen. Stainless-steel surfaces, glossy red doors, slate floor. Twice the size of his mum's. Three times the size. His dad opened the bulky silver fridge.

'Orange, apple and mango, or pineapple?'

'Got any Coke?'

His dad shook his head. 'Banned substance, mate.'

'Orange then.'

Stick stood and watched his dad fuss about, pouring the juice into two thin glasses, then pulling things out of the freezer, puffs of cold air escaping around him.

'Goat's cheese and sun-blushed tomatoes?' He held up a pizza box. 'Whatever that is. Or, hang on.' He took out another. 'Pepperoni, that's more like it.'

'Fine.'

'Two hundred degrees, twelve minutes.' His dad peered at the box as he read – mouth slightly open, eyes scrunched. He looked like a dickhead. Stick jigged his foot against the floor and stared at the girls' drawings stuck to the fridge with magnets shaped like strawberries and bananas.

His dad shut the oven and shoved the pizza box into a plastic container by the back door. He turned to Stick. 'Jen was hoping to see you.'

Jen. Call-me-mum Jen. Who smiled even when she was saying she was angry. Who thought it was best for everyone to keep their voices down and act like adults, even when they were kids. Who sent Stick's mum a bunch of flowers every birthday – expensive flowers, with fancy wrapping and ribbon – that would sit in the ugly vase next to the TV for weeks, refusing to die.

'The girls too. They're at swimming after school, till five or so. Jen's picking them up.' He eyeballed Stick. 'You couldn't be around then?'

'Got to get to Mac's.' Stick stared at the huge kitchen clock so he didn't have to meet his dad's gaze. It was one o'clock. 'Like two, two thirty?' He glanced at his dad, who didn't look like he was buying it. 'We've got to check the ferry times,' Stick said. 'And there's a party tonight. Like a goodbye thing.' He caught a frown cross his dad's face. 'It's just mates,' he said and then wished he hadn't; he didn't need to make excuses.

'I thought it'd be good for us all to be together. As a family. Before you go.'

A couple of years ago – he must have been about fifteen – Stick had been sent to anger management classes at school. They were run by a woman with gym-toned arms, green eyes and a posh voice, and he'd sat at the back with a hard-on most of the time. He remembered her now, the way her tongue brushed her lips when she spoke. Take a breath, Kieran. Don't react straight away. Stop and think.

'We're not a family,' he said. Like a grenade. He wasn't stupid. He knew how to lob a couple of words and wait for the explosion – a *wumpf* of flame and smoke and dust.

His dad's face hardened. 'You don't make it easy, Kieran.'

You can make a choice, the anger management woman had said. You can choose to manage things differently.

Stick picked up the nearest thing to hand – a cheese grater shaped like a hedgehog, with a blue plastic handle to stop idiots from grating themselves.

'I'm not trying to cramp your style, but you are my son, and the girls are your sisters,' his dad said.

Half-sisters. Stick ran his finger lightly over the grater's sharp-edged holes.

'And Jen—'

'Is not my mum.'

His dad turned away sharply, opened the oven and stared at the half-cooked pizza. Stick listened to the whirr of the fan.

'I don't know why you have to make things so difficult.' His dad closed the door and turned around, his cheeks flushed. 'I don't know what I'm supposed to do.'

Stick pressed his forefinger against the grater. If he moved it up or down it would slice the skin.

'Is this about your mother?'

Stick stared at one of Bea's pictures on the fridge door – two figures with fat yellow bodies, thin blue arms and legs, and massive orange hands. He could hear himself breathing.

'Kieran, I tried. I did.'

Stick thought about her, leaning over the TV, trying to reach the plug socket without knocking over the piles of DVDs. 'Fine,' he said. 'Whatever. Just don't expect me to cosy up to your new family in your fancy new house with your fancy fucking pizzas.'

His dad coughed and then wiped at his lips. He had a fat mouth, while Stick had his mum's thin lips, the top one almost non-existent. 'It's not so new any more,' he said.

Stick slammed the cheese grater down onto the metal worktop. It made a satisfyingly loud noise. He wanted to pick it up and slam it down again. And again. And again.

'She still calls it Sophie's room,' he said, without meaning to.

His dad lifted his arms out from his sides like he was thinking about hugging Stick, and then let them fall. Stick looked at his dad's feet – red socks with a patch of turquoise over the toes. He heard him take a breath as if to say something, but then the oven timer started beeping and he turned away from Stick and took the pizza – bubbling cheese and oily circles of pepperoni – out of the oven.

'I'm not hungry,' Stick said, once they were in the dining room, sitting opposite each other on the overstuffed leather chairs. He saw his dad's jaw tense and waited for him to have a go, but instead he just shrugged and helped himself to a slice of pizza. Stick listened to him chew, swallow, swallow again, kept his eyes fixed on the framed photo on the far wall

– his dad, Jen, Bea and Rosie lying on their fronts, grinning, against a white studio background.

'So, tomorrow,' his dad said. 'The big trip. Are you taking the toll roads?'

Stick shrugged.

'It's a lot quicker.' His dad lifted another slice of pizza, pulling the strings of cheese to separate them. It smelt good. Stick licked his lips but kept his hands under the table.

'A friend of mine ties a rubber band onto the steering wheel,' his dad said. 'To remind himself to stay on the right. You could try that.'

Him and Mac in the shitty Ford Fiesta, windows down, music on, engine roaring. Stick watched his dad eating and had to stop himself from laughing out loud. He was out of there.

'And when you get back?' his dad said. 'Have you thought about what you'll do?'

Stick wriggled his shoulders, like he was trying to escape from a too-tight jacket. 'We talked about this.'

His dad picked up his knife and fork and then put them down again. 'No,' he said, the way he did when he was angry but pretending not to be. 'We said we were going to talk about it.'

'I said I'd think about it when I got back,' Stick said. Which was never, or not for years anyway, not until he had money in the bank, a proper tan, a beautiful girl on his arm – maybe a kid even. He'd come back and they'd see they couldn't boss him around any more.

'It'll be over before you know it, Kieran.'

'Stop trying to make everything shit.'

His dad sighed and rubbed a hand over his face. 'I don't want my son on benefits.'

'I'm not going to be on fucking benefits.' Stick saw his dad's eyes narrow. 'I'm seventeen. I'm going to Spain.'

His dad held up both palms. 'OK. When you're home, then? We'll talk about it when you're home?'

'Fine.'

His dad sat back in his chair. 'I think this trip will be good for you.' He smiled; Stick didn't smile back. 'I think it'll help you get some perspective.' Stick could see bits of pizza dough in between his teeth when he spoke.

'I'm proud of you, Kieran. Heading off on an adventure. Not everyone has the guts to do that.'

Stick ran his forefinger around his empty plate.

'Just make sure you take good care of yourself,' his dad said. 'Keep your phone charged. Don't get involved with any drugs or what have you.' He coughed and then blushed. 'Use a condom.'

Stick rolled his eyes.

'You know we're here if you need us. Jen and me. You just have to call.'

'I'm not twelve.'

'The world's not always an easy place, Kieran. People aren't always—'

'I'll be fine.'

'I'm just saying.'

'I'll be fine.'

# 3

Back home, Stick showered, swapped his trackies for jeans, his T-shirt for the blue shirt; rubbed wax into his palms and then over his hair, flattening it close to his scalp. He fed Babs; left a note for his mum: *Cat fed. Don't wait up. Love you*; took a half-bottle of vodka from the bottom of his wardrobe, and went over to Mac's.

'Boobs!' Mac shouted, standing in the doorway of his flat, a coconut in each hand. 'Am I a fucking genius or am I actually a fucking genius?' He was wearing electric-blue shorts with a white drawstring, his calves fat and pink above white sports socks.

'You're a fucking knobhead,' Stick laughed. He touched his fist against Mac's and followed him inside. 'Hi, Mrs McKinley.' He nodded to Mac's ma, who sat on the sofa, a cup of tea in one hand, her phone in the other.

'Kieran. Looking smart. How are you? All packed?'

'Yup.'

'Your man here's got some dressing-up plans for you both tonight.'

Stick narrowed his eyes at Mac.

'Yeah, yeah, I know. But you're going to love it, seriously,' Mac said.

Mrs McKinley tipped back her head and laughed. She had nice teeth. Stick thought about telling her so, but didn't.

'I've been teaching Ma Bubble Breaker,' Mac said.

She held up her phone. 'I'm better at that than the helicopter one.'

'Got to keep her occupied while we're living it up in Spain,' Mac said.

Maybe Mrs McKinley could be mates with his mum. Stick tried to picture them sitting together on the black sofa, his mum's feet on the hot-pink rug, drinking a cup of tea, a fag in one hand.

'You all right, man?' Mac asked, beckoning Stick towards the kitchen.

Stick shrugged, took the half-bottle of vodka out of his back pocket and waggled it at Mac.

'Don't mind if I do.' Mac cracked the top and took a long swig. Stick did the same and felt the sting down his throat and across his chest. Mac's kitchen was about as big as the one at Stick's, except Mac's had a hatch in the wall so you could look through into the living room where Mrs McKinley was still frowning at her phone.

'You packed then?' Stick asked.

'Ma did it.'

Stick raised his eyebrows, and Mac snorted. 'You never think more than five minutes ahead, Iain,' he said, mimicking his ma; then, in his own voice, 'There's like first-aid kits and I don't even know what in there.' He took another drink, placed both coconuts on the draining board and took a knife out of the drawer. 'Do you know birds sunbathe topless in Spain?' He gave an exaggerated sigh. 'It's, like, compulsory.'

Stick reached around Mac and took one of the coconuts, threw it up and caught it, rough and dry against his palm. 'Your ma's all right then,' he said. 'About you going?'

Mac started moving his knife across the remaining coconut. 'Yours kicking off?'

'She's back doing that thing with the plugs.'

Mac pulled a face. 'She'll be all right,' he said. 'Seriously, she'll be fine. You worry too much, man.'

Stick looked through the hatch at Mac's ma. The sun was directly on her, lighting up the edges of her hair – the same pale blonde as Mac's. He took a swig of vodka. 'And my dad's on my case, like it's any of his fucking business what I do with my life. "You've got to have a plan, Kieran. You're nearly eighteen, you need to think about the future." Mac, you can't cut it like that.'

'Well, how the fuck else do they get them in half? Come on, I need a drum roll.'

Stick tapped his fingers on the top of the fridge.

'Ladies and gentlemen.' Mac raised his voice. 'You are about to witness something never seen before.' He took the second coconut from Stick and laid it next to the first on the draining board, then lifted the knife in both hands, the handle level with his eyes. 'I will create not one but two sets of beautiful squeezable titties from these ugly, brown, hairy fruit.'

'Nut.'

'What?'

'It's a nut, and I'm not wearing them if that's your big plan.'

Mac screwed up his forehead until his pale eyebrows almost met and brought the knife down hard. A coconut ricocheted away and the blade clashed against the draining board.

'Fucking hell.' He held out the knife towards Stick. 'Shitty tools.'

Stick laughed. 'You going to pull Lainey then?'

Mac grinned. 'If she's lucky.'

'If you're lucky.'

'I'm a catch, man.' Mac retrieved the coconut and went back to his sawing, his whole body wobbling with the effort of it.

'You're a chubber,' Stick said.

Mac grabbed his stomach with both hands. 'The ladies love it! Plus I am going to look hot once I've sorted these fuckers out.'

Stick drank vodka and listened to the *scratch scratch scratch* of the blade.

'He's all right, your dad,' Mac said. 'Least he tries.'

Stick put the bottle down and started opening and closing the cupboard doors. 'You need something heavy,' he said, pulling out a bowl that looked like it was made from stone, or concrete. Weighed a ton. 'You need to whack it with something heavy.'

Mac stepped out of the way. 'Don't wreck anything.'

Stick held the bowl in both hands and brought it down with a thud on one of the coconuts. The whole kitchen shook.

'Iain?' Mrs McKinley shouted through.

Mac pulled a face. 'It's under control,' he shouted back.

Stick slammed the bowl down again. Everything in the cupboards rattled. The coconut rocked, but stayed whole.

'Do you remember he bought you that stuffed rabbit and we torched it?' Mac said, and chuckled.

Stick bashed the coconut again and this time he felt it give a little. 'I was twelve. Who buys a twelve-year-old a stuffed rabbit?' The two of them standing by the canal, Stick's breath high and fast. The smell of burning plastic. The eyes refused to melt, so Mac found a stone and smashed them into tiny orange and black pieces. They'd thrown what was left into the water, watched it float for a second, and then sink, until all they could see was a dark shape like a shadow, down in the green-grey water. Later, when Stick was in bed, he'd remembered the plastic fur singeing and melting, and had to curl himself into a tight ball to stop himself feeling sick.

'It stank,' Stick said.

'Yeah, and you started guilt-tripping halfway through and tried to put it out.'

'Did not.'

'Did too.'

'Yeah, well, he's a dick anyway.' Stick brought the bowl down again and this time the coconut cracked properly. When he held it up, a thin line of water dribbled down his arm.

'Fucker's bleeding,' Mac said and laughed.

Stick bashed at it again, until it split – the curved insides wet and white and perfect.

'Do you reckon the doctor could do something?' Stick said.

Mac took the coconut halves and held them against his chest. 'An enlargement?' he asked, laughing.

'About my mum and the plugs. Do you think it's like a medical thing?'

Mac lowered his hands and shrugged. 'Maybe.' They were silent for a moment and then Mac said, 'Don't think about it, man. Not tonight. Come on, I've got shirts, flip-flops, sunglasses. I've got a fucking blow-up parrot.'

He danced out of the kitchen and Stick followed him, down the dark, narrow corridor to his bedroom, with its long window looking out over the estate towards the jagged buildings of the city centre.

Stick took a turquoise shirt patterned with huge yellow-petalled, red-tongued flowers from the crowded bed. 'Where did you get all this shit?'

'Man's got contacts.' Mac tapped the side of his nose.

Stick picked up a string of blue plastic flowers. 'Is anyone else even dressing up?'

'Course.'

Stick walked to the window, still holding the flowers. Everything looked smaller from up here: the scrappy bit of grass at the back of the block; the flag hanging off the side of the Queen's; the moss-stained roofs of all the houses that looked the same as Stick's – the McCauleys', the Sweeneys', the Stevens's. But the sky looked bigger, bright blue and dotted with white clouds. Sophie used to spend ages staring at clouds then prod him in the arm and shout – an elephant, look, an elephant! Or a cat, or a mouse, or a tiger. They were always animals. He could never see them when she pointed – there, that's the trunk, the tail, its ears, oh, but it's gone. Stick rested his forehead against Mac's window and examined one cloud after another, but they just looked like blobs.

'You want green or red?' Mac was holding up a pair of shorts in each hand.

'I don't wear shorts.'

'We're going to Spain. It'll be boiling.'

Stick glared at him until Mac rolled his eyes and threw Stick a skirt made out of strips of creased beige plastic. 'Put that on over your jeans then.'

Stick threw it back. 'You're gay, you know that.'

'And you're a dickhead. Come on, girls love this stuff. They'll all be in bikinis. We'll drink shots. You might even get laid.' He looked at Stick and then his shoulders dropped. 'Come on?'

Stick looped the blue plastic flowers over his head and Mac grinned.

'That's better. Your mum'll be fine, mate, I promise. And

tonight'll be a blast, and then tomorrow –' he held up his arm in a Superman pose – 'we head for the sea.'

'I ironed this fucking shirt,' Stick said, but he unbuttoned it all the same and put the turquoise one on instead. What did it matter? Tomorrow they were out of there.

The shirt would have fitted Mac but it hung loose on him. Stick chose a pair of glasses with blue plastic rims and smeary lenses. The flowers scratched at the back of his neck. He looked like a knob.

Mac wore three strings of flowers, two grass skirts over his shorts, a straw hat tilted to one side and a pair of pink sunglasses. Stick helped him tie the coconuts on with gaffer tape and string.

'More is more,' he said when Stick started laughing. 'At least I look like I mean it.'

Mac's ma howled with laughter too when they walked into the living room, Mac strutting about saying, 'Hola, senorita bella, veinte cervezas por favor.'

'Can you tell him?' Stick said. 'We can't go out like this.'

'You look cracking,' she said. 'Both of you.'

She made them pasta with a thick creamy sauce and strips of salty bacon. 'Line your stomachs,' she said. 'I saw you with that vodka.' She winked at Stick and he held his hand to his face to hide the colour in his cheeks. He was just like his dad, always reddening up. It did his head in.

# 4

They crossed Queen's Road and cut through the back streets to Rochdale Road, finishing off the vodka at the bus stop. Everyone kept staring at them but Mac didn't seem to give a shit. When a white-van driver blasted his horn, his two mates leaning out of the window, laughing, Mac just fondled his coconuts and shouted 'Want a lick?' Stick wondered, sometimes, how one person could be so different from another.

The vodka helped though, the way it always did, making him softer and easier than he actually was. On the bus, he sat next to Mac and managed to half smile at the people who grinned and made comments. He lowered the sunglasses over his eyes so everything darkened, and looked out of the window: a patch of tall grasses and yellow flowers where there used to be a shop or maybe a house; Cash for Scrap signs in front of a low-slung brick building; a nothingy sort of a park with a path cut through the middle of it and daisies dotting the grass. And then ahead, down the hill – Manchester.

Some idiot had spread sand over the floor of the bar. It might have looked good before anyone arrived, but now it was gathered in thin, dirtied lines and Stick could feel it scratch against the bottoms of his trainers. Mac walked in and roared with laughter. 'Fucking genius. Love it!' he said. Plastic starfish wedged between the bottles of spirits; beach balls set loose amongst the crowd; the bar staff in bikini tops mixing blue cocktails; Ibiza anthems. Pretty much everyone had dressed up. Lainey in a red bikini top and black hot pants, Aaron and Malika with matching pink flower garlands down to their knees. Shooter dressed as a pirate for some reason – eyepatch, black hat, wide-sleeved white shirt. Even Ricky had a cocktail umbrella shoved through his top buttonhole.

Stick headed for the bar. Double shot for the price of a single. He got a quadruple, with Coke, and a thin yellow straw that reminded him of being a kid.

'Gets you drunk faster.'

Stick turned. It was a girl he didn't know in a blue sequinned top, her face already blurred with drink.

'Through a straw,' she said, lurching towards him a little and then steadying herself against the bar. 'It gets it in your bloodstream quicker.' She frowned. 'Something like that. I'm Stacey.' Her hand was on his forearm, Nan tattooed on the bit of skin between her thumb and forefinger.

'Stick.'

'Stick?' She scrunched up her nose.

'Kieran. Whatever.' He'd almost finished his drink, the straw making sucking noises in between the ice cubes.

'Is that cos you're skinny?'

Stick shrugged.

'I've always wanted a nickname. Stace, that's like the best there is for me. You can't just come up with it yourself though, can you? Someone's got to give it to you, or it doesn't stick. Stick.' She grinned at her own joke. 'You getting another one of them?' She pointed at his glass.

Stick shrugged. She tipped her head to one side and batted her eyes at him, fake eyelashes like curling spiders' legs.

'I've got a trip to save for,' he said, but ordered two doubles with Coke and ice all the same.

'Where you going?' She leaned on the bar, both elbows in front of her so her tits squeezed together.

'Malaga.' Stick looked at her cleavage, the soft flesh either side, and felt his cock twitch.

She nodded. 'It's all right there.'

'Yeah?' He handed her one of the drinks.

She put the straw between her lips and sucked. 'Went last year. With my parents.' She rolled her eyes. 'Which was, like, annoying. But I got a tan. Met a couple of nice guys.' She smiled.

'We're driving. Me and –' Stick looked over to where Mac and Lainey were dancing hip to hip – 'him.'

She frowned. 'Why? It's like two hours on a plane.'

Because that wasn't the point. Because the journey was the point. Because he'd never left Manchester, he'd never been anywhere, he'd never even been to the fucking seaside. And if they drove, then he'd have been to all those places, not just Manchester and Malaga, he'd have been everywhere in between.

'It was a bet kind of thing,' he said. 'We were pissed.' Which was also true, him and Mac shit-faced, Mac punching the air and saying, 'Let's go, let's get out of here.'

'We're going for ages,' he said. 'Months. It's like a trip, not a holiday.'

She'd turned her attention back to her drink. Stick looked at the thin gold cross on a thin gold chain falling down between her breasts.

'I'd better go check on my mate.' She scanned the dance floor. 'She's a bit—' She waved the hand with the tattoo, to suggest someone even drunker than herself. 'Later. Maybe.' She did that smile again. That play-it-right-and-I-might-just-give-you-a-blow-job smile.

The place was packed, people squashed against each other, shouting, laughing, holding drinks up above their heads as they tried to push their way through. Stick wasn't good in crowded spaces, and it was hot enough to make anyone queasy. He finished his drink and ordered another, then stood with one elbow resting on the bar and imagined the whole place on fire. It would start at the back, he decided. Someone sneaking a fag, dropping it on the floor – too pissed to notice. Smouldering for a while, and then *whoomph*, catching the carpet, licking up the leg of a chair with a coat slung over the back of it. The smoke was what got people, he knew that, but it was the flames he always imagined, the gentle orange ones and the white-blue roaring ones. How the heat of it could blister walls and soften metal.

'Drink. I am dying for a drink.' Mac crashed off the dance floor towards him, Lainey hanging onto his arm, Aaron and Malika just behind them.

'Shots. Hey, Blondie!' Mac waved at the barman, who scowled but came over. 'One, two, three, four, five,' Mac said, counting them off on his fingers. His coconuts were lopsided and he pulled them straight.

'Jägerbombs.' Aaron slapped his hand on the bar. He was addicted to the gym and had arm muscles to show for it. Stick had been sweating on a building site for six months saving up for Spain, but he suspected he'd never look like that, however many tonnes of bricks he shifted.

Mac shrugged and the barman poured them out, five plastic shot glasses floating in piss-yellow Red Bull.

'A toast,' Mac declared. 'A toast to Stick.'

Stick pulled a face and Mac held up his hand. 'OK, all right. A toast to driving on the fucking right.'

Everyone downed their shots. They tasted like sick – made Stick's head throb. He looked about for the girl with the blue-sequinned top but couldn't see her.

'Again,' Aaron shouted. Malika plucked at his sleeve but he was paying no attention.

They tasted better the second time.

'Photo,' Stick said, the word coming out thick and loud. He got his phone from his jeans pocket and waved at the four of them to stand closer together. He stepped back to fit them onto the screen and tapped. A bright white flash lit them for a second. It was like something you'd see in a film: everyone frozen, grinning, Mac's arms around Lainey and Malika, Aaron waving his empty glass to one side. When Stick lowered his phone Mac was kissing Lainey, Aaron was kissing Malika.

'Get a room. Fuck's sake,' he said, but none of them were listening.

He turned away, about to walk to the toilet, even though he didn't need to go, when there was a scuffle to his left, people stumbling towards him and someone shouting. Stick stood on tiptoe to try and see. Ricky. Of course it was Ricky – he couldn't have a night out without decking someone. He had more anger knotted up inside of him than the rest of them put together, and that was saying something. Stick watched a bouncer in a black suit get Ricky in a headlock and drag him towards the door. Around him, people swore and tutted and repositioned themselves. Five minutes later it was like nothing had happened.

'Should we go?' Stick shouted to Mac. Ricky was a tosser, but he was their mate.

'Shooter's gone,' Mac said. 'He'll sort it.' Mac felt about in his pockets and pulled out a fat brown cigar. 'From pervy Mr Dunne,' he said.

Stick took the cigar. It had already been cut and when he held it to his nose it smelt of honey and dust. Mr Dunne lived in Mac's tower block, on the floor above. He was the fattest man Stick had ever seen – his legs and stomach so big they reckoned he wouldn't be able to find his cock in amongst the folds. 'You wank him off?' he said.

'Twice.' Mac headed for the door.

The bouncers didn't let you smoke in the covered bit – even though it was made up to look like a proper street, with cobbles and lamps and fake old shop signs – so they went outside. It was just about dark, the tall drooped street lights on, the glass office blocks down the end of the road lit up too. Stick felt the air chill the sweat on his face and forearms. He looked around for Ricky and Shooter, but couldn't see them.

'Lap dancing over there.' Mac pointed at the building opposite – orange brick and fancy arched windows. 'Seriously. I've seen the pictures. Girl on girl. The lot.'

Thick curtains hung in folds against the windows. Stick tried to imagine it inside. Cones of light on a dark stage. Women with polished skin and massive tits. 'You're pulling Lainey then?' he said.

Mac grinned. 'She's into me, don't you think?'

'She's not coming to Spain.'

Mac laughed. He held his lighter to the cut end of the cigar until the smoke started. 'Mr Dunne's advice,' he said. 'Don't inhale.'

'I mean it.' Stick took the cigar and put it to his lips.

'I know she's not coming to Spain. Now, just breathe it into your mouth, swirl it round a bit, blow it out.'

'What's the point of that?'

Mac shrugged.

34

Stick sucked on the cigar and felt the smoke pool on his tongue. He pulled it into his throat without thinking and ended up coughing and spluttering.

'What did I say?' Mac took it off him and smoked without coughing, puffing pale rings towards Stick. 'Maybe we should be going to Cuba,' he said. 'That's where they make these babies.'

'I'd rather have a joint.' Stick jigged his foot against the ground. 'Are you sure your mate'll definitely let us crash at his?'

'He's fixed us jobs – I told you. Washing-up and that, but there'll be bar jobs coming soon, he reckons.' Mac jabbed the cigar towards Stick. 'Sea, sand, sex,' he said. 'And once we've got some cash we'll get our own place. Have ourselves some parties.'

Stick took the cigar back, gulped a mouthful of smoke and looked up. Beyond the street lights, the sky was a washed-out grey and he could see just one star shining like its batteries were about to give up.

'You should make nice with your dad,' Mac said. 'Before we go.'

Stick inhaled again – coughed like he was an old man.

'Seriously,' Mac said. 'Imagine if he has, like, a heart attack.'

'I do,' Stick said. 'All the time. I do.'

'You'd be gutted.' Mac took the cigar. 'You'd be gutted about it forever.'

'He's a cunt.'

Mac shook his head. 'He's just trying to help.'

Stick kicked his heel against the pavement. Mac's dad had walked out on Mac and his ma around the same time Sophie had died. Which was how come they'd moved onto the estate. Mrs McKinley called him the Bastard. Mac didn't talk about him all that much.

'This tastes shit,' Mac said. He dropped the cigar onto the pavement and ground it out with his toe.

They both stared at it. 'Maybe I'll send him a postcard,' Stick said, but Mac was already walking back towards the bar.

'Come on. More shots. I can still see,' Mac shouted back to him, pretending like he wasn't bothered any more. And once they were inside, it was too hot, too crowded, too noisy to talk.


Drunk. Proper drunk. All the words gone too big for his mouth, the edges of them shoving at his cheeks, catching on his tongue. Mac dancing like a prick, clutching his coconuts. Shots: peppermint; coffee; tequila; flaming sambuca – beautiful blue fire. The girl in the sequin top – blue, beautiful blue. She didn't step back when he put his hand on it. The sequins scratched his skin, but she was soft. Her tits soft. Her mouth wide and wet and red.

And then Mac was there. Coconuts, grass skirts, grey trainers. He looked like a twat. You look like a twat, Mac. Fuck off. Lainey's having a paddy. She's being psycho. Stick's head thumping, like the whales – *dumpf, dumpf, dumpf*. His mum, checking plugs. He wished she'd stop that. The bar hard in the centre of his back. And Mac – I'm going home. You coming? Home. But the girl with the top. Blue sequins. She was licking her tongue around her lips and leaning against him, her breath in his ear. Don't go. Not yet. Got a treat for you. And then kissing his cheek, and he was hard. Drunk as a fucking newt, but hard. He took off the plastic flowers and put them around her neck.

Come on, mate. Mac was pulling at his arm. But the girl.

Give us a minute. Ten minutes. Mac was shaking his head, saying, I'm going home. I'm going now. Walking out the door without looking back. Grass skirts all bunched up over his shorts.

The girl took Stick's hand and walked, snake-hips, into the toilets. Up against the door. Lock digging into his spine. Jeans down to his knees. Someone banging on the partition. Get a fucking room. Don't need a room for this, baby. He wanted to come in her mouth. He wanted to come in her hair. Yes. Like that.

And then he was done, and she was wiping at her lips, pulling herself up from the floor. He grabbed at her tits. Ripping her top. Fucking be careful, man. The thin gold cross stabbed at his chin. Soft flesh. And then she was moving his hand under her skirt and he was tired all of a sudden. Done. Drunk. He could curl up here, he thought, on the toilet floor, with the scraps of paper and the dribbles of piss, and sleep.

She was rubbing herself against his fingers. Got to go, he kept saying. No – come on, you want to put it in? Her hand on his cock. You can put it in. Got to get back – look out for Mac. He's not looking out for you. Almost falling out of the cubicle, her storming after him, lips puckered, angry. Enjoy your trip. Cheers. Cheers for not much.

And then he was out on the street. Cold. His stomach churning. Everyone else gone. Well, fuck them. He got on the bus. Fell asleep. Missed his stop. Walked back down Rochdale Road. Left onto Queen's Road. The whole world in a haze – street lights and booze. Stopped at the end of his street. He'd wake his mum up, stumbling in. She'd be halfway down the stairs before he'd sorted himself out. He couldn't be doing with that.

He climbed up to the railway tracks at the back of Pitsford Road. Half fell up the steep slope. He'd sleep there. Could sleep anywhere. He'd brought Mac here when they were kids, to show him the trains, how the tracks hummed and you had to hold yourself steady when they came past – a rush of metal sucking up the air and shouting in your face. Mac had shouted back and Stick had stood next to him and opened his mouth, but hadn't let out any noise.

Up by the knackered fence, Stick kicked at the ground to clear it, sat with his back against a tree. Manchester. Birmingham. Dover. Calais. Tours. Bordeaux. Bilbao. Madrid. Malaga. Shit-bucket Ford Fiesta. Push the seats back and you could almost lie down. Sleeping bags. Pillows. Mac's shitty pound-shop window blinds suckered to the glass.

His eyes were heavy as rocks. Head thick with sleep. Booze. That girl's hair. Someone banging on the toilet wall. Mac and his coconuts and the grass skirts. Lainey with mascara halfway down her face. He was tired enough to lie down on the ground, in the soil and the fag butts and the bits of paper and crisp packets and fuck knew what else, and sleep. He rested his head on his arm. Tomorrow. Tomorrow they'd get in the car and drive. Tomorrow they were out of there.

# 5

Aching like a bastard. Soil on his face. Someone calling his name. Stick opened his eyes to sunlight pouring through the leaves, closed them again and watched the colours dance on the backs of his eyelids. He listened. A bird, somewhere; a car; faint footsteps on concrete. A line of drool had dried at the corner of his mouth. He wiped it off, dug the plastic sunglasses out of his pocket and put them on. He could smell himself: sex and stale booze and sweat. He imagined Mac kicking him in the side – get up, you dirty bastard, we're going to Spain. But his phone said it was only 6 a.m. – Mac'd still be snoring away and there was no one there but Stick, the tree, the rusted fence and the train tracks, grass and weeds growing in between the slats like there wasn't a hundred tonnes of metal running over them every five minutes.

He took the glasses off again; tried to get some moisture into his mouth by running his tongue around his gums. Tasted bad. The evening came back in sharp bright fragments. The bar, sticky with spilt drinks. Yellow straws trampled into the floor. The cocktail umbrella in Ricky's buttonhole. A blue sequinned top under the lights. Mac and those fucking coconuts.

It hurt when he stood up. It hurt when he moved, step by cautious step, down the slope, onto the pavement, round the corner towards home. He felt like he needed one of those massive neck braces to keep everything still, like Aaron's cousin had worn after his car crash.

Stick was so focused on putting one foot in front of the other, he didn't notice the front door was wide open until he was down the path, reaching for his key. His brain did its skip-jump-to-disaster move. His mum lying in a pool of blood, or gagged and bound on the kitchen floor. All their stuff gone.

'Mum?' he shouted into the hallway. His voice came out cracked and phlegmy. He cleared his throat. 'Mum?'

Nothing. Then footsteps, and his dad with his shirt buttoned up wrong, standing in the doorway.

'Oh, thank the merciful Lord. Thank you.' His face was blotched red, his eyes bloodshot.

'What the fuck? It's like 6 a.m. Where's Mum?' He felt his stomach clench. 'What's she done?'

'Your mum is walking the streets in her dressing gown, pulling her hair out, trying to find you.' Stick's dad took hold of his wrist and pulled him inside. Then wrapped his arms around him. His shirt smelt like the inside of a car – musty, metallic. Stick pulled away.

'We need to call her.' His dad fumbled in his pocket. 'You. You call her.' He shoved his phone towards Stick but he didn't take it. 'You're OK? You're not bleeding?'

'What are you even on about?' Stick's head was throbbing and his skin was too hot.

His dad was talking into the phone. 'Mandy, he's here. It's OK, he's here.' He was breathing loudly, like he'd been running. 'She wants you.' He handed the phone over.

'Mum? I was just out.'

She was sobbing.

40

'I'm sorry, OK? I was just out. Mum, where are you?' Stick waited, then gave the phone back. 'I can't hear what she's saying.'

His dad held it to his ear, still watching Stick. 'It's all right, Mandy, come back. Come on back.'

Stick put his foot on the bottom stair. 'I'm getting a shower.'

'I think you'd better wait, Kieran. For your mum.'

Stick wanted to tell him to fuck off and stop sticking his nose in, but he felt too sick, too tired. He needed a drink. He needed to lie down. It was like there was a thick blanket between him and the world.

He was in the kitchen downing a pint of water when his mum barged in, took the glass off him and reached up to hold his face, a hand on each cheek. Stick tried to breathe to one side so she didn't catch the stink of him. 'Kieran. Kieran. Kieran.' She just kept saying his name, like she'd lost it. Like she'd really actually lost it. 'Kieran. Kieran. Kieran.' And then she dropped her hands to her sides and gave him a frightened look, standing there in her dressing gown with her hair all wild.

Stick took the glass off the side and finished the water, drinking too fast so it spilt down his chin. His mum was staring at him. 'Tea,' she said. 'I'll make us all a cup of tea.'

'I don't drink tea.' Stick looked at her. 'You know I don't drink tea. What the fuck's going on?' Something cut through the fug of his hangover. 'Nan? Is it Nan?'

'Your nan's fine.'

Stick glanced at his dad, his shirt still misbuttoned. 'You're back with Dad?'

'We need to talk to you, love. Why don't we go and sit down?' She took a packet of cigarettes out of her dressing-gown pocket, pulled one out, then pushed it back in again.

'Mac?' Stick said.

He knew, from the way she bit at her lower lip, the way her eyes slipped away from his face. Felt the weight of it like a sack of bricks pressing on top of him. He saw his mum's mouth move, heard her say, 'He's dead, love. He died. I'm sorry, I'm so sorry.' But the words stopped somewhere above him, like they were floating on the surface of a dirty swimming pool and he was deep down below them.

He managed to turn and put his hands either side of the sink before throwing up. Thick beige puke, bitter with booze, specked with chunks of pasta from the night before.

'There, love. There, there.' His mum rubbed her hand up and down his back, like he was a kid.

Dead. Mac's dead. It was like there was someone inside his head, shouting: Dead. Mac's dead. But the car was outside the house, full of petrol, ready for them to get in and drive away. His bag was upstairs, packed. Mac's bag was in his flat, packed. There was a sofa and a bit of floor in a flat in Spain, waiting for them.

He threw up again – thinner and yellower this time – and stood staring at the mess in the metal bowl. He didn't want to turn around. He wanted to stay there, with the stink of himself, wearing Mac's shirt with the ugly yellow flowers and their cherry-red tongues. His mum kept on rubbing along his spine.

'I'm afraid he was stabbed, Kieran,' his dad said.

'We thought you were dead too, love. We thought they just hadn't found you yet.' His mum made a noise like someone had let out all the air from inside of her.

Stick laughed. It came out more like a dog's bark. 'Bollocks,' he said. His voice sounded smaller than he'd meant it to. He turned round. They were staring at him like he had a bomb strapped to his chest. 'You're talking shit,' he said, louder. 'This is some shit you've made up so I can't go to Spain.'

'They'll find him.' Stick watched his dad's Adam's apple jerk up and down as he swallowed, noticed the way the skin wrinkled at the sides of his neck. 'They'll find whoever did it.'

'Shut up.'

His mum opened her mouth to speak.

'I said, shut up.' Stick was shouting now. 'Both of you, shut up.'

His mum fretted at her dressing-gown belt with her fingertips.

'Look.' Stick took his phone out of his pocket. 'I'm calling him. I'm calling him now.'

But Mac didn't pick up. Stick listened to it ring and then heard the click as it went to Mac's recorded message: 'Dude, I'm busy. Sing me a tune. Laters.' He hung up.

His parents stood in the doorway looking at him, and it was like Sophie was in the room with them, everyone squashed so close together Stick couldn't breathe. He remembered the night after the fire, the house stinking of smoke and the three of them sitting in the living room with nothing to say. Neither his mum nor his dad could stop touching him, like they had to keep checking he was there. Eventually he'd slipped upstairs, past Sophie's door to his room, emptied his Lego onto the bed and then couldn't decide what to build. They wish it was me, he'd told himself over and over; they wish it was me, not Sophie.

'Sweetheart, they will find who did it,' his mum said.

'No one's done anything.' He'd kill Mac himself when he turned up. Stick pictured it: Mac covered in tomato ketchup, laughing hard enough to choke – I got you, I fucking got all of you.

'Maybe a cup of tea,' his mum said. 'Sweet tea? You're in shock.'

Stick turned back towards the sink where his puke still lay, wet and lumpy and stinking. His head was roaring, like when you open the car window on the motorway and can't hear yourself think.

His dad coughed. 'The police will want to speak with you, Kieran.'

His mum coughed too. 'They'll want to know where you were,' she said.

Stick stared out of the window at the shed door, its hinges brown with rust. He thought of the girl in the blue sequinned top, her lips around his cock, and slammed his fist hard against the draining board. His mum snatched in a breath, but neither of them said anything. Eventually Stick turned around. 'He'll be at Lainey's,' he said. 'Or asleep in a bin.' He tried to laugh but it came out sounding more like a sob.

'Why don't you come and sit down and I'll get you a drink. A Coke?' His mum's voice was low and wheedling, like she was frightened of him.

'I'm going over. I'm going to Mac's.' Stick pushed past them into the hallway.

'Not now, love.' His mum put her hand on his arm but he shrugged her off. 'I don't think now's a good time. I mean, whoever did it's still— And his poor mother.' She started to cry. Stick's dad put his arm around her shoulder and pulled her towards him. Stick half ran out of the house, his legs flushed with adrenaline and his heart thumping somewhere up near his throat. He and Mac were driving to Spain. They were leaving today.

# 6

He got himself to Mac's block, through the double doors to the stairwell and then up to the fifth floor, where he ended up holding onto the rail and dry-retching until his eyes watered. Mac's flat was at the far end of the corridor but even from the stairs Stick could see the door was open, could hear people talking in low voices and a woman crying – a thin, constant wail.

He stared at the dark scuffs on the corridor walls, the painted-over graffiti and the noticeboard with nothing on it. He told himself to keep walking, to go to the flat and get someone to explain. But it was as though his skin had been replaced with ice – the thin kind that covered puddles over but cracked as soon as you touched it. He would break if he took another step.

It wasn't until a policewoman came out of Mac's flat and glanced towards Stick that he turned and walked back down the stairs and out into the too-bright day. Nothing looked right. The grass was wrong. The fence around Mac's block was wrong. The new apple trees with their curled green leaves were wrong.

He retraced his route but stopped at the red Ford Fiesta. Mac had bought it off eBay, like a chump. But it went OK.

There was rust on the doors and they'd had to hoover out the inside; their mess was fine – someone else's wasn't. They'd driven it to Mac's aunt's in Sheffield the weekend before – through the Peaks, over the Pennines, along narrow twisting roads, Mac pretending he was a rally driver, and the hills stretching out on both sides, green and empty.

Inside, the car smelt like wet dog. Or maybe it was him. His phone kept bleeping. Lainey, Ricky, Shooter: *wtf? Have u heard?* He threw it into the footwell of the passenger seat and then punched the steering wheel. In the end it turned out that punching the window was better; it hurt his knuckles and made more of a sound. Except the glass wouldn't break, however hard he went at it.

He was sitting with his head against the backrest and his eyes closed when he heard the passenger door open and someone get in. It was his dad, not Mac. He could tell from the way he was breathing, but he kept his eyes shut all the same and imagined his friend sat next to him, his bag on his lap, his eyes bright, saying, 'Come on, let's go!'

Stick's dad cleared his throat. 'How are you doing?' he said.

Stick stayed still.

'Your mum's worried about you.' He paused. 'I'm worried about you.'

*Manchester — Birmingham — Dover — Calais — Tours — Bordeaux — Bilbao — Madrid — Malaga.* Stick listed the names in his head.

'There's a policeman at the house,' his dad said.

Stick opened his eyes.

'Are you ready to talk to him?'

'I've not done anything wrong.'

'No one's saying that. They just need to get as much information as they can. Build up a picture of what might have happened.'

Stick in the toilets with a girl. Lainey crying. Mac walking out of the bar – I'm getting the bus, I'm going home. Tequila and Red Bull. Vodka and Coke.

His dad opened the car door. 'Will you come in? I'll stay with you.'

Stick stared out of the car windscreen at the plastic tractor still lying on its side in front of next door's house. Everyone was acting like it had happened, like Mac was actually dead, but he couldn't be. Stick wasn't dead so how could Mac be? The car was still there, the estate was still there, the sun was out. It didn't make any sense.

'You're doing really well, Kieran,' his dad said. 'You just need to take it step by step.'

It was the notebook that got him. Not the polished shoes or the uniform or the serious face. It was the notebook – black, hard-backed, the pages crowded with blue biro – that made him feel like he'd fallen over face first, except the ground wasn't where he thought it was and he just kept on falling, his stomach pressed up against his ribs. And then he was shaking, his teeth chattering like he'd been out in the rain and couldn't get warm. The policeman put the notebook into his jacket pocket, like it was a phone or a packet of fags, and said they could do it later, down at the station, when he was ready. That tomorrow was fine. That he should try and get some sleep. But Stick said no, he'd do it now. He held his arms tight across his chest, each hand gripping the opposite elbow as if he was trying to keep himself from falling apart, and he answered the policeman's questions. Who had been where. Who had said what. We were pissed, he said. Everyone was pissed. We were celebrating. We were going away – today; we were supposed to be going away today. The policeman wrote it all down in his notebook. Stick watched the blue words appear on the page and felt they couldn't have anything to do with what had happened.

Once the policeman had gone, Stick went upstairs and stood under the shower with the water almost too hot to bear, examining the tiny blue dolphins on the bathroom tiles as if they might tell him something if he looked at them for long enough. He stayed there until the water ran cold and when he finally got out, there was Mac's shirt lying in a heap on the bathmat. He had to kick it into the corner of the room and get out of there so he didn't do something stupid.

He was almost at the front door, dressed in his grey trackies and a black T-shirt, when his mum appeared. She'd got dressed and brushed her hair but her eyes were still wild.

'Kieran?' She stood in front of him, her arms crossed.

'I'm going out.' He was going to Paget Street. That was the only thing the policeman had been able to tell him: it had happened on Paget Street, a five-minute walk away, on their route home from the bus stop. He'd have gone the same way if he hadn't fallen asleep. Stick pictured Mac running across Rochdale Road and taking a left, walking with his hands in his pockets, whistling to himself – he did that, Mac, like he was an old man.

'I don't want you out there.' She angled her head towards the door. 'Not while that man's—'

'It's like ten thirty in the morning, Mum.'

'It's not safe.'

'I'm going out.' He took a step towards her but she stayed where she was. Stick looked past her at the white front door with its four frosted panes of glass and felt a flicker of panic in his chest. You can't be dead, he said to himself – to Mac. You can't have just fucked off. You wouldn't do that.

'You can't stop me.' His voice sounded crueller than he'd meant it to.

Little circles of red had appeared on her cheeks. 'Your dad agrees. Gary!' she shouted into the house.

Stick heard the toilet flush and his dad's footsteps on the stairs. He saw the two of them exchange a glance.

'Just until they've found whoever did it, son,' his dad said.

'So, what? You live here now? You can't lock me up.' He should be in the car, Mac mucking about with the radio, a bag of crisps open in his lap and a can of Coke balanced on the dashboard. They should be laughing about last night: about Lainey; about the girl in the blue sequinned top; about Ricky getting kicked out. They should be driving with all the windows down, the wind slamming against their arms and faces, heading south.

'I'm not losing you too.' His mum pressed her fingers against her mouth. 'I'm not having it.' Her eyes were red from crying and she looked small, standing there in front of him.

He wanted, for a minute, to put his arms around her, but instead he squared his shoulders and lowered his voice and said, 'Mum, I'm going out. I can look after myself.'

'Kieran, you have to understand—' his dad started.

'No!' Stick swung round. 'I'm eighteen nearly. This is fucking stupid.' He had to get out. The hall was too small. The house was too small. His heart was racing and his skin had turned hot and itchy and tight. Stick reached around his mum and opened the front door – a breath of cool, outside air.

'Have you got your phone?' She spoke so quietly he almost didn't hear her. 'Kieran? Your phone.'

'It's in the car.' He moved past her and out of the house.

'Kieran? Please.'

He made a show of opening the car door, holding up his phone and putting it in his pocket, and then he stalked off without looking back.

It started raining as soon as he reached the end of the road, drops darkening the paving slabs like a child was flicking paint. Queen's Road looked the same as usual – traffic, an empty beer can rolling around in front of the housing office, the traffic lights repeating themselves over and over. A few people ran along with newspapers or plastic bags held over their heads. Two kids stood in the chippy gazing up at the menu, which hadn't changed in forever. Stick walked slowly, the rain soaking into his clothes. It made no difference to anything if he got wet.

Paget Street. Short enough that you could stand at one end and see cars and buses rushing up and down Rochdale Road at the other. A scabby-looking tortoiseshell cat stalking along the bit of grass that was just about big enough for a game of footy. Blue-and-white police tape had been wrapped around thin metal posts to mark out a wonky rectangle. And just next to the tape, half on the pavement, half on the grass, was a caravan with 'incident unit' written across the side in dark-blue letters and the police logo, with the red crown sticking up off the top, almost the full height of it.

A bored-looking policewoman in a black shirt and a bulletproof vest with a radio attached stood by a set of narrow metal steps, absent-mindedly kicking at them – right foot, left foot, right foot. When she looked up and saw Stick she brought both feet together, as though standing to attention. She had neat black cornrows, just visible under her hat, which, as he approached her, Stick saw was beaded with drops of water.

He stepped up to the tape, held the slippery wet plastic between his finger and thumb.

'You're not to cross that,' the woman said.

Stick stared at the ground. Mac: two grass skirts over his shorts; coconuts gaffer-taped to his T-shirt; a pair of pink plastic sunglasses. 'I was his best mate,' he said.

Her hand went straight for her radio.

Stick shook his head. 'I've already talked to them. I don't know anything. Is this where—' He tried to picture Mac with a knife in his chest, falling.

'Do you want to come out of the rain?' The woman nodded towards the caravan. 'Have a cup of tea or something?'

'Is there blood?'

'Excuse me?'

'Blood.' Stick pointed.

'They'll have taken samples of everything.'

'So why's this tape still up?' He plucked at the plastic.

'It'll be down as soon as they're ready for it to be down. I said you're not to cross that.'

The grass was thick summer green, with bright clumps of dandelions. Stick pictured Mac stumbling backwards, hands against his stomach, blood gathering between his fingers.

'Did he have a fight then, or what?' Stick asked.

'I'm afraid I don't have that information.'

'Everyone loved Mac.' Stick heard his voice catch and coughed, pretending he had something in his throat. 'No one would kill him.'

'I'm sorry.'

Stick looked at her. She had dark eyes and a pretty snub nose. 'Are you?' he asked.

She nodded. 'Yes, I am.'

'So tell me what happened.'

She gave him a half-smile. 'I'm afraid we don't know yet. We're trying to get as much information as we can. That's what this is for.' She pointed at the caravan. 'Maybe you could help? Encourage people to come and talk to us?'

'I missed my stop,' Stick said. 'I fell asleep on the bus. If I hadn't missed my stop I'd have seen him, wouldn't I?'

'We've got victim support leaflets inside. There's a number to call if you want to talk to someone.'

'Why'd I want to talk to someone?'

'It's hard to come to terms with something like this. It can help to talk it through.'

'I just want to know what happened. Is there a number I can call for that?'

'We're doing our best, you can be sure we're doing our best.'

'Fuck's sake.' Stick kicked at the metal steps so they rattled against the pavement.

If Mac was there he'd be chatting up the policewoman, getting her to tell them about police stuff – fingerprinting, CCTV, forensics, profiling. Stick glanced past her to the rectangle of tape. Who would kill Mac? He could imagine someone wanting to kill Ricky, or his dad, but Mac?

'You have to find whoever did it,' he said, looking her straight in the eyes. 'You have to.'

She nodded. 'Patience and hard work, that's what my boss always says, patience and hard work.'

'Stick!' Lainey was standing at the top of the caravan steps, a shiny black bag hugged to her chest like a teddy bear. She wore a dress the same colour as the daffodils, tight and low cut. There were big smudges of mascara around her eyes.

'Stick!' she shouted again, and waved, then half stumbled down the stairs and pulled him into a hug, her breasts pressed against his chest. She smelt of sherbet and strawberry lip gloss, and she was crying – he could feel it shaking through her, hear her sniff into his T-shirt.

'I came down cos I didn't believe it.' She pulled back and gestured towards the caravan, shaking her head, her breath coming in short gasps. 'Mac's—'

'I know.'

'He can't be—' She twisted a yellow plastic ring around and around her finger and stared at Stick. 'He was there.'

'Where?'

'Yesterday. In the bar. He was there.' She held her hands out as if she could see Mac and was touching him on both shoulders. 'I kissed him.' She started crying again.

Stick stood with his arms against his sides, looking at Lainey's bag so he didn't have to look at her face all screwed up and wet.

She took a big, shaky breath in. 'It's my fault,' she declared. Stick shook his head but didn't say anything.

'I – I wouldn't go back with him. And then we started fighting about Spain and Spanish girls, and I don't even know, I was that pissed. And he went. And so it's my fault.' She started crying again.

The policewoman had moved away and was looking towards the backs of the row of houses like she wasn't really listening, though he'd bet she was.

'It's not your fault,' Stick said. He sounded like a robot. Lainey just kept on crying.

The tortoiseshell cat had settled itself in the middle of the blue-and-white police tape rectangle, stuck its leg in the air and started licking at its fur. Stick bent down, picked up a stone and threw it. He missed and the cat took no notice.

'What are you doing?' Lainey was staring at him, her breath still coming in little hiccuping sobs, like she was trying not to drown.

'I don't want it licking its arse there.'

'You can't throw stones at cats.'

'Shoo,' Stick shouted at the cat. 'Fuck off.' It looked at him for a brief moment, then went back to its cleaning. 'I said fuck off,' he shouted, louder. He could see the policewoman at the edge of his vision, hand on her radio.

'Stick.' Lainey touched his arm.

'I told him to wait,' Stick said and then walked up to the caravan and punched it, hard, with his right fist. Hurt like fuck. Ridged metal against his knuckles. If Mac wasn't such a stubborn bastard he wouldn't be dead. They'd be past Birmingham now, halfway to Kent.

'It's not your fault either,' Lainey said.

Stick punched the caravan again.

'Will you knock that off?' A different policewoman stood at the top of the steps. Stick glowered at her. 'You've got something to tell us, come on in,' she said. 'Otherwise, scoot.'

'I'm not a dog,' he snapped.

'And this isn't a punchbag.'

Stick slammed his foot into the ground.

'He's upset, Miss,' Lainey said, sniffing.

'I still don't need him here kicking off.'

'I wouldn't be here if you'd tell me what fucking happened,' Stick said.

'You need to leave.' The policewoman walked down the steps and stood in front of Stick.

'Fucking pigs,' Lainey snapped.

'Now,' said the woman, quietly.

'We were leaving anyway. Come on, Stick.' Lainey tugged at his arm.

He followed her, away from where Mac had died, and the whole way back home he kept thinking, did it hurt? Did he struggle? Did he shit himself? Did he cry? Was there a point when he knew that that was it? What the fuck did it feel like to stop being alive?

# 7

He kept the TV on all night because every time he turned it off his heart started racing and his breath got tangled in his throat and he felt like he would explode unless he opened his mouth and shouted, or got out of the house and ran. Plus his mum was up and about again, fussing at the plugs, and the TV covered up the noise enough that he could stop himself going downstairs to help her.

Morning arrived, lightening his room through the curtains. Stick shut his eyes so he didn't have to look at anything, and tried to work out if he'd slept or not. Not, he decided. At some point his mum knocked on his door to say she was going to work; she wished he'd stay in the house, just for the next few days; if he had to go out would he take his phone? Stick lay on his back and nodded and eventually she left.

The news came on the TV – protests in Greece; protests in Syria; Olympics tickets; pensions crisis. He flicked through channels until he found *The Simpsons* and closed his eyes again. They should be in France by now, bleary from a night in the car, trying to find a bacon butty for breakfast, unfolding the map to remind themselves which way to go.

You can't just lie around moping, Mac would say. Stop being pathetic, he'd say. Get up and fucking do something.

Stick tried to think of something to do. An episode of *The Simpsons* later he decided he'd go and buy flowers for Mrs McKinley.

There were two rolls of money sat at the top of his sports bag: fifty pounds, and three hundred euros. He pulled the rubber band off the euros and flicked through them. He and Mac had gone to the post office on Spring Gardens last week and exchanged grubby English twenties for clean, glossy notes – green, orange, blue, red. 'Hard-earned cash,' Mac had said to the woman at the counter and she'd smiled like she didn't believe him.

Stick rolled the euros up again and shoved them back into the bag, put the pounds into his pocket and went downstairs. He opened the fridge and stared inside but there was nothing he wanted to eat – it was as though his stomach had disappeared along with Mac.


He wanted nice flowers, not the sad-looking ones in the newsagent's or a bunch with a Tesco's label, so he got the bus into town, walking the long way round so he didn't have to go down Paget Street. In a shop filled with buckets of flowers, the air thick with scent, he told the man – man! – at the counter that he wanted a big bunch, something that looked classy. He hadn't realised flowers could be so expensive, but he handed over thirty quid and got the bus back. People looked at you different if you were carrying a bunch of flowers – like you were a good person.

He sat downstairs with them on his lap, careful not to crease the purple tissue paper or squash the petals. With his other hand he flicked through his phone to the photo: Mac and Lainey, Aaron and Malika, lit up for a second. Mac, fat-faced, red-cheeked, a pair of pink sunglasses propped up on top of his head. Mac squeezing Lainey's shoulder, his mouth open, top teeth showing. Stick stared at him. What had he been saying? Probably something stupid, but he wished he knew.

At school, Stick's art teacher once got them to make a camera out of a shoebox with a tiny hole in one side. A photograph is a physical thing, he kept saying. The film holds the reflected light from whatever is in the image – it's a mark, from the world. Stick had rolled his eyes and sniggered with the rest of them, but he remembered it now, and wished that he'd taken a picture of Mac with a shoebox camera, not his shitty phone. A digital image, the teacher said, was just a collection of pixels, just lots and lots of tiny squares, and if you blew it up enough then the whole thing would fall apart. It's not physical, he kept saying, it's not the same.


Stick took the stairs up to Mac's flat. To Mrs McKinley's flat. The closer he got, the more he thought about turning back, because what was he going to say? Through the double doors the corridor was dim and quiet and empty. It felt longer than normal, like it was an optical illusion that you could never get to the end of. Except, of course, there he was, standing out-side the blue door with its locks and its doorbell and its sticker with flowers round the outside and *Strangers are just friends not yet made* printed in blue swirly writing.

As he rang the bell, Stick suddenly thought that there must be fingerprints; Mac's would still be on the door. Even with visitors and police and whatever, there'd be one, rings within rings like the inside of a tree. If he had white powder and one of those see-through sheets, he could lift one of Mac's fingerprints and keep it.

Mrs McKinley opened the door and made a strangled kind

of a noise, her hand darting to her mouth and her eyes widening.

'Mrs McKinley.' Stick swallowed. He glanced into the flat, half expecting Mac to barrel out of the kitchen, a coconut in one hand, a knife in the other. 'I brought you these.' He held out the flowers.

Mrs McKinley looked at them as though she wasn't sure what they were and then she reached up a hand and stroked Stick's cheek, her fingers cold on his skin. He stepped back, but she took hold of his arm. 'Come in, come in. He's just left.'

'What?'

'Rob.' Her whole face looked puffy, like she'd had an allergic reaction. 'Family liaison officer, he said that's what they call him.' She sounded drunk. 'Nice man. A bit thin.'

Inside, the living room was stuffed full of flowers. Every surface, it seemed, had a vase or a wine bottle or a pint glass full of them. The smell make Stick's head spin.

He looked down at his flowers. Waste of thirty quid. And how was a bunch of flowers supposed to help anyway?

She took them though, held them against her chest and smiled. 'Everyone's so good,' she said. 'They all come. Bring flowers, and little plastic boxes of food. Make cups of tea.' She let out a sigh. 'I can't eat anything.' She paused. 'Do you want to take some food, Kieran? There's so much of it.'

'You're all right, Mrs McKinley,' Stick said. 'Mum works at Tesco's, doesn't she? She gets discount.'

Mrs McKinley nodded. She was still holding the flowers, her fingers worrying at their petals. She'd ruin them, but Stick couldn't think how to say so, and it didn't much matter.

'Are you— How are—' Stick felt himself reddening. 'I just came round to—' He was trying not to think about Mac, but he was everywhere. Mac stood at the window eating biscuits straight from the packet. Mac with his Wii, dancing round the room like an idiot. Mac with man flu, lying on the sofa with a duvet, screwed-up tissues spread around him.

'Should I put those in water?' he managed to say. He took the flowers off her and went into the kitchen. A bottle of vodka sat on top of the fridge next to an empty plastic bag. The sink was crowded with glasses. He found a jug in a cupboard, filled it with water and shoved the flowers in. It wasn't big or heavy enough to keep them straight so he propped them up against the wall and then turned and looked through the hatch. Mrs McKinley was standing in the middle of the living room staring out of the window. She didn't move, didn't turn and look at him, didn't cough or check her phone or touch her hair. She looked like a statue. He should make her a cup of tea, go back in and say something to her, take her arm and get her to sit down. But he couldn't do it. He couldn't do anything except back out of the kitchen, quietly open the front door and walk down the corridor, his heart up near his throat, telling himself he was a cunt, a coward, a twat, but leaving all the same.


When he got home, the TV wouldn't turn on. Stick flicked the living-room light but nothing happened. The fuse box was in the understairs cupboard, behind a pile of empty cardboard boxes and the gazebo they'd used for his nan's sixtieth the year before. Stick threw everything out into the hallway and got the torch from its hook on the door. He pressed the trip switch down and heard the phone beep, the fridge whir back into life.

Mrs McKinley was probably still standing in the living room, waiting for him to come back in. Or she was looking for him, shouting through the flat, out into the corridor –

'Kieran? Kieran?' Or maybe she hadn't even noticed. Maybe someone else had turned up and she'd forgotten he'd even been there.

Instead of stepping back into the hallway, Stick pulled the cupboard door shut, turned off the torch and dropped it onto the floor. The place smelt of old shoes – dust and rubber and stale feet – and it was hot, or at least Stick was sweating, damp patches starting under his arms and across his back. He opened his eyes as wide as they'd go, so that his eyeballs felt like they could fall out of their sockets and into his lap. His left side pressed against the soft fake fur of his mum's winter coat. His right arm just touched the rough wooden slats of the door. If he stretched out either foot he'd hit the Hoover.

They would put Mac in a coffin and nail it shut. There'd be a funeral and a grave, a stone with his name on it and then nothing. 'You fucking bastard,' Stick whispered into the fusty cupboard air. 'You've gone and ruined everything.'

He'd freaked out once in a lift, when he was a kid – suddenly unable to breathe and terrified he'd never be able to escape. He could feel the same sensation coming now, like a slow, creeping burn. The walls too close. The ceiling too low. The Hoover looming up towards him and his mum's coat like some kind of dead animal, hot against his arm. Stick scrunched his eyes shut but all he could see was Mac falling face forwards onto the grass, and a figure standing over him. As he reached for the door he thought of Mrs McKinley standing in her flat, wondering where he'd gone. He deserved to feel shit, so he shoved his hands under his armpits and lowered himself to the ground, sat in a tight, curled ball. His head felt like it would explode, his brain coming out through his eyes, his nose, his ears; his lungs would close up and suffocate him to death. Get the fuck over yourself, he told himself. Mac's dead. Mac's fucking dead and you can't even make his ma a cup of tea.

When he finally opened the cupboard door and unfolded himself back into the hallway, Stick had made up his mind. He chucked the boxes and the gazebo back under the stairs. They'd left bits of rubbish on the carpet – scraps of cardboard, a leaf, a speck of dried mud. He tried to brush them to one side with his foot but they wouldn't shift.

He wrote his mum a note – *Gone to Spain. Will call. Don't freak out* – and positioned it on the little table in the hallway. Then he lifted the black sports bag off his bed, picked up his keys, and left.

The car coughed and spluttered but started. Stick did a fast three-point turn, and drove down the worn-out tarmac of the cul-de-sac, right then right again, past the school. The steering wheel cool under his hands. He didn't look up at Mac's flat but accelerated past the fenced-in garden at the front of the block, past the neat red-brick houses, past the Clarendon with its ugly walls and scratty wooden benches, hard over the speed bumps. He only stopped, brakes squealing, for the bus, which was taking up the road. A woman with headphones turned to look out of the back window at him and he held her gaze until the bus heaved itself down the road and round the corner.

*Manchester. Birmingham. Dover. Calais.* His mum would go mental, but he'd be long gone by the time she got back from work. Stick turned on the radio. There was a scratchy hiss behind the music when he turned it up, plus they were playing shit; he didn't even know what it was, but it helped to fill up his head with the noise. And it was even better once he got on the motorway, burning down the fast lane, feeling the car groan and strain as he pushed his foot flat against the floor.

Two hours in and he was crawling in traffic near to Birmingham. The car's fan belt kept squealing like a trapped bird. 'Nordausques, St Omer, Aire-sur-la-Lys,' he said, almost too quietly to hear above the radio. 'Bordeaux, Bilbao, Madrid.' And then, 'Hey, dude! What's with the shit music?', trying to make his voice sound like Mac's.

He pictured his mum reading the note, a fag in one hand, the other fussing at her clothes. She'd probably call the police, tell them to chase him down the motorway and bring him home. He was seventeen. He was nearly eighteen. It wasn't illegal to drive to Spain. 'I'm going to Spain,' he said out loud. 'I am going to Spain.' He brought his fist down hard on the steering wheel, his eyes tearing up so he could hardly see out of the windscreen. 'You fucking bastard,' he said, his voice cracking. 'You fucking bastarding bastard. Why aren't you here?'

He took the next exit, drove fast around the roundabout and pulled onto the motorway in the opposite direction. He switched the radio off and the car filled with the noise of the wheezing engine and the buffet of wind against metal. His eyes were tired. His head ached. He had just enough petrol, he reckoned, to get back home.

# 8

By the time Stick got home it was early evening. The note had gone. His mum was by the back door, smoking. She turned to him and he could see the tension in her jaw, her eyes bright and panicked.

He walked across the room and stood next to her. 'Can I have a fag?'

She stared at him, then tapped one out of the packet and lit it.

Stick drew the smoke into his lungs and looked at the paved back yard, the shed, the flower bed with the oversized daisies on their too-thin stems. The kids next door were kicking a ball against the fence.

'You shouldn't smoke,' his mum said.

Stick took another drag. 'I know.'

They stood there in silence, listening to the slap of the football and the rattle of the fence panel.

'I was thinking you could go to the doctor's,' Stick said. He felt her stiffen but carried on. 'So you can sleep better. I think they can help with that. I could make you an appointment.'

His mum stubbed her cigarette out on the wall, hard enough to break the end in two. 'I did lamb chops for your tea,' she said.

'Mum?'

'I can put a plate in the microwave. I'll do that now.' She went inside and Stick stayed where he was, smoking slowly and thinking he'd like Mac to come back from the dead so he could punch him in the face.

She sat opposite him while he ate. Stick waited for her to say something about the note, about the car, but she just watched him eat, and then as he was about to go up to bed she said, 'Oh, I nearly forgot,' and handed him a white plastic bag. 'Mrs McKinley brought it round,' she said, watching him carefully. 'I think she was hoping to see you.'

Stick looked in the bag. A pair of red Nike trainers. Mac's red Nike trainers. He looked at his mum and she shrugged.

'I don't know, love. She said she wanted you to have them. I couldn't say no.'

Stick stared at the trainers. He remembered Mac wearing them for the first time a couple of months back, the strut he always did when he'd bought something new.

'She's in shock. We all are.'

'And the police?'

'She didn't say anything, love.'

Stick touched the inside of one trainer with his forefinger, then snatched his hand away. 'I'm going to bed.'

'You can talk to me, Kieran.'

For one brief moment he wanted to lie on the sofa with his head in her lap, the way he used to when he was little, her stroking his hair and them laughing at the TV. He tried to smile. He tried to say thanks, but ended up just shaking his head and walking upstairs, Mac's shoes banging against his leg.

The whole of the next day the trainers sat by Stick's bed still in the plastic bag. He kept pulling the edges of it apart so he could look at them, but every time he went to pick them up he had an image of Mac lying on a metal trolley – his face covered up with a white sheet and his bare feet sticking out at the bottom.

Tuesday morning though, he sat on the edge of his bed, snatched up the shoes and put them on, yanking the laces tight and trying to keep his brain quiet. They pretty much fitted.

He hadn't been running since school and hadn't really done it then either, Mr Brazey shouting at them, all red-faced like he thought he was in the army. Stick and Mac sauntering along, having a smoke. He waited until he was on Queen's Road before he started. It felt wrong, like he couldn't get one leg in time with the other, but he kept on, listening to his breath scratch at his throat, past the bottom of the park and onto the bridge. He stopped, panting, to look over the low red-brick wall at the trees and the river below. He should be in Spain, sitting on the beach with a beer, listening to Mac chatting shit.

He started running again, turned off the main road and down a shallow hill, along a street of houses that looked like his mum's, except they had little porches stuck on the front and that bumpy stuff on the walls. Down towards a railway bridge with a long wet stain on the patchy red-and-grey bricks – looked like a giant kept pissing there on his way home from the pub; smelt like it too. On the other side, gravel and stubby grass, and then a road with tall brick walls on both sides, plants and trees crowding over the top.

He kept running. Still wheezing like he smoked fifty a day, not three. Stick gathered up the spit in his mouth and gobbed it at the wall to his right. Why couldn't Mac have taken the coconuts off, and the grass skirts and the stupid fucking hat? Why did he always have to draw attention to himself? The trainers were starting to rub at his heels, the skin turning hot and sore. Another railway bridge and now an industrial estate – blue security fences, lines of delivery vans. They hadn't even arrested anyone. Four days and no arrests. A bit in the *Manchester Evening News*, a bit on the local TV, that was it. Both had used the same picture – Mac with his hood pulled up, grinning. If he'd been a girl there'd have been TV appeals and everyone wringing their hands and saying, 'Oh, was she raped? Oh, did she suffer? Oh, what a tragedy.' It was a fucking joke.

Up the hill to his left were the three tower blocks that had got fancied up a few years back. Down where he was: barbed wire, security shutters, window mesh. A sign for bouncy castle hire, another for dog shampooing, another – hand-painted – for car repairs. He spied a path on his right and followed it to the river. It was dirty – bits of toilet paper and rags hanging from the trees either side; a bleached-out crisp packet and a Mars Bar wrapper going in circles. He carried on running along a thin, muddy path by the edge of the river, trees scratching at his arms.

The stitch doubled him up. A tearing pain, sharp in his left side. Couldn't breathe without it stabbing underneath his skin. He pressed his fingers deep into the muscle of his stomach but it didn't help. He sucked air in through his teeth, then blew it out again. Felt like he had a bag of nails pushing into his insides. Mac's trainers were covered in mud. Mac'd be pissed off about that; he was always cleaning his trainers – stopping in the middle of the road to wipe off a bit of dirt.

He was almost in town, near the railway arches, a new lot of flats off to his right. He took slow, cautious steps and tried to breathe deeply. He could see Strangeways' tower at the top of the hill. Red brick, straight sides, a balcony and then a smaller curved top. Looks like a cock, Mac always said. Get in trouble with the pigs and you'll end up in the cock. Stick had googled it once at the youth club. It's supposed to be a ventilation shaft, he'd told Mac, but I reckon it's for observation. Shaft, Mac had said, shaft – and pissed himself laughing. You could see everything from up there, Stick had said. You'd need binoculars, Mac said, otherwise you'd be so high up everyone would look the same.

It was always the threat at school: you'll end up in Strangeways if you don't buck your ideas up, if you don't stop screwing around, if you don't sit down and keep schtum and pay attention. Ricky's dad had been in twice, and his brother.

He tried running again, but the pain was still there, and he was knackered all of a sudden. You need to get some rest, his mum kept saying, you look tired, love. And it was true, he'd not been sleeping, not properly. Every time he closed his eyes he got a picture of Mac in his head – his stomach ripped open. He hadn't even been stabbed in the stomach. It was his chest, straight into an artery, that's what everyone was saying – you were fucked if they got an artery. But still, in Stick's dream-waking it was Mac's stomach, sliced open and peeled back, his insides raw and red and bleeding.

He started walking, ended up on Cheetham Hill Road next to an offie advertising cheap vodka, and went inside. At the till, he put the bottle on the counter and held the cashier's gaze, flicking a creased tenner in his right hand. The man just shrugged and served him. Less than three weeks and he'd be eighteen. Except he didn't want to be eighteen, not without Mac.

Stick walked through the back streets, looking for the river, but he couldn't quite remember how to get there. The pain had gone. Even when he pressed his fingers into his side he couldn't bring it back. He thought of his dad, those weeks after Sophie, slumped on the sofa with dead eyes – beer cans all over the carpet. He thought of Mac, lifting a bottle of Red Square to his lips, laughing and coughing as it burnt its way down.

He walked along a road that was a mess of patched tarmac, cobbles showing where bits had worn away, or been ripped up, or whatever it was that happened to tarmac. On the corner with another, smaller road, he stopped by a bit of badly fenced-in wasteland, full of dandelions and purple flowers and rubbish. There was, he saw, a gap below one of the fence panels where a wall had fallen away. It was as good a place to drink as any. He bent double and squeezed in sideways.

The ground was scattered with cracked bits of plastic, half-smashed bricks and piles of what looked like clothes – wet and dirty. A Budweiser bottle, a video tape spewing its reel, a cheap plastic joystick. Stick picked up a belt buckle. The metal was rusted so the prong bit hardly moved. He pushed and pulled it until it snapped off in his hand.

'Just waltz in and start trashing the place, why don't you?'

A girl's voice. Stick turned around, then round again. Couldn't see anyone. He dropped the buckle.

'That's right, litter the place up.'

There was a high, red-brick wall to his left – the remains of a warehouse or something – and there she was, perched on a windowsill, the glass long since gone. He could see the bottoms of a pair of white Converse, jeans, black hair with a streak of pink and two wide dark eyes.

'You're trespassing,' she shouted.

Stick turned away and walked, not towards the road, but further into whatever the place was. Dirty blue carpet tiles had rotted and curled up from slabs of buckled hardwood. Beneath that, rows of neat wooden blocks were laid out in

Vs. Some had come loose and he could see little ridges on their sides where they were supposed to fit one into the other.

'I'm serious.' She was standing behind him, her thin brown arms folded. She wore a sleeveless puffa jacket and had her top lip pierced with a small silver stud.

'Go.' She pointed towards the hole in the fence.

'You don't own the place.' Stick kicked the toe of his right foot against a cracked brick.

'I'd like you to go.' She tugged at her fringe – the pink half. 'Please?' She stretched the word please a little and lifted the corners of her mouth into a false smile.

Stick looked her up and down. She was almost as skinny as him. No breasts to speak of. No arse to speak of.

'I said, I'd like you to go.' She stepped closer and he caught the smell of cigarettes and something sweet.

He turned again and walked away from her, over a pile of bricks and bits of rotten wood and mushed-up who-knew-what. He sat on a lump of concrete and danced one foot up and down, up and down. She was watching him, he could feel it, but he didn't look over. Opened the vodka instead and took a drink straight from the bottle, like the guys on the street. Washing their troubles away, his mum said. Not much like washing. More like drowning. Hot through his chest. It made you realise you'd got insides. Made you remember there was a tube from your mouth to your cock. He could feel the vodka burn all the way down it. Now his stitch had gone he felt the ache in his legs, his thighs tight and his shins sore. He rolled himself a fag. Then rolled another.

'You want one?' he shouted, holding it up.

She didn't answer.

Stick put the fag in his mouth and flicked his lighter across the end. He tried to blow smoke rings the way Mac did, but he'd never been able to do it.

'You have to keep your tongue at the back of your mouth.' She walked round and stood in front of him.

Stick dragged hard on his cigarette and looked at her through narrowed eyes.

She picked up the second fag and held out her hand for the lighter.

'I'm J,' she said, once she'd lit up and blown a perfect smoke ring that rose slowly upwards before dissolving into the air. 'The letter, not the bird.'

'What's it stand for?'

'Itself.'

'Your parents called you after a letter in the alphabet?'

She blew another smoke ring. 'Can I have some of that vodka?'

Stick held out the bottle. 'What? Jennifer? Julie? Jessica? Jody?'

He watched her lift the bottle to her lips and drink without wincing. She had a pointy chin and a dark, bony face. No make-up. Brown freckles across her cheeks. He suspected she always looked pissed off.

'What's yours?' She handed the vodka back.

'I thought you wanted me to go? I thought I was trespassing.'

'I decided to like you. What's your name?'

Stick hesitated for a minute. 'Kieran.'

J nodded. 'Nice to meet you, Kieran. Welcome to my –' she paused and then laughed, a little snort to herself – 'abode.'

'What?'

'Home.' She swept her arm in a semicircle.

'This is where you live?'

'Course it's not where I live. Come on, I'll show you the best view.' She led him to a red armchair which had been pushed against the wall where he'd first seen her – its leather slashed and tagged with black marker-pen scrawls. Stick stood on its back and pulled himself up onto the window ledge next to J.

'Cool, huh?' she said. 'I reckon it was a handbag factory. You can see them.' She pointed.

Stick looked down over the ruined space. She was right; they were scattered in amongst all the other shit: hundreds of cheap fake-leather bags.

'They look like dead animals,' J said. 'Like they've all been killed and are just lying there.' She took a long swig from the bottle. 'I've seen rats here – big as a cat, one of them was,' she said. 'I feel sorry for rats. Everyone thinks they're evil and all they're doing is living their lives.'

'Ugly fuckers though.'

A white van drove past below, techno blasting out of the driver's window, and they listened until it was out of earshot.

'Where are you from, anyway?' Stick said.

J frowned. 'Here.'

'I mean—'

'You mean I'm not white.'

'I just mean—'

'Dad's from Ghana. Mum's from Cheetham Hill.'

'They together?'

She shrugged. 'Just about.' Their knees touched as he reached for the vodka. When he passed it back, he felt the brush of her hand against his.

Stick looked out at the warehouses with their red-brick walls and triangular roofs. 'I'm going to Spain,' he said. 'With my mate, Mac.' He swallowed and glanced over at J. She was twisting the vodka cap on and then off and then on again. 'We're going to drive,' he said. 'Down to Dover, then Calais, through France: Tours, Bordeaux, then Spain: Bilbao, Madrid, Malaga.'

She didn't ask why they weren't going to fly; she just passed him the bottle and smiled. She was too skinny, but she had a nice smile.

'Mac's got a mate in Malaga with a flat right on the beach. We're going to stay with him and then find our own place.' Stick blinked, swallowed again. 'We're leaving Saturday.'

J rested her head against the wall. 'Sounds good,' she said. 'Better than Cheetham Hill.'

'You should come out,' Stick said without thinking.

She gave him a startled look and then laughed and Stick felt his cheeks burn red. 'I don't mean – I just meant—' He got his tobacco out and rolled two more fags so he didn't have to look at her.

'I'm going to live by the sea,' she said after a while. She took a bit of hair between her finger and thumb and put it into her mouth. 'I love it. All that space, and everything smells different and tastes different and sounds different. Don't you think?' Her hair stuck to her upper lip as she spoke.

He didn't tell her he'd never been to the sea. He didn't tell her that Mac was dead. Instead, he twisted his body to the right and leaned forwards to kiss her. She moved faster than you'd think, jutted her fist into his cheekbone. Hard.

'What the fuck?' He reared back, put one hand to his face and held the ledge with the other – rough brick against his palm.

'I told you to leave, didn't I? I told you to fuck off.'

And then she jumped down and was gone. White plastic soles across the rubble. The fence panel rattling as she shoved her way out. He stayed sitting on the ledge, his face smarting, watching her hurry up the street, hands shoved into her pockets, shoulders up near her ears. He couldn't think what words to shout after her.

# 9

When he got back, the sweat cold under his clothes and his head fogged with vodka, he found his mum all dressed up. White jeans, red sandals, a blue blouse with little flowers all over it. She held his phone out accusingly.

'We agreed,' she said.

'I went for a run.'

'You don't run.'

Stick raised his eyebrows.

'We agreed, Kieran. You take your phone. You keep it on. There's me calling you and it's just ringing away upstairs.'

He should have carried on driving. Stick imagined a ferry swallowing up the shit little red car and him climbing metal steps onto the deck, the wind in his face and water spraying up the side of the boat.

'We're leaving in five minutes.' She rolled her eyes at Stick's expression. 'I've told you ten times, Kieran. Your nan's. And yes, you do have to. They invited you especially. Your nan seems to think it might help.'

'With what?'

His mum just shrugged. 'I've made a cake,' she said. 'Chocolate.'

She always used to make chocolate cake for his birthday

– two dark sponges stuck together with icing and then more icing over the top. She'd buy things to stick on: Lego spacemen, candles, two racing cars on a sugar-paper track. 'I thought Nan was off sugar,' he said.

His mum laughed. 'I can't imagine that lasting more than five minutes, can you? Come on.' She clapped her hands at him. 'Shower. Get changed. We'll be late.'

At his nan's flat on the Ashton Old Road, Stick and his mum let themselves into the communal entrance and walked up the shallow, carpeted stairs, Stick with the cake in a cardboard box, his mum clutching a bottle of white wine. Two tree branches had been taped to the door frame to form an arch – the bottom half of each was criss-crossed with thick yellow ribbon.

'Lainey said if they haven't caught anyone in the first twenty-four hours that means they're, like, fifty per cent less likely to arrest someone,' Stick said.

His mum had been about to ring the doorbell. She lowered her hand. 'They'll catch him,' she said and then turned to him and said it again, louder, like that might sound more convincing. 'They will. They've got forensics and all that clever stuff. They're bound to.'

Stick stared at the pale bark and the green leaves already curling in on themselves. 'That's just on telly, isn't it?'

'No, love. They'll find him. They will.' She put her hand on his cheek, where J had punched him. 'Have you been fighting?'

Stick twisted away from her.

'Kieran?'

'It's fine.' Stick rang the bell and they both listened to the electronic scale echoing into the flat.

His nan answered the door wearing a long yellow skirt and an orange top with embroidery all over it. She was sixty-one but liked to tell Stick she still felt eighteen, and since she'd met Alan she'd started wearing these weird, floaty things you could see her underwear through. Bracelets halfway to her elbows, and three or four necklaces at a time.

'Cake.' Stick held the box out towards her. She looked inside and pulled a face.

'Oh, you are good, but today we eat only fresh fruit and vegetables.' She glanced at Stick's mum. 'I did tell you.'

Stick's mum smiled thinly. 'Shall I hold onto the wine then?'

His nan made an apologetic face. 'It's all about new beginnings, you see.'

Stick balanced the box on the white wooden chest in the hallway.

'Careful.' His nan sprang forwards, lowered the box onto the carpet and bent to rearrange some stones on the chest. 'Amber and quartz,' she said. 'Healing, purification, new energy.' Then she turned and pulled Stick into a hug. She smelt of washing-up liquid and incense. He'd cleaned his teeth for ages but odds were she'd still smell the vodka on him. She held on longer than usual, then gripped her hands around the tops of his arms and looked into his eyes.

'But Iain. Poor Iain. I can hardly even think about it,' she said, shaking her head. 'And you. And your trip? All those plans. Oh, my sweet boy.'

Stick looked down at the carpet.

'Today is the solstice, the longest day. Your mum told you that?'

Stick shook his head.

'Alan does a ritual. That's why we wanted you to come.

It's about joy and power and courage. We banish negativity.' She flung her arm to one side.

Stick looked at his mum. She opened her eyes wide and lifted her shoulders, and for a moment he wanted to laugh.

'Fellow travellers.'. Alan appeared at the door to the kitchen. He was older than Stick's nan, a small man with a tanned, wrinkled face. A long white top reached over his beer belly and he had strings of beads and strips of leather around his neck and wrists. He held a glass bowl – the one Stick's nan used for whisking eggs – filled with water, a yoghurt pot floating on the surface. As he approached, he dunked the pot so it filled with water and before Stick could dodge, he had reached up and tipped it over Stick's head.

Stick reared back, hand to his scalp. The water splashed down onto his nose, into the crease behind his left ear, over the front of his T-shirt.

'Sun water.' Alan smiled. 'Opens the crown chakra. Clears the aura. Amanda?' He turned to Stick's mum.

'It's Mandy,' she said. 'And you're all right.'

'We were up at sunrise to make it,' Alan said. 'Feels good, doesn't it, Kieran?'

'Alan, I'm not—' Stick's mum protested, but Alan had already filled the yoghurt pot and now half threw it towards her. Water splashed against her face and she spluttered and swore, wiping her hands across her eyes.

'Now,' Stick's nan announced, as though everything was going to plan. 'Come through.' She led the way into the sitting room. 'Sit, sit.'

Alan sat in the armchair by the electric fire, put his hands on his knees and leaned forwards. 'Now, let me tell you about today. Today is about looking ahead, into tomorrow and everything that will come. Kieran, we wanted you here because of Iain, because of what's happened.'

Mac was dead and no one had a fucking clue who'd done it. Ricky said he'd been asking around but no one knew a thing.

'This is a powerful time of the year. Things seem insurmountable. The world feels broken and terrifying and wrong. But we are powerful. We reach inside of ourselves and we find we are powerful.'

Stick thought about J sitting up in the empty window frame, pointing at the rotting handbags – *they look like dead animals* – and him bollocking on about driving to Spain. He couldn't even hold it together to get past Birmingham.

'Do you really believe this shit?' he said, looking at his nan. Her cheeks flushed red and he felt immediately bad, but he couldn't seem to stop himself. 'Sun water and shakers and bits of rock?'

'Chakras,' said Alan. He shook his head at Stick's nan. 'He's angry, of course he's angry,' he said and then turned to Stick. 'Of course you're angry, son.'

'I'm not your son.'

'Look, I'm not sure this is really a very good idea. Kieran's still in shock. I shouldn't have—' Stick's mum sat forwards on the sofa, but Alan held up his hand and carried on.

'Your friend Iain has simply passed over. He's still close, just on the other side.'

Stick imagined Mac floating around on the other side of the window, farting and pulling faces and moving his mouth like he was trying to say something but knew Stick couldn't hear through the glass.

'I know you think you're helping, Alan—' Stick's mum tried again.

'It's a continuum, that's what most people don't realise.' Alan pushed his palms against each other. 'He's been lifted from his body, but his spirit—' He moved his hands up and apart, fingers spread. 'His spirit is free. That is a wonderful thing – to be released from time, from anxiety.'

'Wonderful,' Stick said, his voice quiet, his eyes fixed on Alan's.

He could sense his mum watching him. 'Maybe we should go. Love, do you want to go?'

'It is really, actually, fucking wonderful that my best mate got stabbed and bled to death on his own in the dark, five minutes from his flat. And now he's in a morgue and I'm stuck in Manchester. That is pretty much the most wonderful thing I have ever heard.'

Alan just shook his head. 'No, a tragedy. A terrible, terrible tragedy. But I want you to know that he's here.'

Stick stood up. He could feel himself shaking. 'He's not fucking here. If he was here then I wouldn't be here.' He waved his arm to take in the room. 'I'd be in Spain, sat in a bar drinking beer, not here listening to your shit.'

'Kieran, come on. We'll go.'

Stick shook off his mum's hand. 'No,' he said. 'If Alan knows so much about everything, maybe he can tell me who killed Mac.'

'Kieran, come on. We'll get pizza. Watch a film, take your mind off it.'

Stick stared at Alan. 'If Mac's still here then he can say who killed him, right? So who did it?'

'I'm afraid that kind of work's a touch beyond my capabilities, young man,' Alan said, like Stick had been joking. 'I've a friend though, who—'

'Enough.' Stick's nan stood up, hands on her hips. 'Enough.' She pointed at the ugly brass clock sat on top of the electric fire. 'It's time,' she said. 'And I for one have every intention of doing this. Kieran, I would very much like you to stay.'

Stick's mum had started ushering him towards the door, but Stick looked at his nan, all dressed up and hopeful-looking, and imagined Mac stood by the electric fire shaking his head, saying, *Stick, dude! Chill out, man.* His anger leached away as quickly as it had arrived and he sat down heavily on the sofa.

'Will you stay?' his nan asked.

Stick shrugged.

She smiled. 'We'll do it in the kitchen,' she said. 'I thought that would be best.'

It was, Alan explained, a compromise: a metal bowl of water with red and yellow food colouring dropped into it. 'To represent the fire,' he said. 'Usually, there'd be a fire. But we thought—' He glanced at Stick's mum and then smoothed his hair against his neck and stared at the water. 'Fire symbolises the sun. We jump over the fire and strengthen the power of the sun.'

Stick's mum put her arm around his shoulders and squeezed. He didn't step away. The food colouring did look a bit like swirls of smoke in the water, turning orange where one crossed the other. The bowl was balanced on a wooden chopping board in the middle of the floor.

'We jump,' he said. 'And then we write what we need – our wishes – and we burn them in the flames. You first, Kieran.' Alan waved Stick towards the bowl. 'Feet up. Knees up. Feel the power of the sun.'

Mac would be pissing himself at this: red-cheeked, his stomach wobbling under his T-shirt, a hand slapping at his side. Mac would jump; he wouldn't think twice about it. And so Stick jumped. Feet up. Knees up.

Alan clapped his hands together. 'Great stuff. Mandy?'

Alan beckoned but she shook her head. Stick's nan stepped forwards and jumped.

It was Alan who knocked it over. His heel catching the edge, coloured water spreading across the pale floor.

'Fucking hell,' he snapped. Stick and his mum backed towards the cupboards.

'Not the end of the world, nothing a mop won't fix. Go on, do your wishes.' Stick's nan hustled them into the dining room.

Four pieces of paper – pale pink, with faint flowers printed across them – had been laid out like place mats on the glass table, four sharpened pencils next to them.

'Sit, sit.' Alan looked pissed off. 'You're to write something you want to invite into your life.' He pointed to the pieces of paper.

Stick's mum wrote something on hers and folded it in half before Stick could read it.

Stick stared at his paper for a long time, listening to his nan in the kitchen – the slop and slap of the mop and her humming under her breath.

'Ready?' Alan said.

Stick folded his piece of paper in half and then half again.

'I suppose we'll just have to put them in the water.' Alan didn't sound convinced.

Stick's nan reappeared in the doorway. 'All good as new,' she said.

'We'll go first.' Alan beckoned to Stick and he followed him into the kitchen. Alan closed the door behind them. The bowl had been refilled with non-dyed water. Stick could see a faint orange stain on the floor.

'Let's use the cooker,' Alan whispered.

Stick wondered what he'd been like as a teenager. A bit of a geek. A bit of a goth. Bullied, probably.

Alan lit the smallest gas ring and held out his hand for Stick's paper. 'I won't read it,' he said, and so Stick passed it to him, watched him hold it against the burner until it caught, the flame creeping upwards. He waited until it was close enough to scorch his fingers and then dropped it onto the cooker top, where it burnt itself up into nothing but soft grey ash.

'Now don't tell me what you wrote,' Alan said. 'You mustn't tell your wish to anyone.'

Stick looked at what was left of the paper. Ashes to ashes, dust to dust, isn't that what they said at funerals?

'Now mine.' Alan repeated the process with his own folded paper. 'And then I'll get rid of this.' He took up a cloth, scooped up the ash and the burnt scraps in a soggy grey clump and rinsed it out in the sink. 'And we're done.' He looked at Stick and smiled, and Stick didn't tell him that his piece of paper had been blank, because even though he'd tried to work out how to put it, which words to use, he hadn't been able to.

# 10

People had started leaving things on the fence outside Mac's block almost as soon as it had happened – didn't take news long to travel round there. Nearly a week on and it was packed, top to bottom, left to right: a riot of colour – flowers and teddy bears, photos and cards.

It had taken Stick this long to decide what to put up himself, and now he stood breathing in the thick, sweet smell of the flowers, looking for a space. He should have brought Sellotape, he thought, moving a bunch of yellow roses from Tesco's – the price tag only half ripped off. He tried to wedge the road map of Europe in between two fence struts. It stayed there for a moment and then slipped through, falling onto the grass on the other side so he had to trek all the way around to get it back. He wanted to unfold the map, spread it out on the ground and wait for it to rain so the paper would soften and fall apart. Instead, he balanced it on top of a framed photo of Mac wearing a Santa hat, and tugged a blue teddy bear down a little to fix it in position.

He stepped back to see what it looked like and wondered if the ugly fence outside his mum's house would be covered with this much stuff if it had been him, not Mac. It would be harder to attach things to, definitely, but that wouldn't be the reason. Everyone knew Mac. Everyone loved him.

He'd never worked out why Mac had picked him out as a friend. Because that's what it felt like. They were both ten. Sophie had been dead two months and Stick's house felt like the funeral home he'd gone to with his mum – quiet and awkward and not quite real. Stick had started going up to the railway after school, sitting by the tracks and waiting for the trains to come past and blast him. His mum didn't seem to notice he was coming in late, that he pushed his dinner round his plate instead of eating it. His teachers kept asking if he was OK, if he needed some time out. The other kids either ignored him, looked at him weirdly, or asked him questions he couldn't answer. What happened? Did you start it? Did you see her? Was she, like, burnt up?

And then Mac had arrived, all noise and confidence. He was fat. That should have been enough to make him a laughing stock. But he was bolshie and brash and funny and quick to make friends. And for some reason he wanted to be friends with Stick – who was still Kieran at that point. One lunchtime, Stick was slouched by the window of Year Five's classroom scratching his fingernail into the mortar between the bricks. Mac came over and stood watching him. 'What are you doing?'

Stick dropped his hand to his side. 'Nothing.'

'I'm Mac. Well, Iain, but Mac to my mates.' He held his hand out, like he was a grown man. It was a trick, surely. He'd be into karate or something, take Stick's hand and flip him over onto the concrete. 'Shake,' he insisted, and what could Stick do but reach out his own hand?

Mac shook. 'Want to see something?'

Stick nodded.

Mac opened his other hand to reveal ten silver ball bearings. 'Bullets,' he said. 'They're bullets for small people.'

'They're those things for cakes.'

'Uh-uh.' Mac put one between his teeth and bit it, spat it out again. 'That's metal, that is.'

Stick looked at the tiny silver spheres, and then up at Mac. 'My sister died,' he said.

Mac's face turned serious, his pale eyebrows coming together into a frown. He didn't say anything for a long time, and then he opened his arms and put them around Stick, who had to bite his tongue really hard to stop himself from crying into Mac's shoulder. He made himself pull away, even though he didn't want to.

'Are you a gay?' he asked.

Mac laughed. 'I've touched a girl's boobs.' And then he took one of the tiny silver bullets between his fingers and threw it at the classroom window. It made a noise bigger than itself; a crack like a gunshot. Mac offered one to Stick and he did the same. A teacher appeared on the other side of the glass and started shouting.

Mac held his hand to his ear. 'I can't hear you,' he said, loud and slow, exaggerating each word. 'Sorry, I can't hear you.' And then they turned and ran, laughing, across the field towards the tall metal fence that separated it from the road.

And that was it, they were friends. Stick had never asked Mac why he'd picked him, and now it was too late. Mac was dead and there was a fence covered in flowers and teddy bears to prove it. Stick stared at a bunch of white lilies just opening to show their violent pink insides. It didn't even matter, except that he couldn't ask him, and so he wanted to know.

'Kieran!' It was Mac's ma, walking down the street towards

him. She looked like she hadn't washed her hair for days. Stick fought the urge to run away.

'Mrs McKinley,' he said and tried to smile.

'Isn't this—' She waved towards the fence. 'I've read all of them. All the cards.'

Stick reached out to touch the edges of the map. 'I'm sorry about the other day,' he muttered.

'They've arrested him,' Mrs McKinley said.

Stick stared at her.

'A man called Owen Lee. He killed my boy.' She said it like she was a kid in bottom set trying to read. 'Rob says they'll charge him.' She looked at Stick and nodded. 'Rob says they'll be charging him tomorrow. They'll go for murder.' She laughed and then pressed her hand over her mouth. 'That's what he said. They'll go for murder. That's instead of manslaughter. And the papers. It'll be in the papers tomorrow. He said I shouldn't buy one. I shouldn't look. But—'

Stick could hear the roar in his head. The world felt suddenly fragile, as though if he moved it might shatter into tiny shards.

'Why?' he asked.

Mrs McKinley had a white leather handbag over her shoulder and kept opening and closing the big gold clasp. *Click. Click. Click.* 'They've found things.' She nodded. 'They've found things in his flat.'

Stick wanted to throw up. 'Why did he kill him?' he asked. 'Who is he?'

'And then they charge him, and then –' she let out another little laugh – 'and then they do a post-mortem. Another one.' She looked at Stick. 'I don't know why they have to do that.'

He couldn't look at her. Stared instead at the blue metal grid of the balconies; bikes and mops and plants and furniture pressed against frosted glass; rows of pleated net curtains. He remembered the first time he visited Mac, standing high up on the fifth floor, throwing peanuts down into the street.

'And then if – if it all – I don't know. But then they release him,' Mrs McKinley said.

Stick's head cleared for a second. 'They can't release him. A murderer?' The word sounded wrong – like he'd just made it up.

'My boy,' she went on, as if he hadn't spoken. 'They release my boy. The funeral will be Wednesday.' She nodded. 'That's a good day. Wednesday. Isn't it?' She looked at Stick, waiting for him to say something.

He tried to smile, tried to say, yes, Wednesday's fine, but what came out was, 'Owen Lee? Owen Lee killed Mac? Who the fuck's Owen Lee?'

'And I'm going to town to buy a dress.' She grabbed his elbow, tight enough to hurt. 'A dress for my boy's funeral. Can you believe that? I don't have anything black.' She drew in little gasps between the words.

Stick thought of his mum at Sophie's funeral, in a neat black dress. His dad in a suit Stick had never seen before or since. Stick in his school uniform with a black tie around his neck, walking behind his parents. They wouldn't look at him, or at each other, wouldn't hold hands – each of them close up together and entirely on their own.

Mrs McKinley leaned her face closer to his. 'You'll come.'

'Sorry?'

She was nodding now. 'You'll come and help me choose. You'll know what he'd like.'

Stick felt the panic under his skin. 'Mrs McKinley, I can't, I'm sorry.' He shook his head and tried to step back, but she was still gripping his elbow.

'I need you,' she said. 'To help me choose.'

'My mum might?' Stick said. 'Or your sister. They'd be

good for that, wouldn't they? They'd be better than me at that.'

She was shaking her head.

'I don't know anything about dresses, Mrs McKinley.' He could lie – tell her work had taken him back on and he had to go down to the site, but before he could, she said, 'I need you,' again, and he remembered her standing in the flat, staring out of the window and him creeping off like a coward.

'All right, then,' he said, and managed to smile this time. 'I can drive if you like.'

She shook her head. 'It's half a week's rent to park down there.' She sounded, for a moment, like herself again. 'We'll get the bus. I'll pay.'

So they walked across the grass at the back of the Queen's, dodging the dog shit and bits of broken glass, Mrs McKinley half leaning on his arm. He took her the long way around and she didn't seem to notice, except that once they got to the stop she said, 'Do you think it hurt? Do you think he suffered? Rob said probably not, but I don't know.'

Stick stared across the road towards Paget Street. 'No,' he said. It was like his voice was breaking all over again – couldn't trust it. He swallowed. 'It'd be quick, I'm sure. They say it doesn't hurt.'

They say it doesn't hurt straight away. They say it's like being punched and sometimes you don't even notice until you see the blood. It must hurt after a bit though, once your brain's caught up with what's going on. And Mac hated blood, turned green and woozed about at the sight of it.

'Who's Owen Lee?' Stick asked.

She didn't answer him.

'Mrs McKinley?'

She blinked and looked at him as though she'd forgotten he was there. The bus turned up before he could ask again.

They sat downstairs, Stick by the window staring out at Rochdale Road unravelling like a slow, jerky film. Past Paget Street; past the school and the car park and the storage place; past the fenced-off flats waiting to be knocked down. They'd got inside one of them once. Mac's mate Faisal was always breaking into empty houses. Camping out with a couple of spliffs, a tab of acid, cans of cheap lager. He slept there sometimes and no one seemed to bother much about it. He'd broken into the Rochdale Road ones and Mac and Stick had gone to meet him in one of the ground-floor places – the windows boarded up and the electrics off. It smelt of damp, and piss, and weed. Faisal lounged on a tattered-looking sofa, a fag crackling red between his lips.

'I could kill the pair of you and no one would find you for months,' he said, laughing. They sat and smoked and talked about every case they could remember where people had been murdered and then built into walls, or buried in cellars, or hidden in lofts, to be unearthed years later as skeletons with bits of rotting flesh still clinging on.

'Did the police say why he did it?' Stick said.

He thought she hadn't heard him, but when he turned to ask again she said, 'He won't tell them anything.' Her voice shook. 'Wrong time, wrong place, they say. They don't think he knew him.' She looked at Stick. 'You don't know him, do you?'

Stick shook his head.

Mrs McKinley scraped a fingernail over her jeans. 'There was an argument on the bus,' she said quietly. 'Maybe it was the dressing-up. Some men get –' she hesitated – 'bothered about things like that, don't they?' She sniffed and wiped her hand across her face. 'He just liked a joke though, Iain, didn't he?'

Stick leaned his head against the window and tapped one foot on the floor. He thought about Mac's bed covered with shirts and shorts, flowers and flip-flops and plastic sunglasses. If he could go back, he'd wear the lot – leave nothing for Mac.

Mrs McKinley put her hand on his thigh.

He froze.

'Makes me nervous,' she said. 'When someone jiggles their leg like that.'

'Sorry.'

She left her hand there – *one, two, three, four* – and then the bus lurched to one side and she pulled it back onto her own lap.

'Would you look at my nails,' she said, holding up both hands. 'I'll have to get them done, for Wednesday.'

'He wouldn't mind,' Stick said. He kept his gaze on the floor, tried to keep his leg still.


Saturday afternoon in town. It reminded him of being a kid. Crowding down Market Street with his mum, begging for sweet money; later with Mac, smoking weed and laughing at the guys with their white-painted faces, pretending to be made out of stone; spending Stick's dad's money on cider and fags. Stick called it guilt money; Mac said he should stop being a cunt and have some gratitude.

'Would you look at that,' Mrs McKinley said, stopping by the curved brick wall of the Arndale car park and pointing at a red circle of metal with white writing on it. 'Food riots. 1757. Four died. I did not know that.' She stood there staring at it, like she'd forgotten she was in town, like she didn't realise she was in the way.

Stick and his mum used to come to the Arndale Centre on the weekend, when he was twelve or thirteen. A tenner to spend on whatever he wanted, if he'd been good enough and his mum had the cash to spare. Traipse round the shops and then a McDonald's for lunch. His mum sitting and watching the girls – she'd always fix on one, about the age Sophie would have been, and watch her hungrily. Stick would see and say nothing, sit chewing his burger and feeding fries into his mouth, his stomach clenching.

'Are we going Arndale?' Stick asked and she looked at him like she was surprised he was there next to her, waiting.

'Harvey Nichols,' she said. 'I've never been in.'

Stick shrugged and followed her along the side of the Arndale Centre, keeping his eyes left and holding his breath as they passed Dantzic Street and the Printworks. Owen Lee. Who the fuck was Owen Lee? Maybe he'd been in the bar, staking Mac out like a psycho. Maybe he'd seen Stick stumble into the toilets with the girl in the blue sequinned top. Maybe Stick had seen him.

Harvey Nichols was in the posh bit of town – by the tarted-up Corn Exchange and the open area with the sloped concrete benches and a dug-out stream of water, the whole place full of pale-grey stone and massive glass windows. A security guard in black trousers and a black shirt narrowed his eyes as Stick walked towards the door, but he didn't say anything. Inside, the air was choked with perfume; the lights so bright everything glittered.

Mac's ma seemed to shrink a little next to him.

'You sure this is where—' Stick said.

'He was a good boy.'

'Yes.' Stick stretched out the word. 'But—'

'Least I can do is wear something decent.'

Stick followed her through islands of make-up, where

women in white doctors' coats fussed about with pots and brushes. Up three steps and then an escalator into the women's section. Stick kept his eyes fixed on the thick grey carpet.

'There aren't many clothes, are there?' Mac's ma said.

It was pretty empty, with short silver rails arranged at angles. Mac's ma walked from one to another like she was in a trance. Stick followed, head down, listening to the coat hangers clack as she picked things up and then put them back again, tutting.

'What do you think?' She held up a black dress made out of shiny material, with a low neckline.

Stick felt himself blush. He shrugged.

'A bit slutty?' She put the dress back and pulled out another. 'This one?'

It didn't look that different.

'You find me one, Kieran.'

Stick grabbed the first black thing he saw, except it had shoulder pads and silver studs around the neck and sleeves. He thought about the girl, J, with the stud in her top lip. He'd gone back to the space a day or two ago but she hadn't been there, or if she had she'd hidden herself away somewhere.

'Do you think?' Mac's ma said.

Stick shoved it back on the rail. He needed Mac. Mac could do this kind of thing. He'd dance round the shop fetching things, chatting up the assistants. He'd try a bloody dress on himself if they let him.

'They need to get him to confess,' Stick said. 'Need to pull his fingernails out or something. Mrs McKinley, the police must have said something about why he did it?'

She just shook her head.

'There'll be a court case though? He'll have to explain?'

'That's right.' She half smiled.

92

Stick picked out a long-sleeved, plain-looking dress and held it up.

'Have they got it in a sixteen?'

He fumbled with the label. 'It's an eight.'

'Who's an eight? Look if there's another one.'

He looked, but couldn't find her size.

'Will you ask someone for me?'

Stick chose a shop assistant who was wearing a bright-orange dress and yellow shoes. She didn't react as he walked up, and he felt his cheeks colour.

'Have you got a sixteen?' he said.

She took the dress off him, looked at the label then looked at him.

'It's for her.' Stick gestured to Mac's ma with his head.

The assistant didn't even look over. 'I'll go and see. We don't always stock the larger sizes.'

She stalked off and Stick stood with his head down, shuffling his feet against the pale-grey carpet, which was stained from people's shoes – a bit of mud here, something spilt there.

She came back with two dresses and held one out to him. 'You're in luck.'

He snatched it and retreated back to Mac's ma. 'They're not nice in here.'

'They're just bored, the loves,' she said. 'Standing around all day, nothing to do.'

Mac's ma worked in a care home. Wiping old people's arses all day, Mac used to say. They must have given her a week off.

'Come on, I'll try this one, and I've found another.' She draped both dresses over her arm and walked to the changing rooms.

'He's helping me choose,' Mac's ma said to the woman at

the entrance, and then she laughed like she was a girl, like she was drunk. Stick pictured himself inside a changing cubicle with her. There wouldn't be enough room for the two of them, not without touching. Stick swallowed hard.

'I'll wait here,' he said.

'Don't go anywhere. I need you to tell me.'

'It's all right,' Stick said. 'I'll be here.'

And then she was gone and it was just him and the woman, who turned her back on him, started picking clothes off a pile on the table next to her and putting them back onto hangers. It was too hot, too bright. They should have gone to Primark.

He heard a cough and looked up to see Mac's ma in a dress that was too short and too tight. He glanced at the shop assistant and saw her hide her smirk. Bitch.

'Did you try the other one?' he said.

Mrs McKinley's face fell a little. 'You'll wait here?'

'Sure.'


The next dress was a bit better, but what the fuck did he know?

'I look fat, don't I?' Her voice wobbled.

'You look nice,' he said, then blushed like an idiot.

'It's three hundred quid.'

'Fucking hell,' he said, before he could stop himself. The assistant snatched in a disapproving breath. Stick lowered his voice. 'I mean, it's expensive isn't it? For a dress.' She didn't have that kind of money, he knew that. He thought of the euros still rolled up in the sports bag in his room. Even all of them wouldn't buy the dress.

'It's for Iain.'

'But he's—' He stopped himself. 'Don't you think some-where cheaper would be just as good?'

She smoothed her hands over her hips. The dress had a low V-neck and he could see the top of her tits. He tried not to look.

'I haven't worn black for years,' she said. 'I used to. When that excuse for a husband was around.' She let out a little laugh. 'Soon as I got rid of him I started wearing colours. Tells you something, that does.'

That was not Mac's version of events. 'She says she chucked him out but she never,' he told Stick once. 'He left, and then came back and she let him stay, and then he left again, and came back, and again. It was only when he got one of his other girlfriends pregnant he stopped it.'

'Maybe we should go somewhere else, just to look?' Stick said.

She was like a child, he thought, looking at him and nodding.

As she handed the dresses back to the assistant, she said, 'Will you keep this one for me? I'm going to think about it.'

'I can hold it back for an hour.'

'Thank you.' Mac's ma smiled, like she hadn't noticed what a stuck-up cow the woman was, and Stick guided her back outside.

'M&S,' he said. 'It's just there. They'll have something.'

'I'm not old,' she said, but they went in and did the same thing again, just this time the price tags were less. And this time she did cry, standing outside the changing rooms in a dress that kind of bagged in the middle, with the whole world looking. Stick stood with his arms suddenly useless at his sides and his face burning. This time the assistant wasn't a bitch and when Stick looked at her, desperate, she smiled and stepped in, patted Mac's ma on the back, sat her down on a stool and sent him off to buy a bottle of water. By the time he got back her face was blotched red but she'd stopped crying. She took the water but didn't open it.

'I'm going to get the other one,' she said.

'Are you sure?'

'It's for Iain.' She squeezed the bottle so hard it made a cracking noise.

Mac would know what to say. Stick's mum would know what to say. Probably that girl J would know what to say. He looked about for the assistant but she was talking to another customer.

'OK,' he said.

And so they went back to Harvey Nichols. The assistant at the changing rooms was a different woman, smaller and smilier. The other one hadn't kept the dress back at all, and Mac's ma was in a flap trying to find it again. Three hundred quid. It would have been better if someone else had bought it, but they hadn't.

The woman at the checkout spent ages folding up the dress and then wrapping it in tissue paper, using little bits of Sellotape like it was a birthday present.

'For a special occasion, is it?' she said chirpily.

'It's for a funeral,' he said, before Mac's ma could speak. The woman dropped her gaze and muttered, 'I'm sorry.'

'It's for Iain,' Mac's ma said.

The checkout woman put the dress into a posh bag with string handles and rang up the amount on the till. He knew he shouldn't be letting Mrs McKinley spend that much, but he watched her fit her credit card into the machine and punch in her PIN and then it was done. Maybe if he told his mum, or Lainey, they could talk her round, take it back for a refund.

Mac's ma cradled the bag in both arms instead of holding it properly. They walked without speaking up towards

Shudehill bus station. Past the big wheel and the spinning metal sculptures, round by Next, right past Printworks. And there he was: Mac – a girl on each arm, two grass skirts one on top of the other, three strings of plastic flowers, and those fucking coconuts – turning for a moment and smiling. Stick wanted to run after him, shouting: you cunt, where've you been, you scared the fucking life out of everyone. Except he wasn't there, and Stick was just looking at a street full of people he didn't know.

# 11

There was a photo in the newspaper the next day. A man with dark hair and a long, sharp nose. Owen Lee. Thirty-four. Father of two. History of violence. Recent divorce. He was smiling, not at the person holding the camera, but at someone next to him – one of his children, Stick thought, or his wife – but whoever it was had been cut out of the photo. Of course they had.

Stick read the article three times. There had been an argument on the bus, it said, they had CCTV footage and people who remembered, people who'd seen them get off and the older man follow the younger across Rochdale Road. When he knew each word off by heart, Stick ripped around the photo and the text and Blu-Tacked it to his wall, in the middle of where the map used to be.

On Sunday morning, his mum had knocked on his bedroom door and he'd opened it to her telling him he'd be late if he didn't get a move on. She looked past him and he saw her spot the article stuck to the wall, but she said nothing. Before he left, he prised it off, folded it up and put it into his pocket.

———

His dad's house – which in reality was Jen's house – smelt of gravy and roasting meat and cake.

'Shoes,' Jen said in her shiny, overenthusiastic, everything-is-fine voice, and Stick stooped to pull off Mac's trainers, dropped them one on top of the other.

'Your dad's just carving,' she said. And then, 'I'm sorry, Kieran. I was so sorry to hear.'

Stick felt for the folded-up newsprint in his pocket and smoothed it between his fingers. He followed her into the dining room and sat down where he always sat, next to Jen, opposite Bea, diagonal from Rosie. His dad had the end seat, head of the table, the chicken in front of him on its spiky metal tray. Stick avoided meeting his eye.

'Wing, leg or breast, Kieran?'

Stick shrugged. 'Whatever.'

Bea put her hand over her mouth and giggled, looking at Stick with goggle eyes. He smiled back at her. They were all right, the girls. Bea talked too much in her posh voice, and Rosie was too little to say anything that made much sense, but they were all right.

His dad poured him a glass of red wine, nodded at him as he passed it over, as if they had some kind of secret. Stick wanted to knock it over onto the horrible white tablecloth with the fancy embroidered edges. His dad never used to drink wine before he met Jen.

'Just the one, yes?' Jen said. When Stick looked at her she gave him a forced smile. 'Don't want to give him bad habits, do we?' she joked.

Stick drank half the wine in one go. Jen pulled a face but said nothing.

They were halfway through eating when Bea looked up from her plate and said, 'Mum said your friend got killed.'

'Beatrice,' Jen snapped, her face reddening.

Stick could feel his dad watching him.

'Why did he get killed?' Bea said.

Stick jabbed his fork into a roast potato. 'I don't know, Bea.'

'Now, Bea, why don't you tell Kieran about your swimming lessons?' Jen said, her voice high and forced.

Bea stared at Stick, frowning. 'Will you get killed?' she said.

'Beatrice, will you stop that?'

'Stop what?'

'No, I won't get killed,' he said.

'Why not?'

Jen flapped her hand in front of her face, like she was trying to cool herself down. 'Gary, please.' She glared at Stick's dad.

'More chicken?' Stick's dad almost shouted. 'Come on, girls. Eat up, eat up.' He clapped his hands. 'We all know what's for pudding.'

'Because I don't think anyone would want to kill me, that's why,' Stick said. Because I don't wear coconuts taped to my T-shirt; because I don't mouth off to strangers when I'm pissed.

'More potatoes?' his dad said.

'But someone wanted to kill your friend?'

Stick had tried to work it out. He'd gone back to Paget Street, walked the route from the bus stop to where the police tape had been. Made himself picture it – the yellow glow from the street lights, the trees throwing dark shadows. Footsteps behind him. Mac must have turned towards Owen Lee, must have seen his face as the knife went in. And then the blood. Could you feel blood coming out? You must be able to if there was so much coming out that there wasn't enough left for you.

'I do not want you talking about this at the dinner table,' Jen snapped.

Stick put his fork down and looked at Jen. A thin plastic headband held her hair back from her round face. There were pink patches on her cheeks and blotched across her neck. He picked up the bottle of wine and refilled his glass, even though he didn't like the taste. And then he took the piece of paper out of his pocket and smoothed it flat on the tabletop.

'This is the man,' he said, turning it around so Bea could see.

'Your friend?' she asked.

'The man who killed him.'

Bea's eyes filled with tears.

'Kieran, honestly.' Jen reached across the table and put her hand over Bea's. 'Beatrice, don't cry. There's nothing to cry about. The bad man's in jail now, honey.'

Stick took a large mouthful of wine. He caught Bea's eye and winked at her but she didn't smile. He thought about Owen Lee sat in a police cell with a smirk on his face, refusing to answer questions. Jen refolded the paper carefully and handed it back to Stick.

Bea sniffed, wiped her hand across her face and then said, 'I'm a penguin.'

'Is that right?' Stick said.

'At swimming,' Jen said. 'She's in the penguin class. She's doing very well, aren't you, Bea?'

'And in the summer I do a course and then I turn into a dolphin,' Bea declared. 'And there's a show and we all swim and then we get medals. Will you come, Kiery?'

Stick didn't say anything and her eyes started to fill up again. 'OK,' he said. 'OK, I'll come.'

Jen had made a lemon cake with thick white icing, which

Bea and Rosie had decorated with tiny silver balls in the shape of smiley faces.

'This is to cheer you up,' Bea said, putting it in front of Stick. 'Because of your friend,' she whispered loudly.

'Smiley,' Rosie said, pointing at the cake. 'Smiley.'

Stick thought of Mac that day in the playground, opening his palm to show the tiny silver ball bearings.

'Don't you like it?' Bea's voice wavered.

'Course I like it.' He punched her lightly – maybe not lightly enough – on the arm. 'I love it. Look.' And he pulled a clown's-face grin.

She leaned in towards him, cupping her hand up to his ear. 'Does being killed hurt?' she whispered. He felt bits of spit going onto his cheek.

'I don't know,' he said, and then looked at her worried face and said, 'Not too much, I don't think. You don't need to worry about it.'

The cake was sharp and sweet at the same time. Stick ate two slices and drank another glass of wine.

'Well, you two want to talk.' Jen stood up. 'Come on, girls.' She lifted the wine bottle and took it out into the kitchen, the girls trailing after her. Bea glanced back at Stick as she left.

And then it was just him and his dad.

'That was not my fault,' Stick said.

His dad pushed his chair back from the table. 'I didn't say it was.' He shook his head. 'Jen's just – it's difficult with little ones. She doesn't want Bea getting scared.'

'Can't hide her from the big bad world though, can you?'

His dad raised his eyebrows. 'You wait till you've got kids,' he said. 'You'll see.'

Stick and Mac had talked about kids once – Mac wanted five, Stick wanted three.

'How are you?' his dad said.

Stick closed his eyes. He didn't need this. 'Fine.'

'It's hard, I know, but you're doing great, and it'll get easier; you just need to take it one day at a time.'

He didn't want it to get easier.

'I hear they've charged someone?'

'Can I use your Internet?' He needed more than a shitty news article. He wanted to find Owen Lee's Facebook page. He wanted to know what people were saying about him. The court hearing was still five days away; he couldn't wait until then. Stick stood up, scraping his chair over the floorboards.

'Hang on a minute. Sit, sit.' His dad patted at the table. 'I want to ask what your plans are. Now the trip's not—' He rubbed his finger against his chin. 'Not happening. I want to know what you're going to do next. Sit down, Kieran. Please. The Internet's not going anywhere.'

Stick sat back down, jigged his right heel. 'I don't have any plans,' he muttered.

His dad nodded. 'Because –' he drew out the word – 'I have a proposition.'

Stick stared at the remains of the cake, half the plate just crumbs and smears of white icing, a stray silver ball.

'How do you feel about working for GC Windows?' He said it like he was announcing the lottery.

Stick remembered Mac's ma walking out of the changing rooms in her too-expensive black dress. *Ta da!*

'A trainee post,' his dad carried on. 'I've talked to John and he's good with it. Six months' trial. Chance for a pay rise after that.' He was talking quickly, like he was excited. 'Because I can see college wasn't right for you. I get that – you want to be out in the world, earning your way. You don't want to be coming asking me for money every five minutes.' He gave a nervous laugh.

Stick folded his arms.

'And that job with those cowboys over in Gorton – it's not a long-term solution, is it?'

Plus they didn't want him back. He'd gone down to the site last week, because he couldn't think of anything else to do, couldn't stand being at home with his mum fretting at him, and the cat being sick, and Lainey messaging him, trying to get him to come out. And even though he'd explained about Mac and everything, the head guy had just shrugged and said they'd got someone else in – 'plenty more where you came from, mate'.

'You'll be shadowing me first, out doing sales, visiting people's homes,' his dad said. 'We'll have you in the shop for a while, then out with John measuring up, then with the lads doing the fitting. You'll get a taste of everything. Like one of those company schemes. No special treatment cos you're mine.' He held his palms up and grinned. 'But it'll be good. You'll do just grand.' He put his hands down on the table and looked at Stick. 'What do you say?'

He said no. He said get me the fuck out of here. He said, window salesman, are you fucking joking? He pictured Mac with his chin resting on his fist saying, 'Yeah, you could do that, window salesman, why not?'

His dad held his hands up again. 'I know. It's sudden. You've a lot going on. I mean, Christ, you're still in shock, of course you are. But I thought it might help, now things have changed.'

Stick stared at his empty wine glass.

'You'll want to think about it.' His dad cleared his throat. 'I mean, it's not an offer that's going to be there forever. But, yes, take your time.'

Stick reached forwards and scooped a bit of icing off the side of the leftover cake. 'I don't want to sell windows.' He sucked his finger, the sugar dissolving against the top of his mouth.

'You don't need to decide now.'

'I don't want to do it, Dad.'

'I spoke to your mum.' He hesitated. 'She thought it was a great idea. And Jen – she thinks it'll be good for – that it'll be a good thing.'

'No.' Stick shook his head. 'No.' He took another bit of icing.

'Can you not do that?' his dad snapped.

Stick sucked his finger and then wiped it on his trousers.

His dad sighed. 'It's a good, respectable, dependable business – the windows trade.'

'I said, no.'

His dad picked up the knife and cut a thin slice of cake, which crumbled into pieces. He piled it all into the palm of his hand and ate it in one go. 'So perhaps you can enlighten me,' he said, when he'd finished chewing.

'What?'

'If you're going to just dismiss this offer without a minute's thought I'm guessing you must have another idea.'

Stick glared at the table – the cake and his empty wine glass, the stupid salt and pepper grinders which lit up when you used them.

'I know you've got a lot on your plate, Kieran.' His dad kept his voice low, like he was trying to calm an animal. 'But you're eighteen in, what, three weeks? And I know, I know Iain's dead and it's awful, but the world's not going to stand still for you. I'm just trying to help.'

Stick scratched at his cheek, didn't look up. 'I don't need your help,' he muttered.

'I can't hear you when you mumble, Kieran.'

'I said, I don't need your fucking help.' Stick met his dad's gaze and held it, his jaw set.

'Everything all right in here?' Jen stood in the doorway. 'You told him about the trainee job?'

Stick's dad nodded.

'Exciting, right?' She looked between Stick and his dad and stopped smiling.

'Tell her, Kieran,' his dad said, and when Stick didn't speak he turned to Jen and said, 'He doesn't want to do it, apparently,' in a hurt-sounding voice.

'Your dad pulled a lot of strings to sort that out, Kieran.'

Stick pushed his chair back and stood up. 'When you two have finished organising my life, and making out I'm too shit to do anything except sell fucking double glazing, let me know, won't you?'

'Kieran.' Jen glared at him. 'Apologise to your father.'

'I'm going home.' He leaned on the word home.

'I said, apologise to your father.'

'And I said, I'm going home.'

Jen was stood between him and the hallway. He was taller than her.

He pulled his hood up. 'I need to get past.'

She looked at his dad, as if to say, come on, do something, stand up for yourself. But he wouldn't, he never did. He'd be sat there with his hands on the table and a poor-me expression on his face. Jen blinked and stepped to one side and Stick walked slowly down the hallway to the front door, putting on a deliberate swagger.

'Bye, girls,' he shouted.

Bea ran out of the front room and grabbed him around his knees. 'You haven't played tickle.' She frowned up at him. 'You said you'd play tickle.'

Stick glanced back towards the kitchen; Jen was watching

them. He unwound Bea's arms from his legs. 'I've got to go, buzzy bee,' he said.

Bea grinned and started running up and down the hall, making buzzing noises. 'I'm a buzzy bee, buzzy bee,' she shouted, but when he undid the latch on the front door she ran back to him and said, 'Play tickle, Kiery. You said.'

'Next time.' Stick gave her a weak smile. She pulled a face. Stick glanced up at Jen, who was still watching. 'I'm sorry, Bea, I am,' he said, and left.

# 12

Mrs McKinley asked Stick if he'd carry the coffin from the hearse to the grave.

'Not on your own,' she said and tried to laugh, but it ended up more like a sob.

Stick nodded. 'Yeah, course, it'd be an honour.' And then he bit at his lip because he sounded just like his dad. They were on the balcony in her flat. She stood with her back against the living-room window, her hands wrapped around a cup of tea. Stick leaned on the rail, facing her.

'We're having the service by the –' she coughed – 'the grave. I can't be doing with –' She shook her head. 'There'll be six of you,' she said. 'You, Aaron, Keith, Mikey, his Uncle Tim.' She hesitated. 'And Paul.'

'Paul?'

'His dad,' she said. 'Iain's dad.'

Stick frowned.

'I know,' she said. 'But I couldn't not call him.'

Stick turned and looked down at the estate: the Queen's with its St George's flag snapping in the wind and three guys he didn't recognise puffing away by the back door; someone pinning up a notice outside Talbot House; washing hung out in a V in the Sweeneys' yard. He could hear the diggers working on the tram line behind the block. It was as though nothing had changed. Stick wanted to shout, 'He's dead. He's fucking dead, do none of you know that?' loud enough to echo off the houses, loud enough for them to hear in town.

His mum asked if his dad had given him money for a suit and when Stick said no she'd pulled out her purse and made him take fifty quid. It was enough to get one from Primark. The jacket was a bit tight under his armpits, but it was all right. It'll do for job interviews, even, his mum had said – with a different tie. Stick tried to imagine himself in an interview but he could only think of the common room at the college he'd stuck out for a single term: frayed chairs, dark-blue carpet, cork noticeboards. He couldn't even think of a job he'd want to apply for.

On the day of Mac's funeral, Stick sat in his suit, staring at the black-and-white newspaper picture of Owen Lee, which he'd Blu-Tacked back onto his bedroom wall. Mrs McKinley had called to ask if he wanted to talk to Rob about the court hearing, about what to expect, but he'd said no. He was going to see Owen Lee. He was going to get some answers. That's all he needed to know.

'Will you be OK on your own, love?' his mum said as he came downstairs. The front door was open and Stick could see the taxi pulling up outside.

'I won't be on my own, will I?'

'I just meant in the taxi. I would have come, except you know what work are like.' She tugged at his jacket, smoothed her hands down the lapels. 'You look smart,' she said. 'You look right smart.'

It was the same place Sophie was buried, a big, well-kept place north of town. Stick stared out of the taxi window and watched the houses get posher: bay windows and loft conversions and repointed brickwork. He recognised the cemetery as soon as they got there: gold lettering on a black board at the entrance; low gates that wouldn't stop anyone from climbing over; the road snaking up between neat grass verges. The whole place was neat – he remembered that too. It looked like someone had gone round with a ruler and a pair of scissors, making every blade of grass exactly the same height. They passed the bit full of trees, flowers tied to their trunks or in vases shoved into the circles of soil around their bases. Sophie was in that bit, but Stick realised he'd never find her grave even if he spent all day looking.

And then the taxi turned a corner and Stick saw not trees and plaques but gravestones, in small groups on a shallow hillside like they'd clustered together for safety. He wanted to leave – open the car door and walk back to town, let them all get on with it without him. He wanted to go back to the place near Strangeways and find J and say he was sorry and then drink vodka with her until he could forget that Mac was dead. But she thought he was in Spain, and he didn't even have her phone number.

Outside the car, the air was cool on his cheeks, a breeze fussing at his hair as he walked up towards two massive black Mercedes and a hearse with a white coffin lying in the back. He headed straight for Aaron and Shooter, who were both in smart black suits, their hair slicked. They touched fists and nodded, then stood in an awkward silence.

'Is his dad here?' Stick whispered and Aaron tilted his head towards a tall man with balding blond hair, a beer belly, features too big for his face. As Stick looked, Paul lifted his hand up and out, gesturing into the sky as he spoke, the same way Mac would have done, and something inside Stick pulled tight.

'His mum's proper drugged up,' Shooter hissed, flicking his eyes left.

Mrs McKinley stood propped up on either side by her sister and Lainey. She was wearing the too-expensive dress and had painted her lips a bright, bloody red. Her eyes were dull, her mouth slack. She looked like she'd fall if either of them let go.

A man from the funeral home gathered the six of them together and handed out pairs of white cotton gloves. 'Just take one handle each,' he said in a low voice. 'Up on the shoulder. Walk slowly. Follow the person in front.'

Paul ground his cigarette out with his toe and turned to the group. 'Check your shoelaces, lads,' he said. 'We don't want anyone falling over.'

Stick looked down. He was wearing his old school shoes, polished by his mum but they still looked knackered. The laces were tightly knotted.

'And bend at the knees. You should always bend at the knees when you're lifting something heavy.'

Mac would have laughed at that – 'You're right, I'm a heavy bastard.' Stick saw Shooter's mouth twitch. He almost laughed himself but if he started maybe he wouldn't be able to stop, so he held his face tight and turned with the rest of them to where the coffin now sat on a flimsy metal table with thin concertinaed legs.

It must have cost a fortune. Polished white wood. Each panel edged with a carved border. Gold handles. He imagined white satin padding inside. And Mac. In the dark. Nailed in. Stick turned to the man from the funeral home. There are stories, he wanted to say, where people are still alive, even though everyone – doctors, parents, everyone – thinks they're dead, and they get put in a coffin and then wake up and can't get out. Fingernail scratches on the inside.

He didn't say it, but as he curled his fist around the handle – which felt fake, which felt like it would break – he pictured Mac punching his way out, the wood splitting and him sitting up, roaring with laughter.

'One, two, three. And lift.'

He was a heavy bastard. Stick wavered and fidgeted with the rest of them. Got it on his shoulder, the wood pressing hard onto the bone. A slow shuffle up the narrow road to the left of the grassy slope. He was behind Mac's dad, and stared at the back of his head, the neat line of newly cut hair, a red spot on his neck.

They turned right, along a strip of concrete marked with painted numbers and lines, the coffin hard and unstable between them. He'd have a bruise on the top of his shoulder – they all would, the blood colouring beneath their skin. Mac was there, in the box, he was right there. Dead, Stick told himself. Dead. But it made no sense.

He didn't see the hole until they were almost standing in it. Deep. Straight-edged, with wooden shuttering flat against the sides to stop the whole thing collapsing. Almost worse than the hole was the massive pile of earth next to it. Someone had covered it over with a sheet of bright green fake grass, as though then people would think it was just a hill rather than however many tonnes of soil ready to be shovelled back on top of Mac in his expensive white coffin.

Another crappy metal table had been set up on the concrete strip and they lowered Mac onto it. Without the weight of him on his shoulder Stick felt too light – untethered. He glanced at Mac's dad, who had a fag in his mouth, clicking the lighter against its end and sucking the smoke in hard. The drivers, with their grey suits and black leather gloves, carried the flowers from the hearse and laid them to the left of the grave. And then other people started walking up and adding more flowers and the pile kept growing – red, yellow, pink, purple – like Mrs McKinley's living room. Cellophane and handwritten cards. Stick looked down at his white gloves. He hadn't brought anything.

Next to the hole were three new graves. Two still had flowers heaped over the mounds of dry soil, dead stems in water-stained wrappings. Stick thought about the coffins underneath, choked with earth. There was a wooden cross with a cheap-looking brass plate at the head of each. Stick peered down at one: *Alice. Fell asleep, April 2011*. Why did they write that kind of shit on graves? *Iain McKinley, fell asleep, 18th June 2011*. They wouldn't write *stabbed by some cunt while wearing coconuts and two grass skirts*. They should write that.

There must have been fifty, a hundred people jostling to get around the grave. And more kept arriving, standing close together and craning their necks to see. The man from the funeral home looped straps through the coffin's handles and motioned the six of them to step closer.

'Take a strap. Keep it slow and steady. It'll rock a bit but don't panic. You just need to line it up with the grave and then slowly lower it down. OK?' He looked each of them in the eyes.

Stick tried to stop his brain from freewheeling. He took the strap and tried not to think that it had been used for this before, for other people: old people, kids – it happened all the time, death, didn't it? He let out a noise as he took Mac's weight, didn't mean to, but a couple of the others did the same, a kind of grunt. Slowly. Slowly. There wasn't much room between the side of the hole and the coffin. Down. Down. It was deeper than six feet. Must be dug deep so they could bury his ma on top of him. Stick let the strap slide a bit too fast and the coffin lurched and wobbled. He gripped his hand into a fist and it steadied.

And then it was done: Mac at the bottom of the hole, and the funeral-home man gesturing to Stick to drop the strap so it could be pulled out, rolled up, ready for the next poor dead bastard who needed it. Stick took off the gloves – his hands felt cold and naked without them.

A priest was standing at the head of the grave with his Bible open and ready. He looked up at them all and then started bollixing on about the uncertainty of life and the certainty and comfort of death. Stick wanted to jump down into the hole with Mac, but he kept himself upright, kept himself still, listened to a bird trill away to itself in the trees up at the top of the hill.

'Iain was a popular boy with lots of friends.' The priest had a posh voice; he sounded like he'd said the same thing a thousand times before. 'A good student, a loving son, Iain was about to embark on a trip to southern Spain before his life was tragically cut short.'

Before he was stabbed to death by a twat called Owen Lee. Stick wanted to push the priest to one side and say, 'He wasn't a boy. He definitely wasn't a good student. He was my best fucking mate.' But the priest was on to the prayers now. Heavenly Father. Soul of Christ. Mac didn't even believe in God, so what help was all of that now?

The priest closed his Bible with a slightly too-enthusiastic snap, took a handful of soil from a white box and dropped it onto Mac's coffin. The sound made Stick jump. Crappy Manchester soil on polished white wood. It looked like spilt coffee. It looked a mess.

Mrs McKinley took a handful of soil and did the same as the priest. *Thump. Spill.* They were taking it in turns, clockwise around the grave. Stick didn't want to be there. He wanted to be down by the canal with a joint, throwing stones at some target Mac had chosen – a plastic milk bottle, a rotting piece of wood, a bloated condom.

He wanted that girl J to be there, standing next to him, her hands in her pockets, her skinny shoulders hunched up towards her ears. The silver stud on her top lip. The bright stripe of pink hair.

They were waiting for him – someone he didn't know offering him the box. He took it, got a handful of soil, dry and gritty in his palm. Everyone was waiting for him. Fuck them. Fuck all of this. He wanted to turn and throw the soil at the priest, with his softly-softly voice and his smug face. Or at Aaron who was standing there crying like that was OK. Or lift his arm and let the earth fall onto his own head. Instead he did what everyone else had done – held his hand over the grave and opened his fingers. *Thump. Spill.*

Stick rubbed his hands together to get rid of the dirt. He stared down at the coffin. *Don't have died.* They should be in Spain, drinking beer, washing dishes, clubbing until the sun rose. *Don't have died, you bastard.* The first court hearing was on Friday. Owen Lee in the dock. A load of bloody clothes in clear plastic bags with paper labels tied on with string. *Don't have died. Please. Don't have fucking died.*


Everyone was going to the Queen's. Free bar and a buffet. Stick wanted to stay at the cemetery, watch them fill in the grave with all the soil hidden under the fake grass and then catch a bus home and get into bed, put his duvet over his head and try to make his mind go quiet. But Mac's uncle offered him a lift and it was easier just to go than think up an excuse.

They got lost on the way back and the pub was already on the way to drunk-loud when they arrived, the sandwiches half gone – stray bits of cucumber and lettuce littering the trays. Stick took a handful of crisps and chewed without tasting them.

'Kieran!' Mac's ma was sat at the bar with two glasses of white wine. She beckoned him over.

'Kieran, love,' Mrs McKinley slurred, her voice still raised even though he was standing right in front of her. 'Give us a hug. Come on.'

He let her pull him towards her. She squeezed him tight, then sat back and put her hand on his head, stroked his hair.

'So nice,' she said.

'Need to get it cut.'

She shook her head, kept her hand where it was. 'You used to have such nice hair. Smart. You and Iain with your smart hair and your uniforms, off to school.'

They'd dump the ties soon as they got out of sight, scuff up their shoes so they didn't look like knobheads.

'Come on, sit here, by me.' She dropped her hand and felt into her bag, took out a scrunched-up tenner and half threw it at the barmaid. 'I put three hundred quid behind the bar,' she told Stick. 'They said it's done, though. What'll you have? Come and sit here, talk to me.'

Stick ordered a pint of Foster's, sipped at it and tried not to stare at the smear of egg mayo on her dress.

Mrs McKinley finished her wine and started on the next glass. 'Iain was going to drive lorries,' she said, as though Stick had asked her a question. 'Like his dad,' she said, looking over towards the fruit machine where Paul was feeding in another quid, his fingers dancing over the lit-up buttons.

Stick frowned. 'Is that what he does?'

Mac's ma nodded vacantly.

Last summer, Stick and Mac had found a fucked-up door down by the canal. Half of it was burnt black, but they got it in the water and it stayed afloat, even with Mac standing on it. Stick had run along the path and Mac had paddled with a branch he'd yanked off some tree, his arse hanging out of his trousers. 'I am transport and logistics,' he'd shouted. 'Anyone need any transport or logistics?' And then later, drinking cans of warm beer and watching the sun dye the undersides of the clouds pink, he'd told Stick he was going to have his own truck; no, his own fleet of trucks, 'Mac McKinley' printed in two-metre-high letters across the side of each one.

Mrs McKinley tapped her fingernails against the bar and said, 'Talk to me, Kieran. Talk to me some more.'

The pub smelt of farts and cheese-and-onion crisps and old carpet. Framed black-and-white photos lined the walls – pictures of the estate being built, some party at the pub with flags and bunting. The food table looked depressing: limp bits of salad, half an egg sandwich, biscuit crumbs and something yellow spilt across the paper tablecloth.

'I was going to have a cake,' Mrs McKinley said. 'Because it's a celebration, isn't it? It's a celebration of his life.' She took a large gulp of wine. 'I couldn't think which one to get though. They don't do funeral cakes.' She laughed.

Stick watched Mac's dad, stood with two other men now, waving his arms about as he spoke, resting them on an imaginary steering wheel and then lifting them up again, fingers spread. Mac never said he drove a lorry. Mac never said anything except he was a lazy twat who couldn't keep his dick in his pants.

Stick started rolling a fag and Mrs McKinley patted his arm. 'You go on, love,' she said.

Outside, he smoked slowly. The estate was quiet. A man stood watching his dog run in crazed circles on the grass behind the pub. Ricky's little sister and a girl Stick didn't recognise pushed a pink plastic doll's pram up the street and round the corner. A white van with spots of grey under-coat along one side sat with its engine idling – a man in the driver's seat with a newspaper spread over the wheel. Stick thought about Owen Lee standing in a courtroom, handcuffs cutting into his wrists.

'You didn't write on his Facebook page.' Lainey stood in front of him. She wore shiny black leggings, baggy at the knees and stomach. Black high heels and a tight black top. False eyelashes and big rings of eyeliner. Her hair was piled up on her head like one of those film stars from forever ago. He hadn't even heard her come out.

'You're supposed to be his best mate,' she said.

'I am. Was. I just haven't—'

He'd spent enough time thinking about it. Lay in bed typing versions over and over in his head, but none of them sounded right. He'd thought about uploading the photo from his phone of Mac and Lainey, Aaron and Malika, but he hadn't done it.

Lainey wiped her forefinger under one eye and then the other. 'It was all right, wasn't it?' she said.

Stick dropped his cigarette butt on the concrete and ground it under his foot. 'The priest was a twat.'

Lainey frowned. 'I thought he was sweet. And nice Mac's dad came.'

Stick scowled. 'Not much use coming once he's dead, is it?' Stick thought about Mac stood outside the Printworks, jabbing the end of the cigar towards Stick, saying *you should make nice with your dad, before we go.*

'Everyone's inside,' Lainey said, and Stick shrugged and followed her back into the pub, to the large booth opposite the bar where Shooter, Ricky, Aaron and Malika were sat, talking about riots in Greece – firebombs, tear gas, street fights with the police. Stick sat with his head down and said nothing.

'Hey, Stick.' Aaron tapped his shoulder. 'I had an idea, about Ranger.'

'Not now.' Malika hit him on the arm.

'Thought I'd change his name,' Aaron said. 'To Mac. You know, like a tribute.'

Mac would kill himself laughing at that, Stick thought – I die and they name a dog after me.

'That's fucked up.' Lainey leaned over the table, her breasts ready to spill. 'That is proper weird.'

'Nah, it's a compliment.' Aaron pretended to tug at a dog's lead and said, 'Hey, Mac. Sit.'

Malika hit him again.

Stick picked up a beer mat and turned it round and round between his thumb and finger.

'You all right, mate?' Aaron asked.

He wasn't about to cry. He wasn't about to lose it. He just wanted to drink his pint and have everyone leave him alone.

'I've been making enquiries,' Ricky said. He had his black Yankees baseball cap perched on top of his head. 'Should shoot the bastard if you ask me.' He lifted his right hand, fingers out like a gun barrel, and pretended to shoot, making quiet explosions with his mouth. 'But there are other ways.' He grinned.

Stick nodded. 'Hearing's Friday.'

'Hearing smearing. Got to sort that shit out yourself.' Ricky was shadow-boxing now, *right, left, right, left.*

Stick stared at the tiny amber bubbles racing up to the surface of his drink and wondered where they came from, and if he sat there for long enough whether they'd ever stop.

'Why did he do it?' he said.

No one responded. Maybe he'd said it in his head, not out loud. 'Why did he do it?' he repeated.

'Hate crime,' Lainey said. 'It was a hate crime.'

'No one hated Mac,' Stick said. 'That cunt didn't even know him.'

'Because he was different,' Lainey said.

'He wasn't different,' Stick said.

'Maybe he bad-mouthed the guy on the bus,' Shooter said. 'Said he'd shagged his mum or whatever.'

Stick shook his head.

'Or that Lee guy's a proper psycho,' Aaron said. 'Like he goes out on a weekend with a knife, looking for someone to bang.'

Lainey tutted and nodded. Stick ripped the beer mat in half. Shooter coughed and said, 'Drink? The man needs a drink.'

'You're all right, I'm going,' Stick said, standing up.

Aaron stood too, trying to get Stick to meet his eye. 'Mate. Mate? You all right, mate?'

Stick kept his head down and made for the door.

'Mate?' Hand on his shoulder.

'Crybaby,' Stick said and pulled away from him. Outside it was still light, but the sky had clogged up with clouds and the air had turned cool. He went up to the railway tracks and sat on the ground, even though it'd mess up his suit. Tipped his head back against the fence post and listened for the whisper of a train. When one came, he opened his mouth and shouted every swear word he could think of, one after the other. He carried on even when the train had passed, lowering his voice to a whisper.

# 13

The envelope from his dad came the day after the funeral. Brown. A4. His name and address in neat capital letters. Stick kicked it off the hallway mat onto the carpet.

He was tired. He'd been in bed by nine but had lain awake for hours, thinking about Mac in his coffin and the weight of all that soil on top of him, and then thinking about the court case, and what it would be like to be in the same room as Owen Lee – whether he'd be able to get close enough to touch him. Around three he'd heard his mum downstairs. He'd pictured her in her blue dressing gown and her rabbit slippers, her hair scuffed with sleep, her fingers worrying at the switches, but he'd not got up to help her. He must have fallen asleep eventually because he woke with a start, from a dream he couldn't remember, except for an image of himself sat on a coach looking out of the window – a coach, not a bus, and there were fields outside, not buildings.

That morning, before the post arrived, he'd sat opposite his mum at breakfast and seen the dark smudges under her eyes and he'd felt bad. Even though he wanted to feel angry, he felt bad.

He told her he was going back to the site, to give it another go, see if the other bloke had fucked up or fucked off. But he went the opposite way, into town. He wanted to buy her one of those burners, with the dish where you put the scent and a bit underneath for a tea light. And a little bottle of lavender oil. His nan said lavender was good for relaxation.

Market Street was packed. Legs and arms. Cleavages. Knees. Everyone's tattoos on show: butterflies and horses, hearts and arrows, words in fancy writing: *love, Kyle, forever, Mum*. A man stood outside Miss Selfridge holding a massive bunch of silver-edged helium balloons: SpongeBob, Homer Simpson, and a pink horse covered in stars that Sophie would have loved. HMV blasting Lady Gaga. Some bald guy with a sound system and a crappy electric guitar singing 'Heartbreak Hotel'. The trams toot-tooting. Dummies looking blankly out of shop windows with their perfect clothes and flat white faces.

Stick ducked into TK Maxx. The shop was too bright – all strip lights and shiny floor tiles – it made his head hurt. He kept thinking about the coach. It felt like a memory, but he was pretty sure it wasn't. Grey fabric seats. The smell of carpet cleaner and feet. Rain on the windows. The hum of the engine and the *tsk tsk* of other people's iPods. The comforting rock and tilt as they drove, and the sense that he could just stay there, going forwards, to nowhere in particular, forever.

He was standing by the low shelves packed with boxed-up toiletries and bags of cosmetics, note cards and china vases, when he saw J. Her hair was pink. All of it this time. Violent pink. She had a black bag and wore the same tight black jeans and white Converse. Stick held his breath, as if that would stop her from seeing him. But she wasn't even looking his way. She was stood by a rack of sunglasses, trying on pair after pair, frowning at her reflection in the small square mirror just above her. Stick moved over a couple of aisles so he could see her better, but kept his distance. Her hair didn't look real – looked more like a doll's than a person's. He wondered what it would feel like to touch.

He almost missed it. A practised move – the glasses disappearing into her bag instead of back onto the shelf without her missing a beat. Stick glanced over to the security guards, but they were eyeing up three girls in hot pants standing by the rows of handbags.

J was still trying on sunglasses, frowning and shaking her head and pressing her finger against her lips as though she was wondering whether to buy this pair or the other. And then she walked out, past the security guards and onto Market Street.

Stick hurried after her, caught her by the arm as she rounded the corner onto Spring Gardens. She launched into a run.

'J!'

She half stumbled to a stop, turned. 'You?' Her cheeks darkened a shade.

'You didn't pay for those glasses.'

Her hand went immediately to her bag, as if she was shielding it from him. 'Aren't you supposed to be in Spain?'

'Yes.'

J stared at him for what seemed like ages, and then she started laughing, still holding onto her bag, her face creasing up, and Stick started laughing too – he couldn't help it.

When they stopped, the silence felt sharp and difficult and Stick wanted to laugh again, but it would just sound forced and stupid, and there wasn't even anything to laugh about. He was about to say he had to go and look for the oil burner when she said, 'I owe you a drink.'

Stick touched his cheekbone where she'd hit him. 'It didn't even bruise,' he said.

'I know a place,' J said. 'I'll get vodka.'

Stick listened to the hubbub of Market Street behind him. Tomorrow Owen Lee would stand in a courtroom and Stick would be there, breathing the same air, close enough to touch him.

'Kieran?'

'It's Stick,' he said.

'What?'

'My name. My real name. My mates call me Stick.'

The morning with the tiny silver bullets, Mac and he had run all the way to the edge of the school playground and Mac had turned to him and said, 'What's your real name?'

'Kieran.'

'No, your real name.'

He hadn't understood.

'You can't just have the name they give you,' Mac had insisted. 'You've got to make your own.' And then he'd looked Stick up and down and said. 'How about Stick, cos you're a skinny bastard? Stick. That'll do.'

J nodded. 'Stick,' she said. 'Will you come drink some vodka with me?'

He followed her between the tall windowless buildings of Spring Gardens, past the post office, through the quiet shaded back streets, the posh cobbled streets with their overpriced shops, and then out into the hurry of Deansgate – a crowd already gathered outside the Wetherspoon's, pints and fags in hand, a stale-pub smell leaking onto the street every time the doors opened.

Stick waited outside the supermarket while J went in to buy vodka. He watched the city getting on with its day, people rushing about as though whatever they were doing was important. There was something about it that made him feel desperate. Like he might cry if he let himself.

J came out with a plastic bag and a grin and they carried on along Deansgate, towards the Beetham Tower with its sharp edges – all the tiny flats like little glass-fronted rabbit hutches.

She took him down past the crap Roman fort Stick remembered having to draw on a school trip once, down under the massive bridges, their arches soaring above them and J swinging the bag with the vodka in it, twisting and turning her body through the shaded space. He followed her along a thin cobbled path by the canal until they reached a low bench tucked up against the wall, under a curved pedestrian bridge.

J sat down and plonked the vodka bottle next to her. Stick stayed standing, watching two fag ends dance together in what looked like a gob of spit on the surface of the water.

'This place used to be a shithole,' J said, twisting the top off the vodka and holding the bottle towards him.

Stick took a drink, swirled it around his mouth and felt his skin tingle. He watched the fag ends touch and then drift apart, touch and then drift apart, and wondered what was making them move.

'It was all dirty and stinking, my dad says,' J said. 'Before they did it up.' She held out her hand and Stick passed her the bottle.

They were on the bend of the canal, the water – a soupy green-brown – heading off in four directions. The three bridges crowded next to each other on their right, metal and brick, arches within arches, the electric tram lines strung up like washing lines. Stick watched a man tying up his barge, looping thick rope around a metal post. Behind the man were warehouses with neat brickwork and arched glass windows – a beer garden with red and yellow flowers, huge linen umbrellas, a stone fountain. 'They did my estate up,' he said.

'Started the year I was born.' The year good things began to happen, his mum used to say; he hadn't heard that in ages.

'My mum reckons it's better,' he said. 'I reckon they should knock it down.' He imagined Mac's block of flats falling to the ground. He'd seen a programme about demolition once – men in yellow jackets and hard hats talking about how they laid the explosive here, and here, and here, so the building would collapse without killing people, without trashing everything else around it. They'd shown the same block of flats go down again and again, in slow motion, the whole thing crumbling like someone had punched it in the stomach and it had sunk to its knees in defeat. 'Nah,' he said. 'It's all right. Is what it is.' He sat down next to J. 'Where do you live?'

'In a house.' She took the sunglasses out of her bag and put them on. 'I say, have you seen my latest Hollywood blockbuster, darling?' she said, standing up and flinging her pink doll's hair left to right.

'You're a nutjob,' Stick said, and then, when she pouted and pulled a face he said, 'They're nice. You're a nutjob with good taste.'

J pushed the sunglasses up onto her head and sat back down, her knee not quite touching his. 'What happened to Spain anyway?'

Stick opened his mouth and then closed it again.

'Fell out with your buddy?' J asked.

Stick took the article about Owen Lee from his pocket and handed it to her. He regretted it immediately, but then he saw how carefully she unfolded it, and the way her nose wrinkled a little as she squinted her eyes to read.

'He killed someone?' J pointed at Owen Lee and glanced at Stick. 'No?' She examined the paper again. 'No. Your mate's Iain McKinley,' she said.

'Mac. He's called Mac. Was.' Stick rubbed at his nose, and then thought that that was what his dad always did and so he shoved both hands under his thighs and stared at the canal.

'Serious?' J said.

A goose cut a V through the water, honking loudly. The man who'd tied up his barge earlier came out onto the tow-path, wearing a green jumper and a white shirt underneath with the collar turned up. Stick watched him walk towards the pub, talking into his mobile phone, and wished for a minute that they could swap places. The man looked like he had a job and a house, a wife and a kid, a boat and a wallet full of cash, a best mate who was still alive.

'They got this guy though, Owen Lee. That's good,' J said.

Stick swallowed. 'They should hang him,' he said. 'It's not right, is it? You kill someone and then you get given some-where to live and have your meals cooked for you every night.'

J laughed. 'Eye for an eye.'

'What?'

'My dad's into the Bible. He fights with my gran about it – my mum's mum. She says too much bad has come from people who hide behind God. She's into politics and justice and writing to people in prison.' J stopped. 'I mean – people who – fuck, I don't know, but not people like your guy. She wouldn't write to him.'

'It's the court case,' Stick said. 'Tomorrow.'

'Already?'

'A hearing or something.' Stick took out his tobacco and papers, rolled two cigarettes and handed one to J. He lit his and sucked at it, hard, so the tobacco crackled and the paper disintegrated fast.

'So you'll see him,' J said. 'Owen Lee?'

'I want to hear him say it.' Stick took another mouthful of

smoke, another mouthful of vodka. 'And why. I want him to say why.' He stared at the light reflecting off the water onto the bottom of the bridge – shimmering white lines and shifting patches of dark in between. 'They'll send him down. Life, I reckon.'

J scratched at the vodka bottle's label with her finger.

'They've got evidence,' Stick said. 'But he won't talk, that's what Mac's ma said. He just sits there like a twat and says nothing.' He looked at the canal. The fag ends had gone and a plastic cup floated in their place, catching the sun. 'Not that she's seen him. She'll see him tomorrow. She's not, like, been at the station with him, but there's this police bloke called Rob, and he tells her what's going on.' Stick stopped talking.

They sat in silence, watching the light on the water; a yellow tram whisper across the bridge; a woman with a wheeled suitcase struggling over the cobbles on the opposite side of the canal.

'I lied,' Stick said.

J glanced over at him but said nothing.

'That other time I met you. Mac was dead then.' Stick thought about the rotting handbags and the broken-down walls and J sitting up on the brick window ledge. 'I said I was going to Spain but he was already dead.'

J nodded and said, 'Malaga. Costa del Sol.' She smiled. 'I googled it when I got home. Looks nice.'

Mac would have liked her, Stick thought. Mac would have definitely liked her.

'You got a boyfriend?' he said, and then felt himself blush. He scraped his foot against the ground.

J shook her head. 'Why?'

'Just wondered.' Stick bit at his bottom lip, hard enough to hurt. He stared at the boat with its black sides and red painted flowers. 'Can I have your number?' he said, trying to get the words out fast. 'I just thought – I could message you. See if you're about.'

'I don't have a phone.' J aimed a kick at a pigeon pecking by their feet and it backed off, flapping its wings.

'How can you not have a phone?'

She opened both palms.

'I don't know anyone who doesn't have a phone,' Stick said.

'You do now.'

'You're not normal, do you know that?'

J smiled like he'd paid her a compliment.

'So if I want to see you again then I just have to hang around that dump and hope you turn up?' Stick said.

'Do you want to see me again?'

Stick looked at the ground – tiny green ferns growing up between the stones. 'Whatever.'

'People didn't used to have mobile phones,' J said.

'Well, what the fuck did they do?'

J shrugged. 'Organised stuff in advance.'

Stick looked at her.

'So, like, I say, I'll meet you at Piccadilly Gardens, one o'clock, Saturday,' she said.

'And I turn up and you're not there.'

'Or you turn up and I am there.'

'Or I turn up and you're there but I can't find you because you're sat in one bit and I'm in another bit, and by the time I've trekked the whole way round the place you've got bored and decided I've stood you up and you've fucked off home.'

'Or I say we'll meet at the statue.'

Stick frowned at her. She was pretty and at the same time not, he thought, with her pointy face and her freckles and her too-tight clothes and her too-thin body.

'One o'clock Saturday?' he said.

'Yeah.' She shrugged. 'Why not? You can tell me about the court thing.' She stretched out her hand. 'Deal?'

He shook her hand, made sure he didn't hold on to it too long in case she socked him in the face again.

'I've got to go,' she said, getting up. 'You can keep the rest of it.' She pointed at the bottle, and then she was gone. Stick made himself wait a minute before he twisted around. When he did, kneeling up on the bench to get a better view, she'd already disappeared.

The envelope was still lying in the hallway when he got back, half pissed. He sat on the bottom of the stairs and ripped it open. A GC Windows catalogue and a note from his dad: *Kieran, Something to whet your appetite! Let's discuss on Sunday? Dad x.* The catalogue was printed on thick glossy paper. The front cover had a photo of a blonde woman standing in front of a house, her hand touching the living-room window, her mouth stretched into a false smile.

Stick shoved the catalogue and the note back in the envelope and carried it through to the kitchen. Babs stood by the sink, looking hopeful. There was still food in her bowl, but he shook in some more dry stuff and crouched next to her, stroking her head and neck as she inspected it.

'I've met a girl, Babs,' he whispered.

The cat selected a brown biscuit shaped like a fish and crunched it between her teeth.

'Got a date,' Stick said. 'Sort of.' He smiled and then stopped himself. 'Plus they're going to nail the fucker that killed Mac. They're going to send him down.'

Babs pushed her head against his palm and purred. Stick

looked at the envelope on the floor next to him. His dad had written his return address on the back like an idiot.

'He wants me to work for him,' Stick said. 'Thinks I'm some kind of charity case. Thinks I can't sort my own shit out.' Babs lowered her nose and started eating again, then turned away from her bowl and wandered into the hallway.

Stick picked the envelope off the floor and took the catalogue out again. He tried to imagine himself in a suit, holding a briefcase and ringing a stranger's doorbell. *Hello, can I interest you in new windows?* He shook the thought away, folded the catalogue and the envelope in half and shoved it into the bin.

# July 2011

# 14

The hearing was in the old court building, which stood like an ugly sister next to the new one with its jutting green and yellow glass cubes. Stick walked along a low covered walkway, past tinted windows blocked by vertical blinds, into a foyer spattered with photocopied signs. *Mobiles off. Empty your pockets through security.* Stick put his phone in a plastic box and walked through the metal detector arch. No one pulled him aside or asked why he was there.

The building was dimly lit and smelt of dust; long blue carpets trailed along corridors and up stairs; matching blue chairs sat in lines against the walls; and more notices: *No mobiles in court, No food or drink in court.* Stick walked slowly. He'd woken up with a fizz in his stomach, like a kid at Christmas. This was justice. Owen Lee wouldn't be able to say 'no comment' in court. They'd make him explain and then they'd send him down.

Mac's ma and Rob the police guy sat outside court twelve. She was wearing the black dress from Harvey Nichols – the egg mayo stain cleaned off, but still visible. Stick had his Primark suit on again, with the blue tie his mum had brought home for him the day before. He didn't like it, but it was nice of her. Plus she said she'd thought about it, and she would call the GP about the plugs, and then she'd laughed in a panicked way, so Stick had taken the tie and smiled and said, great, thanks.

The hearing was scheduled for three, but they sat on the blue chairs until twenty past, when the court door opened and a man wearing a suit and a black gown leaned out and said, 'The case of Mr Owen Lee. Court twelve,' without even looking at the three of them sat there waiting.

The courtroom was smaller than Stick had expected, like a crap school hall, rather than somewhere grand where people got made to account for themselves. He searched the room for Owen Lee amongst the people in gowns and suits but couldn't see him. The dock was empty. Stick pictured him being led in wearing an orange boiler suit and cuffs, a guard's hand on each arm, gripping hard enough to leave a bruise.

'Officer?' A man, sitting at a table in front of the judge, spoke into a desk microphone. Next to the microphone, a digital clock with large red numbers counted off the seconds. 'Can you bring Mr Owen Lee?'

'I'll get him now,' a voice said, and Stick saw something move on a huge plasma screen mounted on the far wall. It showed an empty room: the curved edge of a table, a plastic chair, and behind that a dark-grey curtain.

Stick turned to Mrs McKinley, who was staring straight ahead. 'He's coming here, right?' he whispered. 'He's here?'

She didn't respond and Stick turned back to see a man walking into the camera's frame and lowering himself onto the chair behind the table.

Owen Lee. He looked the same as in the newspaper photo, only in colour, and wearing a suit. His face pale. Small dark eyes. A sharp nose. Nothing special about him. He just looked like some man you'd sit next to on the bus.

'Are you Owen Lee?' the man at the desk said into his microphone.

The man nodded. 'Yes.' His voice was flat.

Stick felt the skin on his cheeks burn red, his whole body itching like there were ants crawling over him. He turned back to Mac's ma and hissed, 'Why's he not here?'

Rob leaned forwards and put his finger to his lips. 'Video link,' he mouthed.

'Video link?' Stick raised his voice and one of the gown-wearing men glanced over at him.

'It's normal,' Rob whispered. 'For a preliminary.'

In the bottom right-hand corner of the screen, a small square showed a view of the court. The man at the desk was listing the name of the judge, then the lawyers. Each time he said a name someone moved the camera so it pointed to the relevant person. He didn't introduce them though. He didn't point the camera at Mrs McKinley.

Stick was sweating now and shaking his head, his hands clenched into damp fists on his knees.

One of the lawyers, a man with grey hair and stooped shoulders, stood up. 'This is a preliminary hearing,' he said. He had a soft, posh voice. 'The court suggests a provisional trial date of 14th February 2012. A plea and case management hearing on Thursday 11th August, with papers served on Monday 1st August.'

February? Stick tapped Rob on the knee. 'February?' he whispered.

Rob nodded, glancing up at Mrs McKinley, who was sitting, staring straight ahead like she was made out of stone. 'It takes time,' he whispered back. 'They have to get their case together.'

Stick counted in his head. February was six months away.

'And could you outline the issues in this case?' asked the

judge. He was perched on a high-backed chair, raised up above the court, a small, serious-faced black man wearing a white wig and a gown with a purple stripe down the front. He sounded bored. Stick pushed his hands under his thighs and pressed his lips together, tried to make his breathing quieter.

'The defendant has been charged on the basis of strong circumstantial evidence. We have CCTV placing him very near the scene and witness statements confirming an argument between the defendant and the victim on a bus minutes before the attack.'

Paget Street. Stick had gone back again yesterday. Apart from the lamp post with a couple of bunches of dying flowers taped around it, there was nothing to show that anything had happened. No scraps of police tape, no squashed grass, no blood.

'Very near?' the judge said.

The man fussed at his papers. 'We have no CCTV of the incident, your honour, but we do have footage of the defendant approaching the scene and then hurrying away, which matches the estimated time of death. We are also awaiting forensics for blood found on the defendant's shoes and fibres found at the scene and on the victim's clothes, which we believe match a jumper retrieved from the defendant's home and which is also identified on the CCTV footage.'

Stick stared at Owen Lee, who sat with his hands on the table in front of him, his eyes blank. That's just pixels, Stick thought. That's just pixels on a screen. That's not really him.

'Any early plea?'

A red-haired woman whose gown was ripped at the shoulder got up and shook her head. 'No, your honour.'

The man stood up again. 'We have had no cooperation from the defendant.'

The judge sighed, as though personally annoyed. Owen Lee's face seemed to register nothing. Not a flicker. Stick stared until his eyes hurt, as if by doing so he could get Owen Lee to see him.

'So we have a provisional trial date of 14th February 2012.'

Mrs McKinley let out a quiet cough and Rob turned, whispered something in her ear.

'PCMH on Thursday 11th August,' the judge continued. 'We'll have the prosecution go first. Evidence to be served on Monday 1st August. Let's hope it's good. Defence papers on Friday 5th.' He spoke slowly, writing as he did so. Then put his pen down and raised his face to the screen. 'Mr Owen Lee, can you hear me?'

Owen Lee's eyes widened a fraction. 'Yes.'

'Your next appearance in court will be via video link on Thursday 11th August. Do you understand?'

The man nodded. 'Yes.'

The judge brushed his hand down over his mouth and chin. 'That is the end of this hearing,' he said.

'What?' Stick stood up, shaking. 'The end?'

The judge glanced towards him, his eyebrows raised a little. 'We will move on to the next case,' he said.

Stick saw Owen Lee pushing his chair back and standing up, a man in a brown uniform stepping towards him.

'You haven't asked him,' Stick shouted.

'Come on, Kieran.' Rob was ushering Mac's ma out of her seat. 'Come on.'

Stick shook him off. 'All you asked him was his fucking name,' he shouted. 'Everyone knows what his name is.'

'If the gallery could be cleared?' the judge said.

Rob took Stick's arm and pulled him towards the door, just as a tall wide man in a black suit came in, looking stern.

'We're going. He's going,' Rob said. 'He's just upset.' He got behind Stick and pushed him out of the courtroom.

'Seven minutes?' He should have found the camera, got his face right up against it and spat in the lens. 'They didn't ask him anything.'

'It was just a preliminary,' Rob said, keeping his voice soft. 'It's just the business part of it.' He was looking at Stick's face, but Stick kept his eyes fixed on the blue carpet. 'That's why they use a video link,' Rob said. 'To save them driving prisoners around. I'm sorry, I should have explained it all to you as well.'

'It's a fucking joke.'

'It's the way it works.' Rob looked over to where Mrs McKinley was staring out of the window at the building site below. 'You're not helping her,' he said quietly.

It felt like something breaking, as though he could almost hear the snap inside of him. 'Well, no one's fucking helping me either,' Stick said, his voice cracking, and even when Mrs McKinley turned from the window, her face pale and miserable, he couldn't stop his breath coming out too fast and his eyes blurring and his legs taking him out of the shitty court building into the too-bright afternoon, and his mouth saying, 'fuck you, fuck you, fuck all of you,' over and over again.

It started raining just as he ducked under the railings. The space looked the same. Empty. Full of shit. He kicked at a piece of broken plastic that might have been a bucket once, the kind kids build sandcastles with. It bounced across the ground and then settled on its side. He couldn't breathe straight. Couldn't think straight. The rain tapped a quiet rhythm on the leaves of a plant with purple cones of flowers, on the metal fence, on the piles of rubbish. Damp patches gathered across Stick's suit, the material pressing cold and wet against him. He wanted to climb out of his skin and go somewhere quiet, get rid of the noise inside his head, but he couldn't work out how.

Why would a man like Owen Lee – an ordinary, boring man with an ordinary, boring face, wearing an ordinary, boring suit – want to kill Mac? It didn't make any sense. Mac was just doing his Mac thing – being a knob, a bit pissed, a bit gobby. He was just being Mac. Stick kicked one of the dead handbags. It hardly moved, so he stamped on it instead, brought his foot down again and again into a squelch of fake brown leather.

It wasn't enough. Stick roamed over the wasteland, his breath still too fast and too loud, his hands shaking. In the far corner he found a building he hadn't noticed the first time, even sitting up on the window ledge with J. It was small – a brick shed – nearly the whole of the inside taken up with three metal boxes, each with grey mesh along the front, and inside, fans that looked like propellers. They were spinning, even though they couldn't be attached to anything any more. Just the wind, blowing through the broken-down entrance, turning the blades.

Stick kicked at the mesh, hard enough to hurt his foot. The noise echoed around the small space. He kicked it again. And again. And again. It didn't help. It made his body feel like his limbs weren't connected together right. The noise made his head hurt. But he carried on doing it, kicking and kicking until the sheet of mesh caved and split, and he could kick at the crappy propeller fan until it stopped turning, and then he could pull and kick at the blades. They wouldn't break, but he carried on trying, tugging until his arms ached and his hands hurt, and the sweat ran down his back, kicking with the heel of his foot, his toe, getting down on his knees and shoving at it with his shoulder. And all the time his breath like a steam train and his head roaring with white noise.

He didn't hear J calling him. She must have said something before she stepped inside the shed and put a hand on his shoulder, but he didn't hear her and her touch made him jump. A little cry came out of his mouth before he could stop it.

'Kieran? Stick?' Her hair was blue, the edges curled from the rain. Her eyelids were coated with shiny blue powder and a thin black line ran around each eye with a tiny flick where the lids met. 'Are you all right?' she asked, over the noise of the rain battering the metal roof. She was looking at him like she felt sorry for him. He didn't need her pity.

He turned back to the nearest fan and kicked it hard.

'I don't think that's going to help.'

Stick kicked the metal again.

'You'll break your foot.'

'Fuck off.'

She put her hand on his shoulder again. He pulled away from her. 'I said fuck off. Fuck off. Fuck off. Fuck off.'

J's eyes widened, her eyebrows lifting, but she stayed where she was. Behind her he could see the piles of rubbish and broken-down walls, and behind that, the angled warehouse roofs and the bulk of Strangeways. His insides were too big for his body – his heart and his lungs and his stomach blown up like balloons – he could feel them, squeezed against his skin so hard he was shaking with the pressure.

'Did it not go well?' she asked.

Stick laughed, a loud harsh laugh.

J nodded like she understood. But she didn't. She couldn't. No one could except Mac and he wasn't fucking there.

'They didn't ask him anything,' he said.

J nodded again.

'They asked his name and then said the trial's in fucking February. February?'

'They'll get all the evidence together, right? Get a good case against him.'

'He was supposed to—' Stick felt like the block of flats on the TV programme, the building collapsing from the inside in a storm of dust and rubble. It must have made a noise, but when they'd shown it – filmed from a distance – it had seemed silent: one minute whole, the next minute gone.

J pulled a pack of fags out of her coat pocket. 'Lawyers and police and all that takes for ages.' She held the pack out. 'You want one?'

Stick shook his head. He watched her light one, draw in the smoke and puff out three perfect white rings. It made him think of Mac, stood outside the bar dressed like a twat, smoking Mr Dunne's shitty cigar.

'I said fuck off, didn't I? I said fucking get out of here.' His voice cracked around the words but he kept on shouting because otherwise he'd cry.

But J didn't go. She stepped forwards, opened her arms and hugged him, her hair wet against his cheek. He tried to back away but his legs were already up against the metal box. He could feel the tears just beneath his skin. It helps to cry, his mum had said after the funeral, it can really help. But if he started he'd never fucking stop. He couldn't breathe with her holding on to him.

'Get off me!' He was just trying to get her to let go, but he ended up shoving her backwards and she stumbled, crashing into the door frame.

He opened his mouth to say, 'Sorry, I had to, did you hurt yourself?' but nothing came out. She held her shoulder and glared at him, waiting, but he couldn't speak. After a minute, she turned and walked out into the rain. He wanted to stop her, he wanted to say, *No, I'm sorry. I didn't mean— I never would— I've had a shit day. It wasn't what it was supposed to be. I'm sorry.* But he just stood and rubbed circles with his finger into the dusty surface of the smashed-up box and felt his chest heave, and then he squatted down, his hands cupping the top of his head, and held himself tight, rocking a little on his heels.

# 15

Saturday. One o'clock. That's what they'd agreed. She wouldn't come now, surely, but he'd said he'd be there, and maybe she'd realised he hadn't meant to push her like that.

There were four statues in Piccadilly Gardens. How did he not know? How did J not know? Or maybe she did, Stick thought, pacing from one to the other – the fat woman wearing the crown, the man with a book on his knee, the two others standing with their hands on their hips.

He picked the statue of the fat woman in the crown, because it was the one set furthest back into the gardens and seemed the most obvious. There were stone steps the whole way around it, crowded with people. Stick did a circuit. A pigeon sat on the woman's head, and a line of them queued up on the top of her throne, white streaks of shit all over.

It was busy. People with their hands full of shopping bags: Primark, Debenhams, Boots, Schuh. The fountains were going – gobs of water shooting up from the concrete like someone spitting, and the kids going mental for it. J wasn't there. Of course she wasn't.

Stick found a space on the stone steps and sat down. He watched two girls, twins – with their hair in thin black bunches – playing in the fountains. One kept holding out her hand to touch the water and then pulling it back. The other ran straight through the columns of water, laughing. They were both wearing the same dress – bright pink with little pinafore straps – and the same shoes – black and shiny. How weird, Stick thought, to have someone exactly the same as you. To look at another human and see yourself.

He waited until quarter past, then looped round the other statues again. Sat back on the steps and waited until half past. Quarter to. Two o'clock. Scanning the gardens for a glimpse of blue hair; a pair of skinny black jeans; thin brown arms.

Mac would have said he was a dick and deserved it. And then he'd have said, *Forget it. Forget her. Plenty more fish in the sea.* And if Stick told him he just wanted to apologise, to explain, Mac would say, *Get over it, move on, why bother?*

Stick had woken up that morning feeling like someone had washed out his insides with the cleaning stuff his mum used in the bathroom, the one that made your eyes sting just from the smell of it. All the pressure of the day before, the noise in his head, the feeling he was going to explode, all of it was gone and he was white and empty and weightless. Which meant that if J did turn up, he'd be able to explain. He'd be able to get the right words out in the right order, and she'd listen and nod and then smile at him, and he'd buy a bottle of vodka and they'd go back to the canal and drink it, and he'd ask her to tell him jokes, he'd lean his head against the rough stone wall and listen to her talk, with the geese honking and footsteps on the bridge over their heads.

At quarter past two his phone bleeped with a message and he fumbled it out of his pocket.

*Spoke 2 Shelia (psychic) 2day. Iain's doing just fine! Ur nan sends her luv. Looking 4ward 2 the big bday bash! Alan.*

Stick cupped his hand around the screen. He didn't want

anyone sitting near enough to read it to think that he was a nutjob too.

*Iain's doing just fine!* He read the line again, then glanced up at the people milling across Piccadilly Gardens in shorts and T-shirts and sandals. It struck him that they must all know someone who was dead too.

*Iain's doing just fine!* Is he? Are you? Stick fixed his eyes on the jumping fountains, the sun reflecting off the water as it leapt across the concrete. He wondered what Shelia looked like – if she was into floaty clothes and bangles and crystal balls, or maybe she wore a suit, had her hair cut short and her lips painted bright red. He shoved his phone back into his pocket, rested his chin on his hands and looked for J.

She didn't come. He waited until half past. Quarter to three. She wasn't going to come and he didn't have her phone number, or know where she lived. So that was that, as his nan would say. Move on.

At three, Stick stood and walked down Market Street, turned onto Spring Gardens and changed his euros back into pounds at the post office. He put the crisp banknotes and handful of change into his pocket and went to TK Maxx, where he chose the least girly writing paper he could find – creamy A5 sheets with zebra print around the edges. He stood in the queue, his eyes roaming the store, but she wasn't there either.

No harm in it, he told himself, sitting on the bus back up Rochdale Road. No harm in trying. Except he hated writing. Except she'd never read it. But fuck it.

*Dear J,*

He crossed out *Dear.*

*I waited in Piccadilly Gardens today.*

Which sounded like he was pissed off with her rather than

the other way round. He scrunched up the paper and took another sheet.

*J, I'm sorry. You were being nice and I was being a cunt.*

He reached for another piece of paper.

*J, I'm sorry. You were being nice and I was being an idiot. I went to court and Owen Lee wasn't even there, he was in prison and they had a camera and then a screen in the court so I didn't properly see him. The trial's not until February but I thought it would start then and I felt like I was going to explode, if you know what I mean.*

*I'm sorry*, he wrote again and then stared at the zebra stripes and his shitty handwriting, all cramped up and spiky-edged. *My mum always says 'sorry isn't good enough' but I can't think what else to say, except I'm an idiot, but you know that.*

*Stick*

He wrote his phone number underneath, then reread the note and added:

*PS. I like your hair blue.*

He folded the sheet in half, stuck it into an envelope with a picture of a zebra's face on the back flap and wrote *J* on the front. It looked lost in the middle of the paper so he drew a circle around it and then another circle around that.

Back at the wasteground, he picked up half a brick, stood on the back of the ripped leather chair and hauled himself onto the window ledge. There was a smear of cigarette ash in the mortar between two of the bricks, which was probably from weeks ago but it made him feel better all the same. He put the envelope over the ash and put the brick on top of it, making sure the J was visible.

*Think you're fucking Romeo*, is what Mac would say. *Think you're some kind of romantic.* Stick looked at the envelope and without warning the noise was back in his head, his skin hot, his heart leaping in his chest. He made himself jump down onto the chair and get out of there, before he ripped up the letter, before he smashed anything else, before he fucked up more than he already had.

# 16

The letter stayed there a whole week. Stick kept going back to check, and each time the envelope was softer, grubbier, still unread. And then the weekend after he'd left it, it disappeared.

Stick climbed up onto the window ledge to make sure. No letter. It meant nothing, he told himself. Some scumbag had probably found it and would start texting him porn any minute. Or a bird had picked it up in its beak and dropped it somewhere. Stick straddled his legs over the sill and peered left then right but couldn't see the envelope. And then he saw the piece of glass sat on top of the half-brick. Not just any piece of glass, but one of those that has been smoothed off by the sea, all the sharp edges gone, the surface scuffed by sand into a pale, opaque green.

He was going soft in the head. But still he pocketed the glass, and when he got home he put it on the table in his room next to the writing paper with the zebra pattern, and then he picked it up and held it in his left hand as he wrote another letter.

*J. Thanks for the present. If it was you. If not, ignore that.*

He nearly screwed the paper up again, but then he opened

his left hand and looked at the glass, which had turned darker with the sweat from his palm, and carried on.

*It made me think about the sea. You said you liked the sea? I want to invite you to Blackpool, for my birthday. Will you come? Saturday, 10 a.m., Piccadilly station, outside Thorntons. I'll pay. Stick.*

He folded the paper in half, wrote *J* on an envelope and circled it twice, then unfolded the paper and wrote:

*PS. It's my 18th. I'm not a loser with no mates, but I was going to be in Spain, with Mac. He's 18 three days after me. We'd got big plans. Not big big plans. Beer and beaches and nightclubs, that kind of thing. Anyway, we're getting Chinese at mine Saturday night. You could come (my nan's boyfriend is mental – be warned).*

Mac had been desperate to turn eighteen. *Responsibility, respect,* he'd say, puffing out his chest. *No more fake ID cards and staring down bar staff, and people thinking they can pay you shit-all for working as hard as anyone else.* Stick couldn't help thinking he'd rather be back at school. Not that he liked school – he didn't – but at least it was pretty straightforward. At least you didn't have to make decisions the whole time.


He left the letter in the same place as before and then hung around for a bit, but J didn't show. He wandered over to the brick shed and looked at the smashed-in metal boxes. Two of the fans still turned lazily. He'd managed to damage the third so it stayed stuck in one position.

Stick rubbed at his eyes. He hadn't been sleeping – spent the nights lying in bed staring at the crack across his bedroom ceiling, and the dust on the light shade, and the cobweb in the corner that swayed sometimes as if someone was blowing it. As soon as he closed his eyes he'd start thinking about Mac – blood staining his shirt; or Owen Lee sitting at the table, his eyes blank; or J holding her shoulder, her eyes tearing up.

When he got back home the house smelt of chocolate cake. His mum was at the sink, washing out the mixing bowl.

'I thought I'd make two,' she said. 'And then you can take one over to Iain's mother. What do you think?'

Stick shrugged.

'It's nice to keep in touch with her, love. That kind of thing's important. And chocolate cake's comforting, don't you think?' She lifted the bowl onto the draining board and turned round. 'Are you at your dad's tomorrow?'

Stick pulled a face. 'Might not go.'

'Has he talked to you about—' She narrowed her eyes like she was trying to read his mind.

'I'm not selling double glazing.'

'I thought it was a great offer. Training. A decent salary. Local.'

He was supposed to be in Spain, working in a bar, getting a tan. He was supposed to be enjoying himself.

'You could try it out,' she said.

Stick shook his head. He waited for the lecture – you're eighteen next week; you need to have a plan; you can't just mooch around here for the rest of your life; most people don't get an opportunity like that; look what's happening in Greece, Kieran, you should count yourself lucky – but it didn't come. Instead his mum took two chocolate sponges out of the oven, stuck a knife in each to check they were done and turned them onto a metal cooling rack.

'Did you make the appointment?' Stick asked.

His mum tipped icing sugar into a sieve and shook it over a clean bowl, the sugar coming down in fine white drifts.

'With the GP?' Stick said.

'Oh.' She laughed, like that would make his question go away.

'Mum?'

'I haven't had a moment, love. I'll do it. I will.' She dropped a spoonful of butter into the bowl and started stirring it into the icing sugar. 'These'll be cool enough to ice in a minute. Will you drop one round? Give her my love?'

Stick turned and went up to his room without saying anything. He opened the drawer in the narrow desk he used to do his homework on and pulled out the roll of banknotes he'd changed at the post office. A hundred was a good amount, he reckoned, counting out five twenties and putting the rest back.


Stick's mum put the cake in a cardboard box, told him to hold it at the bottom and watch where he was walking. Outside, the little kid from next door was wandering about in his pants, chewing on a piece of toast, but there was no one else around. Stick walked slowly. The cake smelt good. The sun was warm on his face. Stick thought about Alan's text message. *Iain's doing just fine!* He imagined ringing Mrs McKinley's doorbell and Mac answering, grabbing the cake out of Stick's hands and running off to cut himself a massive slice.


Mrs McKinley answered the door. She didn't look good – her eyes bloodshot, her hair greasy. She was in a tracksuit that was too big for her. It might even have been one of Mac's.

'Kieran!' She held her arms out wide. He could smell the booze on her breath when she leaned in to kiss him.

'Cake,' he said. 'Mum made it.'

Mrs McKinley stared into the box.

'You said everyone kept bringing food, I know. But—'

'That's lovely.' She looked up at him. 'Isn't that lovely?'

Stick followed her into the flat. It looked like someone had broken in and turned the place over – the living room covered with Mac's stuff: clothes and shoes, DVDs and Xbox games, wires and headphones. Two black dumb-bells sat on the black leather armchair – *I'm going to get fit, Stick Man*, Mac had said; it had lasted a week if that. Five phone chargers. Who needed five phone chargers?

'That boy had so much stuff. You wouldn't believe.' Mac's ma waved her arm around the room, shaking her head. 'I can't stand it,' she said. 'Everywhere. He's everywhere.' Her voice cracked as she spoke. 'I thought—'

After the fire, two guys had come round and repainted Sophie's room, a tiny box room next to Stick's with a narrow window looking out over the school car park. The insurance paid for it. Pale creamy walls. A new white carpet. But the smell of smoke was still there, under the smell of new paint. And there was the faintest of smudges in the corner above the window which no one ever mentioned, or painted over. They got a new bed, wardrobe and bedside cabinet on the insurance too. After the men had finished, Stick and his mum and dad went upstairs and stood in the room, which smelt of paint and carpet and plastic wrapping and smoke, and said nothing.

Weeks later Stick had wandered in, bored after school one day, and found a photo of Sophie in a large silver frame propped on the bedside table, loads of her stuff piled around it. Her toy dog, black with smoke; her shoes; a coat button; hat; dummy; the bracelet their nan had given her when she was born. He'd stood and stared at his sister and then gone downstairs and asked his mum what happened to people when they died, and she stared at him and shook her head and said, 'I don't know, love. I'm sorry, I don't know.'

Mac's ma stood with her arms loose by her sides, crying. 'It's so quiet these days,' she said. 'With Iain not— There's just that dog upstairs. Barking fit to drive you mad.'

'Do you want a slice of cake, Mrs McKinley?' Stick asked.

'I need a drink,' she said.

'Tea? I can make tea?'

'A proper drink.' She looked at him, wild-eyed. 'Would you get me one? Just a nip of vodka. It's in the fridge.'

Stick escaped to the kitchen, put the cake on the side and poured out two large measures of vodka. As he went back into the cluttered living room, he thought of Sophie's room and all the things lined up on the bedside table. They weren't there any more and he couldn't remember when they had gone. He hadn't asked and his mum hadn't said anything. Maybe she'd just decided: enough. Maybe she still had everything, in a box under her bed. Maybe it was the same with not going to the graveyard – she didn't want to look at it any more.

'What would he think of me?' Mrs McKinley held the glass up towards the window as if there might be something to see in it other than vodka. 'Drinking in the afternoon.'

'He drank in the afternoon,' Stick said, and she almost smiled – he saw it, the smallest twitch of her lips.

'I did his room.' She let out a little hiccup and pushed her fingertips against her lips like she'd said something wrong.

'What do you mean, did?' Stick moved towards the hall- way. Mrs McKinley didn't try to stop him; she just stood holding her glass, staring at nothing.

He shouldn't have been surprised, but he heard the noise he made when he opened the door.

The room was empty.

Not just clear shelves and a bare wardrobe. It was no-shelves, no-wardrobe, no-fucking-carpet empty. A grubby square of a room. The window had been stripped of its curtains. The ceiling felt too low and the bare lightbulb too small. The floor was hardboard, the glue which had stuck the carpet down splashed in big, dirty globs across it. It made him think of J's place near the prison – the floor warped with rain and underneath it all those neat blocks of wood too bloated to fit together any more.

When he went back through, she wouldn't look at him.

'Where's the furniture?' he said. 'Mrs McKinley? The furniture?'

'They'll take it away,' she said, her voice brittle.

'Who are they?' Stick couldn't stop his voice from shaking.

She waved one hand as though it didn't really matter, then looked up. 'I did give you his shoes?'

Stick nodded, and she smiled as though everything was as it should be. The dog upstairs started barking. *Yap yap yap*, pause, *yap yap yap*, pause.

'Is this because you're broke?' he said, as calmly as he could.

She frowned.

'You're skint and so you're selling his stuff?'

She shook her head.

'I'm going to put it back. I'm putting it back, Mrs McKinley. He's not been dead two minutes. You can't do this.' It was like he'd drunk three cans of Red Bull – the energy fizzing through his body. He couldn't stand still.

Everything had been piled into her bedroom: the wardrobe; chest of drawers; black-and-silver TV stand; the bed dismantled and propped against the wall. The carpet had been sliced into strips, rolled up and shoved into bin bags.

He dragged the bags back into Mac's room, pulled out the carpet and unrolled the pieces one by one. It was like a jigsaw, except that nothing quite fitted together and he ended up with patches of wood showing and bits of carpet overlaid on top of each other.

He'd replaced the bed and the TV stand and had his arms around the wardrobe, walking it down the corridor, when he saw Mrs McKinley standing in the doorway to the living room.

'I took the carpet up,' she said, and rubbed her fingertips together. 'All those spiky bits round by the skirting boards.' The dog was still barking. 'And the dust, coming up when I pulled it.' She kept on rubbing her fingers. 'It's heavy, carpet.'

'I'm putting this back,' he said, pointing at the wardrobe. 'I'm going to put everything back.'

She shrugged, like she didn't care either way, and wandered into the living room. Stick put everything back the way it used to be. Bed by the window, TV against the wall, wardrobe in the corner opposite the door. He was sweating by the time he'd finished.

When he went back into the living room, Mrs McKinley was perched on the edge of the sofa, her glass and the vodka bottle on the coffee table in front of her, next to a pile of old schoolbooks and a toy plastic giraffe. Stick took the twenty-pound notes out of his pocket.

'I brought this for you.' He held out the money and Mrs McKinley looked at it like it was still in euros, or some other currency she'd never seen before. 'It was for the trip,' Stick said. 'I thought you might— Well, I don't need it now, do I? Go on. Take it.'

She kept shaking her head, kept saying, 'No, no, I can't do that. No.' And then she started picking up things of Mac's – stuffed toys and Xbox games and old T-shirts, and saying, 'You must take something. You must take whatever you want. There's so much stuff.' And it was Stick's turn to say, 'No, no, I can't. I've really got to go, Mrs McKinley.'

Before he went, Stick walked down the corridor and stood by Mac's bedroom door. It looked nothing like Mac's bedroom, just looked like a shit, square room with shit IKEA furniture and a slashed-up carpet. It looked like no one lived there. Stick put the twenty-pound notes in a neat pile on the pillow and left.

# 17

Mac would think he was an idiot, leaving messages under bricks and then standing outside Thorntons at Piccadilly station like a spare part, twenty minutes early, on his own birthday, waiting for some crazy blue-haired girl who wasn't going to turn up. He'd shaved, even though he didn't much need to; sprayed on half a can of deodorant.

After ten minutes he went into Thorntons and bought J one of those chocolate mice, with the peppermint insides, its face long and sleek underneath the plastic wrapping. As he came out he saw her, at the far end of the station, and felt his stomach twist. Her hair was pink again, tied up in a ponytail, and she had a black canvas rucksack slung over her shoulder. Stick put the chocolate mouse in his pocket and left his hand in there. He stared at the floor, at the departure boards, at the people sitting on the benches and coming up the elevators – anywhere, so she didn't see him waiting for her, so he didn't look too keen.

J stopped in front of him. 'Hi.'

He couldn't tell if she was still pissed off with him. 'Oh, hi.' He tried to sound cool, like he hadn't really been expecting her to come.

'Blackpool,' she said. 'Good choice.'

Stick held back a smile. 'I've got cash,' he said. 'Saved it up for the trip, but—'

She nodded. 'Rock, candyfloss, doughnuts, rides.' And then she patted at her rucksack. 'I brought you a birthday present too. But—' She held up one hand. 'Not until we're there.'

On the train, they sat opposite each other at a table sticky with someone else's spilt drink, J going backwards because she said she liked it – seeing where she'd already been, not knowing what was coming up. They chugged through the city. Oxford Road. Deansgate. Castlefield. Past the Beetham Tower and the courts, then east towards Salford – stretches of scrubby grass, bigger roads, the three tower blocks on Rochdale Road.

'You got my—' Stick blurted at last.

J nodded.

'You should get a phone.'

She raised her eyebrows.

'I felt like someone out of a play or something,' Stick said and she smiled then, her face softening. 'I am sorry,' he barged on. 'I didn't—'

J shook her head. 'Doesn't matter,' she said. 'Means we're square, anyway.'

Stick took the chocolate mouse out of his pocket. It looked small and cheap. 'I got you a mouse,' he said and put it on the table in front of her.

J glanced up at him. 'Thanks.' She pulled off the wrapper and nibbled the mouse's nose.

Stick sat and watched her eat it, bite by tiny bite, the landscape changing from streets and warehouses to fields, with hedges and sheep. He felt a lightness, like when you get the swing up high enough to leave your stomach behind for a second. J finished the mouse, licked her fingers one by one and then stood to push the window open. The train sucked in the air and threw it across their faces and they sat listening to the racket of the wheels against the tracks.

'To the sea,' J said, pulling Stick through the bright train station hall out onto the street.

She wore denim shorts with frayed bits of thread hanging down her legs. A black vest top, loose enough to keep showing her bra. Stick walked behind her, noticing how the skin met in dark creases at the backs of her knees, listening to the seagulls screeching overhead.

Eighteen. He was eighteen. He straightened his shoulders and put a slight side-to-side in his step, his shoulders shifting left right, left right.

'You're a man now,' his mum had said that morning, pushing a bacon sandwich towards him. She'd sounded like she was trying hard not to let on that she was sad.

He followed J, past a huge pub with photos of the inside on the outside. Past an electrics shop, its window crammed with toasters and kettles and lightbulbs and TVs showing men with T-shirts wrapped round their heads, guns to their shoulders, running along a dusty road. Past banks, charity shops, a nightclub shut up for the daytime. Posters for body piercing and karaoke and cabaret shows, half of them ripped so you had to piece together leftover bits of words to work out what they were about. Past hoardings with pictures of people in posh flats – a man in a kitchen holding a plate of pasta; two kids sitting on a white rug. Past more charity shops and more banks, Blackpool Tower stretching up on their left. And then there, at the end of the street, was the sea.

Stick stopped and stared. A thin stretch of beach – grey pebbles and a glimpse of yellow sand, and then nothing but water, the waves curling into long white lines, sending up flecks of spray.

'Smell it,' J said, drawing in a breath through her nostrils.

'Smells of chips.'

'No, under that.'

Stick tried to smell it. Maybe there was something – salty, a bit grubby, like wet socks.

They went all the way to the beach and J plonked herself down on the pebbles, her bag between her knees. She pulled out a silver Thermos flask and held it towards Stick. 'You like getting high?' She grinned.

'On tea?' Stick said, sitting next to her as she poured brown liquid into the flask's lid and handed it to him.

'Mushrooms,' she said. 'My own recipe. Happy birthday.'

Stick sniffed at the liquid. It looked like tea but smelt like sweaty feet. 'I don't drink tea.'

'It's not tea.'

'It smells bad.'

'So hold your nose.'

Stick looked out towards the sea and thought about his mum, sat across from him at the breakfast table, biting her fingernails. He lifted the cup to his lips and drank it in one bitter gulp, screwed up his eyes and stuck out his tongue.

J laughed, took the cup back and poured herself some. 'Here's to the sea,' she said, drank it in one and wiped her lips with the back of her hand. 'Let's get doughnuts before we start feeling it.'

'How long does it take?'

J shrugged. 'Twenty minutes? Come on.'

Stick bought them doughnuts from a kiosk, and they went down the pier to eat them. J perched on the back of a long metal bench, her feet on the mouldy-looking wooden seat.

She didn't look safe and Stick wanted, for a moment, to take her arm and hold her steady.

She ate her doughnut the same way she ate the chocolate mouse. Stick sat next to her and swallowed his in two mouthfuls. Now he could smell it – the salty, dark-green edge of the sea.

'Every time we came to Blackpool I'd buy loads of rock and take it home in a big plastic bag and then eat it in like two days. Except I'd always keep one bit. One for each birthday. I've still got them,' J said. A seagull landed on the ground by their feet and eyed them. She aimed a kick at it but it didn't even flinch. 'They're all faded and sticky. Can't throw them away though.' J chucked the end of her doughnut to the seagull, who snatched it up like she might change her mind and take it back. 'I'm like my dad,' she said. 'Except not as bad.'

'He saves sweets?'

'He saves everything. He doesn't just save everything, he spends his life buying shit we don't need. Seriously, our house is so full of crap you can't move. Mum says it's because he grew up with nothing, but I reckon he's just mental.'

Stick looked out across the water to another pier, with a Ferris wheel and funfair rides perched at the sea end.

'My nan's boyfriend's a spiritualist,' he said.

'What's that then?'

'He's got mates who talk to dead people. Do you reckon that's for real?' He kept his eyes fixed on the horizon.

'I think it's bollocks,' J said. 'Dead people are dead, aren't they? I mean – I don't mean to be nasty about it, but—'

'No, you're right.' Stick picked bits of paint off the bench and flicked them onto the pier. 'It's bollocks.'

He stared up at the sky. Pale blue. Almost not blue at all.

Layers of clouds at the horizon, one wedged up against the other. He had a sudden, wild urge to tip himself backwards off the edge of the railings. It was a long way down. He'd break his neck. Have to be dragged out. He wondered if J would jump in after him.

'How's being eighteen?' J asked.

Stick took the last doughnut from the bag, bit it in half and handed the other piece to her. 'I don't know,' he said. 'Same as being seventeen. Except you gave me that dodgy tea.'

'You feeling it yet?'

Stick closed his eyes and listened to the sea bashing at the edges of the pier below. 'Nope.'

'Let's go back.' She pointed towards the beach. 'There's too many people here. It's better to be away from people. First time.'


It started with a pressure at the centre of his forehead, like someone was pushing their fingertip against his skin. Just that for a while. Then a bubbling sense of anticipation.

'You need to stay calm when it comes,' J said. 'Think good things. Don't think about your mate, seriously.'

They were sat, side by side, where the pebbles stopped and the sand started. The air had a cool edge and J had taken a loose khaki-green jacket from her bag and hung it around her shoulders.

Stick blinked. Blinked again. There was a layer of green, blue and red blobs over the sea, over the sand, over his hands when he held them in front of his eyes. He could see, but everything looked like it was on a screen and there was something wrong with the signal. When he closed his eyes the colours were still there. When he opened his eyes they were still there, but squarer.

'I can—' His mouth was dry. He moved his tongue around it to try and make it feel right.

J started laughing.

'It's red and green and blue,' Stick said.

J nodded and carried on laughing. 'Look.' She pointed. 'Like someone's drawn the waves on, with crayon.'

Stick looked. All he could see were the coloured squares and the waves moving in, out, in.

'Like a kid's drawn them,' J said.

Stick looked at her. 'Your hair.' He reached out to touch it. Felt like silk. Felt like Babs's fur. 'It's so pink,' he said. Like paint fresh out of the tin. He could look at her hair forever.

J sat and let him touch her hair and after a while – he had no idea how long – she lay down on the sand, and he lay down next to her. He could hear the sea, the edges of the waves bubbling over the sand, towards them, away from them, towards them, away.

J pointed at the sky.

It was the bluest blue he'd ever seen. He kept looking, at the blue, blue sky and the thin white clouds. After a while, the whole thing started to breathe. Stick stared. The sky breathed. In, out, in, out, moving like someone's chest when they're sleeping, the clouds moving too, slipping up and down, up and down. Stick breathed with it. When he stretched his arms to each side, like wings, his fingers brushed J's jacket – soft as candyfloss. It felt as though if he pressed, his hand would go all the way into it.

'We could go to Spain,' Stick said.

'Eat paella,' J said. Her voice seemed to come from directly above him. The sound of it tasted like gingerbread.

'Get a flat.'

'Learn to dive.' She flung her hand upwards and grains of sand flew out, drawing thin yellow lines through the air. 'I've always wanted to go diving.' Her voice sounded like it was in a tunnel now, echoing off the edges.

The squares were still there, but they'd faded, or he'd got used to them. It just looked like someone had put a fishing net in front of his face. He had a sudden, clear memory of climbing into Sophie's cot, the two of them jumping up and down against the wooden bars and squealing, his mum laughing. He could feel it – the soft, squeaky plastic mat, the hard wooden bars. He could smell the soapy-sweet baby wipes and Sophie's skin, sleepy and hot.

The sadness was like a weight dropped into water. He felt it ripple out towards his head, his stomach, his fingertips.

J leaned over him. 'You all right?' Her eyes were so dark he almost couldn't look at them.

Stick reached up and touched her skin, then snatched his hand away and looked at it. He showed it to J and she laughed and then he laughed too, but it didn't stop the sadness rippling out again, his limbs heavy as water.

'What are you going to do?' he said. His lips felt thick, the words smudged between them, like someone had punched him in the mouth.

J lay down and stretched her arms up over her head. 'Watch the sky,' she said.

Stick closed his eyes. He could see red pulses of light on the backs of his eyelids. 'No, like afterwards,' he said. 'Later.'

'Astronaut,' J said. 'Ballet dancer. Racing driver. Nuclear physicist.'

Stick stared at the sky, and realised after a while that its breathing was in time with his own heartbeat. *Dum-dum, dum-dum, dum-dum.*

———

166

When it had worn off, they wandered around the town, eating sticks of pink-and-yellow rock and drinking cans of warm lager. J took him to Coral Island: dark, low-ceilinged, rammed with slot machines. It was too bright, too noisy, too crowded. Sweat and skin, tattoos and toenails. The sound of falling coins. Kids with plastic guns and stuffed toys, pretend cars rocking in front of TV screens, a woman in a wheelchair feeding two-pences into the coin waterfall. Stick couldn't stand it. He dragged J back to the beach, but that was packed too – kids screeching, the sea dotted with the bobbing heads of swimmers. He could feel his face starting to burn and something like panic simmering in his chest.

'So, Chinese tonight,' J said. 'Cashew chicken, chilli beef, prawn crackers, sweet-and-sour pork.'

Stick picked up a stone and threw it, picked up another and threw that. 'Isn't there any more tea?'

J took the flask out of her bag and shook it. 'You want to go home tripping?' she said.

It was three o'clock. They had to be back by seven – should be leaving already. Stick thought about his mum setting the dinner table. Blowing up balloons like he was still five years old. He thought about the sky turned bright blue and J's eyes like jewels. 'It'll be fine.' He reached out his hand and J shrugged, poured another cup, which Stick drank, lukewarm and sour.

They walked, side by side but not touching, far up the beach, trying to get away from the families and the kids and the ice-cream trolleys. They could do this forever, Stick thought. Just walk and walk.

'Where would we end up?' he said. 'If we just carried on.'

J shaded her eyes with one hand. 'We'd get back here, wouldn't we? If you kept on walking and went the whole of the way around, you'd get back to here.'

He wanted, suddenly, to do that with her. 'It'd take fucking ages,' he said.

'And you'd end up back where you started.'

'Just older.'

J laughed.

'You're pretty when you laugh,' Stick said and then blushed.

J stopped and looked at him. He kept walking and after a minute he felt her hand on his sleeve. When he turned, she was standing close. Too close.

'What?' he said, stepping back. She stepped forwards. He could see the pores in her skin, a tiny dark mole on her right cheek, the line of her lips, the silver stud. 'I'm not going to kiss you,' he said.

'Why not?'

'You punched me in the face last time.'

She smiled without opening her mouth. 'Yeah, sorry.'

'You always punch people who try to kiss you?'

She looked him in the eyes. 'Recently, yes.' She dropped his gaze and pushed her foot into the sand. 'There was this other guy, and—' She shrugged. 'He was a cock.'

'Right.'

'But you're not a cock,' she said.

Before Stick could think it through and decide not to, he put one hand on her cheek and kissed her. She tasted of lager and mushroom tea and doughnuts. Her lips and the tip of her nose were cold against his face. He pulled back, but not far, and looked her in the eyes. Her eyelashes were short and black, her eyebrows plucked thin. She held his gaze but he couldn't tell what she was thinking.

Stick dropped his palm from J's cheek and reached for her hand.

'Your hands are cold,' he said.

'Always are.' She closed her fingers through his. 'Shall we walk a bit more?'

Stick nodded and they started walking, matching their steps to each other, her hand warming against his, waiting for the mushrooms to kick in again.

# 18

They were late. Really late. The train coming into Piccadilly station gone nine o'clock. Both of them groggy and silent.

'You'd better not come,' Stick said. 'She's going to kill me.'

'You don't want back-up?' J asked, pulling her rucksack onto her shoulders.

Stick shook his head. He'd missed so many calls by the time he'd thought to look at his phone, he'd just turned it off.

'How do I find you though?' he said, following her along the platform under the high curved roof. 'I can't spend my life leaving you love letters.'

He saw her smile before she caught it and felt himself blush. 'I mean—'

'I'll give you the house number,' she said, and reached into her bag for a pen. She wrote it in neat black numbers on the back of his hand, and then her address below.

'Don't wash it off.' She stood on tiptoes and kissed him, her tongue darting into his mouth and then retreating. He reached his hand around her back and she let him draw her towards him. For a moment. Then she pulled away and said, 'Go on,' and pushed him gently out of the station door and into the cool city air.

———

It was almost ten by the time he got to the estate – the street lights on, the sky dimming towards black.

He didn't take the cut-through down Paget Street; didn't even turn his head to look at it; didn't let himself think about Mac the whole way home.

He slowed down as he got to his road. His chest felt packed full – as though a wrong move would make everything spill out. He never looked at his house. Never thought twice about it really. But now, in this half-light, it felt unfamiliar. The bricks looked too neat, too flat, like a machine had built it, not a person. The paint on the window frames was peeling, dark bits of wood showing under the black. The curtains were open, the front room alight, and he could just see the top of someone's head.

Stick stood on the doorstep and waited a moment before he put his key in the lock. He imagined the sea creeping up to the front door, coming through the gaps and into the hallway, turning the carpet dark, peeling the wallpaper away from the walls, making the lights fizz, and then rising slowly, slowly up the stairs. He imagined letting himself go into it, how his body would lift with the water.

His mum and dad stood in the living-room doorway, her eyes red, his furious. The house smelt of Chinese takeaway.

'We were about to call the police,' his dad said.

'Well?' His mum had her arms folded, lips thin.

He tried to brazen it out. Stepped forwards with a 'Hi, Mum,' and went to kiss her cheek, but she slapped him, hard, a sharp *thwack* of skin on skin and his face burning with it.

'Mandy!' Stick's nan was at the door now. Behind her he could see Alan, hovering. A plastic *Happy Birthday* banner was pinned up over the fireplace with coloured balloons hanging down either side of it. A small pile of parcels sat on the glass coffee table in amongst stained dinner plates and beer cans.

His mum grabbed hold of his chin. 'Look at me.' She'd been drinking red wine. He could see it on her lips. 'Are you high?'

'No.' Stick twisted away from her.

'You are. You're high.'

'I'm not.' He wanted to go to bed, stare at the ceiling and think about J. He pushed past his nan into the living room, picked up a prawn cracker and bit into it. There was an envelope with his dad's writing on it propped next to the presents. It'd be money, same as every year. Couldn't be arsed to think of something I'd like, Stick said to Mac once. Mac punched him on the arm and said, 'Shut up. He used to buy you all them toys and you just burnt them. You'd hate whatever he got you if it wasn't money, and he isn't stupid.' He had a point.

'Party poppers,' his mum shouted from the hallway. 'I bought bloody party poppers.'

Stick looked at the numbers on his hand. He wanted to call J now and say let's run away. They could follow the railway line back to those green fields, with the cows and sheep and the hedges and the tiny stone houses.

'A phone call, Kieran. All you needed to do was call. I'm late. I'm sorry.' His mum was in the living room now, hands locked on her hips. 'I thought I'd brought you up to have some manners.'

Stick caught Alan's eye, who gave him a ghost of a smile.

'I don't have any credit,' he muttered.

'You don't have any credit?' She stared at him. 'You don't have any credit?' It was as though every word puffed her up, bigger and bigger. 'I don't see what I'm supposed to do, Kieran.' She stopped and shook her head, and he thought she was going to soften, say *I'm sorry, love, you're having a hard time, I know*, but instead she walked over to the fireplace and stabbed at one of the balloons with her fingernail. It was like a bullet fired, the house shocked into silence.

'There,' his mum said, and started crying.

Stick's dad put his arm around her and pulled her towards him. Stick ate the rest of the prawn cracker, took another.

'An apology?' his dad said, looking at Stick. 'Maybe you could see fit to give your mother – all of us – an apology?'

Stick bit into the cracker and stared at his feet. Mac's red trainers. *We'll do it in style*, Mac had said, sat down by the canal, waving his arms as he spoke. *Fried breakfast. Hire a moped and drive about, or get one of those four-wheeled beach buggies. Spend the afternoon on the beach with some cold beers. And then champagne!* Stick had pulled a face and said he didn't like champagne. *Champagne*, Mac had insisted. *And steak*, he'd said, *with those thin, twisty little chips, and then chocolate pudding with strawberries and whipped cream and little drizzles of sauce on the side of the plate. You only turn eighteen once*, he'd said. And now Stick was eighteen and Mac wouldn't ever be. Not in three days' time, not ever.

His dad coughed and Stick looked up.

'We're all waiting,' his dad said.

That snap again, like a ligament breaking. 'You fucking apologise,' Stick said.

'I beg your pardon?' His dad took his arm away from Stick's mum's shoulder.

'I said, why don't you fucking apologise?' Stick kept his voice and his stare as steady as he could and felt a prickle of satisfaction when he saw the realisation on his dad's face.

'I haven't done anything wrong,' he said, quietly.

'Right.' Stick nodded. 'You hear that, Mum? No harm done. He just forgot to come home one day. Could have happened to anyone.'

Stick's nan and Alan started gathering up plates and foil containers; they both slunk out towards the kitchen.

'Kieran, this is not the time,' his dad started.

'No, it never is, is it?'

Another bang, as loud as the first. Stick stared at his mum and the two limp bits of coloured rubber behind her.

'I will not have this. You.' She pointed to Stick. 'Upstairs.'

Stick shook his head. 'So you're on his side now?'

'There are no sides,' his dad said.

'Upstairs.' Stick's mum pointed at the door.

'I'm eighteen!'

'Well, you're not acting that way.'

Stick's head throbbed like it could burst as easily as the balloons. He needed Mac to sit him on the sofa, put a can of beer in his hand and turn the TV on. He needed Mac to punch him in the arm and tell him to get the fuck over himself.

'I'm out of here,' he said, lifting the car keys from his pocket. 'I'm going.'

'Look, we're all tired and emotional, we just need to sit down like grown-ups and talk about this,' his dad said. His cheeks were bright red and he was patting Stick's mum's arm like she was a cat.

Stick shook his head, a laugh snaking up from his stomach to his mouth. 'You can't stop me.' He pushed past his dad into the hallway, his mum following close behind.

'You're high!' she said. 'You are not driving.'

'I said, you can't stop me.'

'I can call the police.' She picked up her phone from the hallway table.

'Everyone just needs to calm down.' Stick's dad held up both arms, like a drowning man.

174

'Bet you wish you were back with your other family, don't you?' Stick said.

'Kieran, you're acting like a child. Your mum's right, you need to go upstairs, sleep off whatever you've been taking and then perhaps you'll see fit to apologise to everyone in the morning.'

Stick opened the front door. He looked back at his parents, his mum standing close to his dad, his hand back around her shoulder, Stick's nan and Alan hovering behind them. They didn't need him and he definitely didn't need them. He half ran down the steps onto the street.

As he approached the shit Ford Fiesta, Alan appeared behind him and snatched the car keys.

Stick held out his hand. 'Give them back.'

Alan shook his head. 'Tomorrow,' he said, then walked to his own car and opened the back door. 'Hop in.'

'Fuck off.'

'Come on.' Alan sounded like he was on some shit chat show. 'You've been taking what, mushrooms? LSD? We don't need any accidents. You can stay at ours, sleep it off. Tomorrow's a new day.'

Stick felt suddenly exhausted. 'Fine.' He got in and slammed the door.

Stick's nan got in too, fussed with her seat belt before twisting around and looking at Stick. He stared at J's writing on his hand, and she turned back without saying anything. They drove to Beswick in silence, Stick gazing out of the window, narrowing his eyes until the street lights and the car lights blurred.

# 19

It was a stand-off. His mum calling and Stick not answering. His dad calling and Stick not answering. Neither of them calling. His mum calling again. And his nan in the middle, saying no, I won't get involved, you can stay for a week, OK two, but then you've got to sort this out yourselves. Alan saying it was like harbouring a fugitive and trying to get Stick to come to his Monday art class – it's fabulous, he said, we're just free, we paint what we like. He came home the first week with an ugly painting of Manchester, the buildings grey and black, their edges at weird angles; the second week with what he called a still life – a pile of fruit on a bumpy tablecloth.

The first two times he called J, no one answered. The third time, a man with a faint African accent picked up the phone.

'Is J there?' Stick stumbled over his words.

'Who?'

'J?'

'You have the wrong house.' He put the phone down before Stick could say anything more.

He waited five minutes and then called again. This time J picked up.

'Stick? Sorry.' She was speaking in little more than a whisper.

'Is J not your name then?'

'Course it is. How did it go, the birthday dinner thing?'

Stick was in his nan's spare room. Everything was cream-coloured – the thick puffy duvet, the bedside table, the lamp and its tassled shade, the wallpaper with its pattern of huge pale ferns. 'Not brilliant,' he said. 'I'm at my nan's.'

'As in living at your nan's?'

'Yeah,' Stick said. He hated talking on the phone. As soon as you stopped speaking the silence started, and he never quite knew how to get out of it. 'It's Mac's birthday,' he said. 'We were going to hire mopeds.'

Another silence. And then J said, 'Do you want to come round?'

'Your dad—?'

'He's going out. Come in an hour.'

Stick caught himself smiling.


J lived in a little bungalow in Cheetham Hill with plaster gnomes and dogs arranged in rows on the front lawn. Inside, it was like an antique shop, stuffed full of crystal rabbits and painted cherubs and plates with pictures of animals, and glass bottles with tiny glass stoppers. It made him nervous he'd make too big a move, too wide a gesture, and send the whole thing tumbling, but she laughed and said not to worry – none of it meant anything, none of it was important.

Her room looked like it wasn't part of the same house. Each wall was painted a different colour: black, purple, green, orange; the ceiling bright blue and dotted with glow-in-the-dark stars. A single bed with plain white sheets. A desk with books and papers stacked neatly around an old-looking laptop. A white wardrobe. A white chest of drawers with a rainbow of nail varnish across its top. Black carpet, black curtains. The walls empty except for an unframed mirror above the chest of drawers and a photo of a blonde woman Blu-Tacked up next to the bed.

J stood by the wardrobe. He wanted to kiss her, but when he stepped forwards she held her hand up and said, 'He was more than just a dickhead.'

'What?'

She hitched her shoulders towards her ears. 'My ex. He was—' She scratched at the top of her arm. 'He was – I don't know, a bully?' She glanced at Stick and then looked back at the floor. 'He put a thing on my phone so he always knew where I was.'

Stick backed away and sat on the bed. 'What thing?'

She shrugged. 'Like a tracker. He could see where I was on a map on his phone.'

'But why would—'

'I had to text him where I was, who I was with, what I was doing.'

He wanted to put his hand on hers so she'd stop scratching, but he stayed where he was.

'He'd flip out if I talked to other blokes.' She shrugged. 'It was shit.'

Stick didn't know what to say.

'So that's why,' she said after an age. 'Why I punched you that first time. Why I don't have a phone.' She moved one hand in his direction and then went back to scratching at her arm. 'I mean, I'm all right, but—'

Stick nodded. 'Sounds like a cock, like you said.'

She let out a laugh.

'I wouldn't do that, you know.' Now he sounded like a cock, but she smiled and nodded and said:

'I know.'

'You dumped him?' Stick asked. 'Didn't he freak?'

She flicked her tongue against the silver stud in her lip. 'My dad got involved,' she said at last. 'It was complicated.'

He stood up, walked across the room and kissed her.

She kissed him back, then pulled away and looked at him. 'I'm sorry about Mac,' she said, and then she slipped her arms up and around Stick's neck. He drew her close. She felt like a bird – her body warm and fragile against his.

Two weeks after his birthday his mum called, and this time his nan came to the door of the spare room, her face grave, and said, 'You'd better talk to her.'

Stick was in bed. He shoved the duvet down towards his stomach and took the phone.

'It's Trish McKinley,' his mum said.

For a minute, he thought Mac's ma had killed herself. He could imagine it – an empty bottle of pills by her bed; or her leaning back from the balcony until she lost her balance and fell.

'Is this a trick?' he said.

'A trick?'

'You just want me on the phone?'

'It's the case, Kieran.'

He felt his stomach dip-dive.

'Hang on.' He could hear someone talking to his mum and the rustle of her hand held over the receiver. 'Something about DNA,' she said, eventually. 'Will you come?'

Stick said he would and then hung up and sat staring at the curtains, the shape of the dream catcher just visible behind them – a circle made out of wood, with red thread like a spider's web, scratty feathers and beads hanging off the bottom. Sophie would have loved that, he thought, the idea that you could filter out the bad dreams and they'd just disappear when the sun rose.

Alan drove him to his mum's house. It's no bother, no trouble, I'm happy to, he said, and Stick said thanks, got in the car and tried not to think the whole way there.

Stick's mum didn't try to hug him, just ushered them through to where Mrs McKinley sat at the table with a cup of tea and a plate of chocolate biscuits, both untouched. Stick and Alan sat down opposite her. She looked at them and ground her lips together like she was trying not to cry. Every time she started to speak the words came out in a tangle of sobs, so Stick's mum had to explain.

'Inconclusive,' she said. 'The DNA tests came back inconclusive.'

Like two ribbons twisted together, that was all Stick could remember about DNA. He watched one tear and then another run down Mac's ma's cheeks.

'They'll still serve the evidence,' Stick's mum said. 'Isn't that right, Trish?'

Mrs McKinley looked up and smiled weakly.

Stick's mum caught his eye. 'On Friday,' she said. 'But it doesn't look good. Not any more.'

Stick tried to make his brain work. 'The threads,' he said. 'There were threads.'

Mrs McKinley sniffed and wiped her hand across her face.

'Marks and Spencer's,' Stick's mum said. 'It's too common to prove guilt. Half the men in Manchester are wearing that jumper, it turns out.'

Stick hugged his arms across his chest to stop himself

from shaking. 'And the blood?' he said. 'There was blood on his shoes.'

'Contaminated.' Mrs McKinley's voice sounded like a bell, like the ones they ring in churches, echoing around the walls. 'He'd bleached them before they picked him up.' She looked at Stick with bloodshot eyes.

'So, what? What now? He just walks?'

Stick's mum took a sharp breath. 'They're still serving the evidence,' she said. 'Then the judge decides.'

'And there are other tests,' Mrs McKinley said. 'Complicated ones. They take months, but—'

'What does the judge decide?' Stick asked.

His mum wouldn't look at him. 'Whether to carry on with the case,' she said.

'And if he says no?' Stick swallowed hard. This couldn't be happening.

'Then they do the other tests and hope to recharge him,' his mum said.

Stick pictured a heavy metal prison door pulled open and that man, Owen Lee, walking out of it, lifting his gaze up to the sky and smiling, like you would at a private joke. He shook his head. 'They can't,' he said. 'They can't let him out.'

'It's not happened yet, love,' his mum said. 'It's not happened yet.'


When Mrs McKinley got up to go, Alan stood too. 'I'll see you out, Trish,' he said, putting his hand under her elbow. 'Give you two a minute.' He nodded at Stick.

Stick's mum sat down opposite him and reached her hand to cover his. She'd been biting her nails, the skin around them red and sore.

'It'll work out,' she said. 'It will.'

Stick stared at the table, the pale, slightly shiny wood, marked with the occasional scratch. The underside must still be covered in felt-tip scrawls from when he and Sophie used to drape a duvet cover over it to make walls around them, sit there together and make shit up.

'You don't know that,' he said.

She patted at his hand.

'They don't care,' Stick said.

'Who don't?'

Stick flicked his hand towards the back door. 'Anyone. Police, lawyers, all those cunts in suits.'

'You care. We care.'

'Fat lot of use that is.' Stick heard the cat flap slap open-closed. When Babs came into the room he put out his hand and blew her kisses; she just looked at him and stalked off towards the kitchen.

'How's your nan?' his mum asked after a long pause.

Stick traced his finger in circles on the tabletop. 'Fine.'

Alan and Mrs McKinley were still in the hallway, talking.

'She looking after you?'

Stick nodded.

'Bacon rolls in bed, right?' His mum gave a forced smile, and when Stick didn't respond she said, 'Are you coming home?'

'Want to rent out my room?' He said it before he could stop himself and his mum jerked back as though he'd slapped her. He drew another circle on the tabletop and imagined sitting on a coach, window seat, headphones on, rain on the glass, the movement rocking him so he was almost but not quite asleep.

'Your dad said the job offer's still there,' she said.

'I told you, I don't want it. I told him.'

'You're going to have to start thinking about the future, love.'

He had been. He'd been lying on his nan's sofa trying to think what the fuck he was going to do with his life but had got all of nowhere. Stick swallowed. 'They can't throw the case out, Mum. How can they do that?'

She stood up then and put her arms around him in an awkward hug, so his head rested against her stomach.

'There's your present still,' she said, after an age. 'Let me get it.'

She came back with a silver-wrapped box, a silver gift tag taped to the top: *Kieran, All grown up! Happy Birthday! Mum xxx*.

It was a watch. Armani. Proper nice. Expensive. Silver and black with green-tipped hands you could see in the dark. It was cold against his wrist. A bit big – he was a skinny bastard – but on the tightest setting it'd do. It had a nice weight.

'Thanks.' He tried to smile.

'It suits you.' She was waiting for him to say he was coming home – he could tell.

'I thought I'd get some stuff from upstairs. Some clothes.' He didn't look at her. She didn't say anything.

Upstairs, he stood at his bedroom window, staring at two footballs and a squashed Coke can stranded on the school roof. Inconclusive. He repeated the word over in his head. Inconclusive. He wanted to punch his fist through the glass. A pigeon landed on the back fence and tipped its head up towards him. He hated it. He hated the fat bastard pigeon. He wanted to kill it, put his hands around its neck and squeeze, or – better – smash its head with a rock until its eyes popped out.

If they let Owen Lee out of jail he'd find him and kill him, Stick told himself. He turned away from the window, ripped the newspaper article off the wall and shoved it into his pocket. Then he lifted up the sports bag, which he'd still not unpacked, and walked back downstairs.

Alan was in the hallway. Mac's ma must have left already.

'Can we go?' Stick said, opening the front door.

Alan raised his eyebrows, then held up his hand and went into the living room. Stick waited, kicking at the plastic pot by the front step, listening to their lowered voices.

'I'll ask Shelia to come tomorrow,' Alan said as he pulled off the estate onto Queen's Road. 'She's busy, but we go back a long way.' He drove slower than anyone Stick knew – seemed oblivious to the cars that came right close to his bumper, the drivers that glowered and swore at him. 'Trish is very open to it.' He lifted both hands off the steering wheel and sighed. 'And Shelia is a truly remarkable woman. She can see people. Really see them.' He lowered his voice and leaned a little towards Stick. 'Your nan's a bit sensitive about it,' he said, nodding. 'Women are, aren't they? Exes and that, they get themselves in a tizz, think it means you don't love them.'

'Shelia's your ex?'

'Five years.' Alan let out another sigh. 'She taught me a lot.' He reached over and tapped Stick on the knee. 'Don't ever think a woman can't teach you things, son.'

Stick twisted the bezel on his watch, listened to the *scratch scratch* of the metal turning. 'She reckons she can talk to dead people?' he said.

Alan nodded. 'Those that have passed over, yes. She has a real gift. Had it since she was a little girl. Five, she was, when her spirit guide came through.'

'Must get a bit crowded,' Stick said. 'With all the dead people.'

Alan smiled, like he knew something Stick didn't. 'Different realm, Kieran, that's the thing.'

'When you're dead, you're dead.'

Alan pulled into the car park below the flats and turned the engine off. 'It's about opening your mind, Kieran. That little leap of faith.'

Mac was dead. Sophie was dead. End of.

'You'll see.' Alan smiled. 'Wait for your reading and you'll see.'

Stick lifted his bag off the back seat and got out of the car.

'She tunes in,' Alan persisted, following him up the stairs. 'Sometimes the spirits will send messages. She can guide you.'

'I don't need guiding.' Stick opened the front door and headed for the spare room.

'We all need guiding, Kieran,' Alan called after him. 'Every one of us.'

# 20

Shelia was fat – soft, fleshy fat – big cheeks, big neck, big breasts. She smelt of talcum powder and perfume and her face was thick with make-up – pale foundation dusting the fine hairs along her jawbone.

She came for lunch, sat at the table pulling bits off her sandwich before eating them and going on about Libya, Egypt, Syria. 'All this unrest,' she kept saying. 'I had a boy come through yesterday. Sixteen. Shot in the head.'

Alan fussed around her like she was a member of the royal family – *more tea? Another sandwich? Anything else you need?*

Mrs McKinley asked endless questions: 'So can you see them? Or just hear them? Or is it more that you just feel they're there?'

Stick kept his head down, didn't eat much.

Mrs McKinley's reading lasted nearly an hour. She came out crying and laughing and saying, 'He's OK. My boy's doing OK.'

And then it was Stick's turn – even though he'd said no, he wouldn't bother but thanks anyway. His nan had leaned over and said, 'Go on, Kieran. She is good.' And he'd ended up saying, 'Fine. All right,' going into the dining room and closing the door behind him.

He sat opposite Shelia at the glass table. 'It's rubbish, right?'

She blinked, flashing patches of pearly white eyeshadow.

'I won't say anything,' Stick said.

'I usually start with these.' Shelia picked up an oversized pack of cards with blue swirled patterns on their backs.

'Do you make a lot of money?' Stick asked.

Shelia shuffled the cards, straightened their edges and then fanned them out. 'Pick six.'

'Because I'm not sure it's right.'

Shelia put the cards down. 'Not right?'

Stick gestured towards the closed door to the living room. 'Her son's dead. They're about to let the bastard who killed him out of jail, and now she's smiling and talking shit about Mac being happy, Mac being safe.'

'He's a nice lad.'

Stick narrowed his eyes. 'You've never met him.'

'He's got a good sense of humour. You must miss him.'

Anger, like a fish in his stomach – a quick flash of silver. Stick snatched the top card off the pack and turned it over. It was upside down. A man dressed in black sat on a white horse, holding a black flag. Stick turned it round. 'Death,' he read. 'Give me a fucking break.'

'Reversed.' Shelia nodded. 'It makes sense.'

'What, I'm going to get stabbed too? Great.'

Shelia shook her head, the flesh at her neck wobbling a little. 'It's about change,' she said. 'When it's reversed it means you're resisting.'

Stick pushed the pack towards her, half the cards spilling off the top.

Shelia restacked them. 'I know you're angry,' she said. 'Of course you are. The anger is all part of it.'

They stared at each other. 'Do you want me to invite the spirits, Kieran?'

Stick snorted.

She looked past him, her forehead tensing up as if she was concentrating, as if she was listening to someone. After a while, she nodded. 'A girl?' she said. 'Young. 2001? Does that mean anything to you?'

'No.'

'Try to go with it, Kieran.' She spoke quietly, gently. 'Try to think. I have a girl here. She's with a woman, an older woman.'

'I thought you were supposed to be talking to Mac?'

'She's smiling. I'm getting an S. Does that make sense to you?'

Stick pushed his hands against the table, shoving his chair back so he could stand up.

'Kieran. Kieran.' She held up both hands. 'She wants to talk to you.'

'You can fuck off.' Stick backed towards the door. 'I'm only here because of my nan. I don't want to be here. I'm not interested.' He could feel his heart in his chest, his legs shaky with adrenaline. 'Let's just wait five minutes and then we can say it didn't work out,' he said.

Shelia was doing the listening pose again, tilting her head so her right ear was higher than her left. 'Sophie?' she said.

'Oh, please! Do you think I'm thick?'

She shook her head. 'No, not at all. Do you want to speak to Sophie?'

'Alan tells you about Sophie and then you pretend a fucking ghost told you? This is rubbish.' He heard his voice cracking around the words, like he was about to cry. 'I told you, it's not right.'

Shelia spread both hands palm down on the tabletop, her bracelets clattering against each other. She had pudgy fingers, like a baby's. 'OK, Kieran. I'll tell her not this time.' She closed her eyes, nodding again, as though she was having a conversation in her head. 'It's a shame,' she said. 'She's a lovely girl.'

'Stop saying that. Sophie's lovely. Mac's lovely. They're dead, aren't they? They're not fucking here.'

Shelia kept her eyes closed and Stick stared at her, waiting. Eventually she blinked a couple of times and smiled at him. 'I'm not asking you to believe anything, Kieran. I just pass on messages. That's all I do. Sometimes people aren't ready. That goes for spirits and those earthside.'

Stick stared past her through the window – white clouds sketched across the sky; lines of traffic crawling along the road. He sat back down. 'So what message did Mac have for me?' he asked.

'I'm tired now, Kieran. It's tiring.'

'If Mac was here he'd have said something to me.'

'It was Sophie.'

'But before.'

'He was here for his Mum.'

It was bollocks. All of it was bollocks.

'I think we're done, Kieran.' Shelia stood up and opened the door into the living room.


Shelia left in a noisy flurry of hugs and thanks and promises.

'Wonderful,' Alan said, turning away from the front door, his hands lifted into the air like he was some crazy preacher guy. 'Isn't she just wonderful?'

Stick's nan ushered them back into the living room, her mouth set.

'She's an angel,' Mrs McKinley said. 'She could see him. Imagine being able to see him.' She looked around the room as if Mac might be there, reaching for a biscuit from the plate on the coffee table – taking three at once. 'She told me the clothes he was in when he died. She couldn't have known that, could she?'

Newspaper reports. There'd have been something somewhere. And Mac wouldn't be wearing the coconuts and the grass skirts in heaven or wherever, everything still covered in blood and shit.

'Did he say anything about the coffin?' Stick asked.

Mac's ma frowned, then shook her head.

If it had been Mac he'd have had a go at her about spending so much money. He'd have told her to stay away from Luke Croft and his dodgy loans. If it had been Mac he'd have stayed and talked to Stick.

'And you, Kieran?' Alan said.

'Nothing.' Stick twisted the outside of his watch round and round. He could sense them all watching him. 'I'm going out,' he said. 'I'm going for a walk.'

He left, marched down the overheated, overscented communal hallway, through the parking area and onto Ashton Old Road. Lorries and cars racing past. An old woman with a tartan shopping trolley creeping towards the bus stop. Stick headed away from town, past the shitty industrial estate, the old red-brick terraces, the crappy shops. He went all the way to J's house, stood ringing the doorbell again and again, but no one answered. So he bought himself wings and chips and ate them sat on a low railing by a scraggy-looking strip of grass, staring at the traffic, breathing in the petrol fumes and the smell of fried chicken, his fingers slick with oil.

And then he took the picture of Owen Lee out of his pocket. He ripped the paper in half, and half again and again, until no one could have known it used to be a face, dropping the pieces on the ground.


The top drawer of the chest in his nan's hallway was stuffed full of candles – had been even before she met Alan. Stick eased it open and took the first two he saw, slipped them into the pocket at the front of his hoody and went into the spare room. There was no lock, so he unplugged the tall metal lamp and jammed it under the door handle. He put the tissue box with its lacy cover on the floor and placed the two candles on the bedside table. Tea lights with purple wax. He put them so close they touched, then moved them further apart. It made no difference, but he still couldn't decide.

He lit the first one. The flame flared briefly, melting the wax from the wick into a small blob on the candle's surface. Then it wavered and shrank, hesitated like it was thinking of giving up, until something invisible happened and it climbed again, stretched tall and yellow, turning the wick from glowing red to black. He lit the second and then sat on the bed, his back against the wall, staring at the two flames: long and thin with pointed yellow tops, the slightest of movements left, right, but otherwise quite still. He strained his ears, but could only just make out the sound of the TV in the living room. No one was going to come in, but he still couldn't help imagining it: his nan and Alan standing in the doorway laughing at him – 'That's not how you do it, Kieran, do you know nothing?'

The flames held their shape. He thought about Shelia, the way she looked at him and then seemed to go into herself. He stared at the candles but nothing happened.

They were making him mental, the lot of them were. His dad was right: he needed a job, he needed to get the fuck away from there. Stick leaned forwards and blew out the candles. He'd call J, see if she was back. See if she wanted to go out. Or stay in.

But he didn't get his phone out. He sat on the bed, and after a while he lit the candles again and the room filled with the smell of hot perfumed wax.

'Come on then.' He said it out loud, but as quietly as he could, hating the sound of his own voice. He coughed, held his hand against his mouth. His stomach didn't feel right.

'Mac?' He coughed again.

'Sophie, then?'

The candle nearest to him flickered like someone had breathed on it. Stick swallowed.

'Sophie?'

Nothing. The flame stayed still.

'Mac?'

It felt the same as it had on Blackpool beach, the sadness like a heavy stone dropped into his stomach, the ripples reaching out to his edges.

'I could do with—' He stopped. 'I could do with getting hammered,' he said and sniffed. 'I could do with sitting on your balcony getting stoned and throwing stuff.' He laughed. 'I'm burning candles, for fuck's sake.' Stick looked upwards, as if Mac was there and could hear him better if he looked his way. 'What is wrong with me?'

All he could hear was the TV in the other room, and, faintly, a Hoover going in the flat upstairs. The candles still burned, a narrow rim of metal visible now where the wax had burnt off, the air shimmering slightly above each flame. It only needed one to burn through its holder, or get knocked onto the carpet, or snatch at someone's sleeve or the edge of a duvet, and the whole place would go up. This flat. The one above. The ones next door. Flames pumping from the windows and everything curling in on itself, melted plastic and scarred wood and thick, choking black smoke. He could pick up both candles and drop them onto the bed, sit there with the flames starting around him. Then he'd know, about the spirit thing. Then he'd properly know.

There was a knock on the door, his nan's voice. 'Are you all right, love?'

'Fine.'

'I thought for a minute I could smell burning.'

Stick blew both candles out. Soft swirls of smoke lifted up from the wicks. He licked his fingers and pinched them and they hissed at his touch. 'No. It's fine,' he shouted.

'Do you want some tea?'

Stick looked at the dark smears of soot on his thumb and forefinger.

'I can bring you some in there if you want.'

He tried to stand up, to pull the lamp away from the door, to look at his nan and smile and say, *I'll come through, I'm fine, thank you.* But he couldn't move.

'I'll do you a plate, leave it out here,' she said.

Stick managed to say thank you, loud enough for her to hear.

'You'll open the window if you're smoking, won't you?'

'Yes, Nan.'

'Kieran?'

'Yes?'

'I love you.'

Stick rolled his eyes.

'Pie and chips on its way, then,' she said.

———

He was eating the last of his chips when he heard it.

*You asked her yet?*

Stick nearly choked. He looked towards the door, but he knew it was closed.

*She's not going to ask you.*

He picked up another chip and chewed it slowly.

*She's all right, Stick. She's a good'un. You'll have a blast.*

The candles sat on the bedside table, the wax hard and cold again. The curtains were pulled shut in front of the dream catcher. Stick couldn't speak.

*Car. Coach. Doesn't matter much, does it? Pick a place and go. Find somewhere to stay, or just keep on moving. She'll come with you.*

He was going fucking crazy. He needed a fag. Stick lowered his plate onto the floor.

*You've just got to ask her.*

J liked him, that was true. She'd said as much the last time he saw her. She pulled off her T-shirt and unhooked her bra and he traced the wide hard bone between her breasts with his forefinger, touched the neat brown circles of her nipples. I like you, she'd said, and he'd blushed and said me too, and then kissed her so he didn't have to think of anything else to say. She liked him, but he knew it wasn't going to last – a bright, sparky girl like her with a shitbag like him: no job, no future; he couldn't even hold it together to drive himself to Spain.

*You're not a shitbag.*

'You're not real.'

Silence.

Stick listened.

Nothing.

'Hi,' he said.

Nothing.

'I didn't mean— You just freaked me out.'

Still nothing.

'Mac?'

A swell of tinny music on the TV. A car horn sounding outside. Stick tried to laugh at himself. Talking to the dead! Alan was making him crazy.

'I fucking miss you,' he whispered. 'I really fucking miss you.'

August 2011

# 21

He was with J when his mum called; the two of them sat up on the window ledge in the wasteground near Strangeways, passing a joint back and forth. He'd got an eighth of weed off Ricky and it was almost finished already – it was the only thing that helped him sit still for more than five minutes. He'd been trying to ask J if she knew what she'd do after college, and if she did, how did she know? How do you decide – he was trying to ask – how do you come up with something that might actually happen? He'd been struggling to get his questions to make sense, and she'd kept flicking her hair and sucking on the joint and saying, 'I don't know. I can't be bothered thinking about all that.'

He knew what his mum was going to say even before she said it.

'Love, it's the case. I'm sorry.'

Stick stared down at the handbags, their colours bleached by rain, their clasps and buckles rusted up and their insides rotting. He could sense J looking at him but couldn't meet her eye.

'The judge said there wasn't enough evidence to go ahead.'

Stick could picture the judge in his stupid white wig,

banging a wooden mallet thing down with a crash. Case dismissed. That meant everyone go home, we're done here. That meant we actually can't be arsed. That meant, who cares, it was only some estate kid – probably drugs, probably gangs, probably the world's better off without him anyway.

'They're doing more tests,' she went on. 'They'll find something, they're bound to. And then they can recharge him. They are sure it's him, Trish said that. They say it happens sometimes, this kind of thing; it just means things take a bit longer. I'm sorry, love.'

He wanted to throw his phone as far as he could – over the piles of rubbish and smashed concrete – hear it land with a crash, its screen cracking, the keyboard detaching itself, his mum's voice silenced.

'Are you OK? Do you want me to come?'

He shook his head. He knew she couldn't see him but he didn't trust himself to speak.

'Love?'

'I'm fine,' he croaked. 'Fine.'

'Do you want to come home, love?'

He wanted to run. He wanted to run until he couldn't run a step further, until his chest burst and his legs burned and his brain stopped thinking.

'Kieran, you're worrying me now.'

'Fine, I'm fine. I've got to go.' He hung up and shoved his phone back in his pocket.

J said nothing but he could feel her watching him.

'Fucking police.' He put a hand on the ledge either side of him because he suddenly wasn't quite sure where the edges of his body were. 'They know he did it and they've let him go. How does that even make sense? How is that even allowed?'

They sat in silence for a long time.

'Do they know why he did it?' J asked.

Stick ground his knuckles into the rough brick. 'He wouldn't say anything. But he was there. There was blood on his shoes. He's got history.'

'But there's not enough evidence?'

'Don't even say that.'

'I'm not saying he didn't do it, I'm asking.'

'He did it.'

J held up both hands, then relit the joint and passed it to him. Stick pulled the smoke into his lungs, but it didn't help.


On Saturday morning, Stick took a knife out of the kitchen drawer – the one his nan used for cutting potatoes – wrapped it in a plastic bag and shoved it under the waistband of his boxers. He walked home with the creased plastic scratching at his back.

Someone had snapped the left wing mirror off the car but otherwise it was fine. Still started, the engine coughing into life, the clutch groaning away to itself. He didn't have a plan other than to find Owen Lee. The fucker would be somewhere. Stick would just have to keep driving until he saw him.

He drove to Paget Street first. He was sure he remembered hearing something about criminals going back to the scene of their crimes, even when it was dangerous to do so, as though they couldn't quite believe they'd done what they'd done and thought going back would give them proof, because they'd be there and remember it and it'd feel real again. Stick parked where the incident unit had been. There was no one about.

Sweat prickled down his back and across his palms. The

trees cast chunky black shadows onto the grass. The dandelions had gone to seed, a few white bits of fluff still hanging on, but the rest gone. He shouldn't have ripped up the newspaper article. The more he tried to remember what Owen Lee looked like the less sure he was – the face from the photo, from the court screen, breaking into tiny squares and falling apart, however much he screwed up his eyes, however much he tried.

Stick sat, tapping his fingers against the steering wheel, and waited. He would know him when he saw him. And when he saw him he'd kill him. A magpie swept down from one of the trees, landed lightly on the pavement and looked at Stick.

One for sorrow.

The bird pecked at something on the ground and then heaved itself up into the air again, flashing its blue-black wings with their bright white tips, an impossibly long twig – three or four times its size – hanging from its beak.

He'd put the knife in the glove compartment. Stick tightened his grip on the wheel and tried to imagine what it would feel like to stick a blade into a living human being. He wondered if you'd have to push hard to get it through the skin, or if it would be like stabbing a block of cheese, or a loaf of bread. It would be easier if he had a gun. Stick pointed two fingers at the magpie, which sat in a tree still holding the twig, and made shooting noises. That would be easiest – click and blow him away.

Stick caught a movement in his wing mirror and tensed. It wasn't Owen Lee, just an old guy on the other side of the road, with a limp and a white plastic bag in one hand. For a split second, he imagined jumping out of the car, running up to the man and shoving the knife into his chest. The man kept walking; Stick locked his door and sat there long after the man had disappeared, his heart pounding and his knuckles white on the steering wheel.

If he didn't do it no one else would. Mac would be dead and there'd be no sense to it. Stick started the engine and felt the buzz of it enter through his skin. He jerked the car back onto the road, his body loose with adrenaline, his breath coming in bursts, his hands jittery on the wheel. He screeched down Paget Street and veered left onto Rochdale Road without stopping to look, stuck a finger up at the car hooting behind him. 'Fuck off,' he shouted. It made him feel better, somehow. 'Fuck off. Fuck off.' His voice rose with the engine's revs and he felt a smile sneak across his face. This was how it was going to work. He was going to find that bastard and make him wish he'd never been born.

# 22

'I'm going to shine this light again.' The doctor loomed closer to Stick, aiming a light into his left eye, then his right, leaving yellow-pink shapes glowing in the air. 'And now I'm going to ask you to follow my finger with your eyes, without moving your head. That's right.' She moved her finger across his vision. She was skinny, Asian, young, with red lipstick and her hair tied up in a ponytail.

'Any double vision?' she asked.

Stick shook his head. It was like the millionth time they'd done this. He remembered the magpie, he'd told the other doctor that – a cheery, ruddy-faced man who looked like he should be a schoolteacher, or a children's entertainer. He remembered the magpie with the twig in its mouth, almost too big for it to carry, but after that, it was blank.

'I just need you to clench your teeth together.' She reached out both hands and felt either side of his neck, then rubbed at his temples. Her hands were cool and smooth. She pressed her finger against his chin. 'And now open your mouth.'

He'd driven into a lamp post, the other doctor had said. Any idea why that might have been? Stick had shaken his head and shrugged. The knife would still be in the glove compartment, along with an empty pack of tobacco and some sweet wrappers. But it wasn't illegal to have a kitchen knife in your car.

The new doctor wrote something on her clipboard, looked at it and then nodded. 'Your mum's on her way.'

Stick stared at the pleated blue curtain the doctor had pulled around his bed and felt the weight of himself, like a lump of concrete on the thin, plastic-coated mattress. Through the gap in the curtain he could see nurses sitting behind a big desk covered in phones and computers and bits of paper, and behind them a white board with people's names and bed numbers in blue marker pen. The place stank of cleaning fluid and ill people. It was too bright, too loud – machines bleeping and people talking. Made his head hurt. Made his brain pound against his skull. He wanted to go somewhere dark and quiet. If he was somewhere dark and quiet, then maybe he'd be able to remember whether he'd found Owen Lee or not; whether he'd killed him.

But the doctor hadn't said anything about anyone else. A lamp post, not a man. And there were no police lining up to ask him questions and take fingerprints. Maybe he'd seen Owen Lee and tried to swerve to hit him. Maybe he'd had his hood up and Stick was leaning towards the window, trying to see his face. He searched his brain but it wouldn't give him anything. Just a magpie with blue on its wing.

'How can it just go?' he asked the doctor, who was opening the curtains.

'I'm sorry?'

'Your memory,' Stick said. 'How can it just disappear like that?'

The doctor pursed her lips. 'It's really quite common,' she said. 'With a head injury, and shock.' She looked at her clipboard again. 'We'll do a few more tests, but I think it's nothing serious.' She smiled as if she'd answered his question and walked away, her heels tapping a no-nonsense rhythm.

Stick carried on trying to remember, but it was like he'd died for an hour or two, and then come back to life.


His mum arrived, almost running down the ward towards him, her hand pressed to her chest.

'Oh my God. Oh, Kieran.' She went on and on, like they were in one of her soap operas. She kept touching him, the same way she'd done after Sophie had died, as if checking he was really there.

Stick lay as still as he could and let her words wash over him. His whole body ached, like someone had given him a proper kicking. *The seat belt*, the first doctor had said, tracing his hand diagonally through the air. *At least you were wearing one, but there was no air bag so you've got the wheel too, and it's bruised deep. It'll take a few weeks. No permanent damage though, not to your torso.*

'I just can't believe you'd do that. I can't.' His mum started crying, her shoulders shaking with it. 'I should never have let you two buy that bloody car in the first place.'

Stick felt like he was watching her through a thick pane of glass. He managed to sit himself up a bit in bed and say, 'I'm not dead, Mum. They're just doing tests.'

'But your head.' She reached up and touched just above his ear. 'And to try and—' She put her hand over her mouth. 'To drive into a lamp post.' She was crying even more now. 'I'm sorry,' she said. She kept saying it over and over. 'I'm sorry, I'm so sorry.' And then pulling herself together, sniffing the tears back, her eyes bright. 'I'll fix it. I will. I'll fix it. We'll be all right.' And then crying again.

He was so tired. He kept thinking about how Sophie had

shrunk to just a handful of memories and he wasn't even sure which of them to trust – which he'd made up, or worked out from photos, and which were actually true. It would be the same with Mac. Ten years from now Mac would be a series of images and phrases and feelings that he'd have to keep rehearsing so they didn't disappear completely.

His mum had stopped talking. She was holding his wrist, looking at the Armani watch, which had a single crack right across the face.

'Shit,' Stick said. His voice sounded like it was coming from a long way away.

His mum shook her head. 'We'll fix it. We'll fix it, love.'


They made her leave when it got to dinner time. She walked backwards down the ward towards the double doors, waving at him, but Stick couldn't find the energy to wave back.

His meal came on a plastic tray divided into compartments – chicken in cheesy white sauce, damp green beans and not-quite-cooked potatoes. Stick stabbed at them until they broke into pieces; pushed the bits of chicken into a line around the edge of their space; told the nurse who tried to get him to eat that he wasn't hungry.

Still, every hour, the same thing. Follow my finger. Shining a light. What day is it? Where are you? What's your name? He wanted to shout *fuck off, fuck off, fuck off,* at the top of his voice. He wanted to go to sleep, but his head was too full of noise. Where am I? Who am I? How can Mac be dead?

He felt exposed – dressed in the stupid, scratchy hospital gown which was basically a dress. Lying on the high metal-framed bed with people rushing past, doctors and nurses, and shuffling slippered patients. He could see one window on the other side of the room. Otherwise it was just bright lights and ugly beds and ugly people in the beds with TVs on extendable arms, and beeping machines and trolleys and sinks and bunches of flowers stuck in plastic jugs and the stink of chemicals and rot.

And then his dad turned up. Stick spied him coming through the doors to the ward and quickly closed his eyes.

'Kieran?'

Stick kept his eyes shut and tried to breathe long, slow, asleep-sounding breaths. He felt his dad's hand on his shoulder and made himself not wince. A little push. Another.

'Kieran?'

He used to read Stick stories. He'd forgotten about that, but his dad's voice reminded him now: Stick tucked in bed with the duvet held at his chin and his dad sitting next to him, the weight and the warmth of him against Stick's legs. Pirates and talking mice and dragons.

He heard his dad settle himself in the chair next to the bed, the slight effort of his breath, the rustle of his clothes against each other and then the *tap tap* of his finger against the chair's arm.

'Are you asleep?' his dad said.

Stick shifted onto his side with a sigh, as though he had almost woken up but not quite.

'It's me,' his dad said. 'Your mum called.' His finger still tapped on the chair. 'In a state. She said you'd tried to kill yourself.' His voice veered upwards.

Stick nearly opened his eyes at that.

'I told her. It's not your fault, Mandy, I said.' He paused. 'I said, if it's your fault then it's mine too.'

Stick concentrated on one high-pitched bleep coming from the other side of the ward.

'Why would you?' his dad said, his voice careering out of control again. And then, softly, 'The case. The court case.'

Stick could imagine him sat there, nodding, the hospital lights shining off his forehead.

'Are you awake, Kieran?'

Stick tried not to react, tried to keep his breath slow and steady. He heard his dad sigh.

'I wanted someone to blame,' he went on. 'God, I wanted someone to blame.'

Stick remembered. His dad pacing the house those months after Sophie died. Hours on the phone to lawyers and consumer watchdogs, whatever they were. *I'll nail someone for this. I'll nail the bastards who made this happen.* And all the time his mum getting smaller and paler, like someone was sucking the life out of her.

Stick wanted to sit up and say, *well this is different, isn't it? The fire was an accident. You can't call getting stabbed five times an accident.* He wanted to say, *there is someone to blame, that's the point, but they've let him go.* He half opened one eye, the hospital ward flickering and blurred behind his lashes, his dad a dark, stooped shape at his side. Stick closed it again and thought about Owen Lee, in the newspaper, on the screen in the courtroom. Maybe it would be harder not having someone to fix it all on, not having someone to hate.

'You told me to apologise.' His dad let out a nervous laugh. 'I don't even know where to start.'

He didn't start at all. He just sat there another ten, fifteen minutes, and then he got up. Stick could feel him standing there, watching him, for what seemed like forever. But eventually the light shifted and his dad's footsteps retreated down the ward.

He tried to sleep, but the nurses kept waking him up to do the tests and anyway his head was too full – his thoughts like fat summer flies bashing at a window. The fluorescent lights dug through his eyelids and made his head hurt even more. He ached like a bastard and when he lifted the gown away from his neck he could see huge red and purple welts across his chest.

On the wall next to the white board, the clock's hands barely seemed to move between him looking once and looking again. Stick twisted the outside of his watch around and around and thought about his mum's face and her fingers worrying at the hospital sheet.

There was no announcement, just a ripple of uneasy excitement across the ward. Nurses whispering to each other. The woman in the bed opposite sitting up straighter and holding the edges of her TV screen as if to steady the image. A swell of voices. He'd asked to watch TV but it turned out you had to pay for it and he didn't have any money. If he craned his neck to the left he could just about see his neighbour's screen but there was no sound, only a static hiss from the man's plastic headphones.

The man, who had wires coming off his chest and into a machine, saw Stick looking and pulled his headphones away from his ears. 'Police shot a black guy,' he said, then shook his head. 'Always starts the same bloody way.'

On the screen Stick could see a van on fire. Bright flames and pumping black smoke. It was like the van was a ghost. You could see the shape of it in amongst the flames, but it was as though it wasn't really there at all, just the memory of it, and all that really existed was the fire, roaring. The camera shifted to a crowd of men with their hoods pulled up, throwing bricks and bottles at armed police. Then another group rocking a police van until it overbalanced and fell. Then a grey-haired white guy with frown lines across his forehead, talking. Then the cameras went back to the burning van. A man Stick's age, maybe younger, ran in front of the fire and was silhouetted, black against yellow, just for a moment. It looked like a film. It looked beautiful. Must be Greece again, Stick thought. Not Libya or Egypt – it didn't look hot enough. The man in the bed kept tutting and shaking his head.

He thought about J lying on the beach in Blackpool, the sand swirled into yellow patterns around her. He thought about Owen Lee walking out of prison, his eyes up to the sky, his mouth twisted into a smile. He thought about his car, wrapped around a lamp post he didn't even know where, and wondered if anyone had set that alight. He imagined a lad reaching through the smashed windscreen, or punching out the passenger window before holding a lighter to the crappy grey seats. The slow burn before it took hold and speeded up faster than you could imagine. He wished he was sat in the middle of it, the flames coming up around him like knives over his skin, and then everything – him, the car, the lamp post – swallowed up in a yellow-orange roar.

# 23

They must have stopped waking him up every hour at some point because Stick woke from a deep sleep to see Jen stood by his bed, Rosie hanging onto her hand.

'I've spoken to the doctor and you are good to go,' Jen said, smiling.

Stick grunted and turned over.

'Which is great,' Jen went on. 'Because it's Bea's swimming gala and we've just enough time to get there.'

Stick stared at the grey armchair next to his bed and remembered the burning van on the TV the night before.

'I've packed your things.' Jen held up a canvas bag with the recycling symbol printed on the front. 'There was a gift.' She dipped in her hand and pulled out something small, wrapped in red paper. 'And a note.'

Stick looked up.

'Maybe you can open it in the car?' Jen said, dropping it back into the bag. She looked down at Stick. 'You'll want to get dressed.'

Stick buried his head in the pillow. He did not want to get dressed. He did not want to go anywhere.

'Kieran?'

'Leave me alone.'

Jen put her hand on his shoulder and gave him a little shove.

'That hurts.'

'There's no cure for feeling rubbish like getting up and getting on,' Jen said.

Stick closed his eyes. His head still throbbed.

'Bea's so excited you're coming,' Jen said. 'She made you a get-well card but I said she could give it to you herself, after swimming.'

Stick screwed his eyes tighter shut. 'That's blackmail,' he muttered.

'Maybe it is, but she'll be looking up to the audience and seeing no one at this rate. Your dad had to go into work.'

Stick felt something drop onto the bed over his legs. He opened an eye and saw a red T-shirt and trackie bottoms neatly folded. His nan must have been in while he was asleep.

Rosie walked towards the head of the bed. She was unsteady on her feet, like she'd been on the beers.

'Hi, Rosie,' Stick said.

She reached up and poked him hard on the cheek with her finger. 'Bea-Bea dof-fin,' she said.

'Oh for fuck's sake.' Stick swung himself round to standing, his feet cold on the hospital floor, his legs sticking out under the gown – pasty-white knobbly-kneed shite that he was.

'Fuck's sake,' Rosie echoed.

Jen glared at him.

'Can a man get some privacy round here?' Stick said, picking up the red T-shirt.

Jen backed off and pulled the blue curtains round the bed. Stick could hear Rosie saying 'fuck's sake' and Jen telling her to hush and it cheered him up enough to get himself dressed.

———

Stick sat in the passenger seat of Jen's little Nissan and lifted the present out of the canvas bag. It was small, heavy, solid. He ripped off the paper to find a stone, green with specks of red, polished so hard it shone. Stick held it in between two fingers.

'What's that then?' Jen asked, glancing across at him.

Stick shrugged. He curled his fingers into a fist around the stone and imagined throwing it at the windscreen, the glass shooting out cracks from where it hit.

'You saw the note?' Jen said.

A white envelope with a plain white postcard inside. *This is a bloodstone*, it read. *For courage, strength and wisdom. It gives courage to overcome obstacles and wisdom to decide how to do so. Be strong, Kieran, and wise. Alan.*


The leisure centre was crowded with kids, shouts and screams and splashes echoing off the tiles. Stick felt the energy seeping out of him.

'I should be in bed,' he said to Jen. 'I should be resting.'

'Nonsense.' Jen led him through double doors into a chlorine-stinking corridor, dragging Rosie along with her. They walked up a set of concrete stairs to a balcony that ran the length of the building. There were five lines of hard red plastic seats, bolted to the floor, each row higher than the one before. It was maybe half full – clusters of families with drinks cans and packets of crisps, looking down at the blue rectangle of water.

Jen ushered Stick into a seat on the back row and sat Rosie in between them. 'She'll be so chuffed you're here,' she whispered.

Stick fingered the stone in his pocket and scanned the water below for Bea. He couldn't see her amongst the crowd of kids running about in swimming costumes, jumping into the water like nothing bad could happen. Rosie was gazing up at him with big blue eyes, chattering nonsense. She had a bubble of green snot in one nostril that bulged as she breathed.

'Bea,' she said, turning to look down at the exact moment her sister walked towards the pool in the middle of a straggly line of kids. Bea wore a red swimming costume, her stomach puffed out in front of her.

'Dof-fin.' Rosie pointed down at the children who now stood solemnly at the edge of the water.

'That's right! Dolphin!' Jen cooed.

Stick couldn't really work out what was going on. It wasn't, it seemed, a race – more a disorganised show of sorts. The kids jumped one by one into the shallow end, doggy-paddled for a bit and then clung to the edge, their faces raised. Adults in red uniforms stood on each side of the pool ready to fish out anyone about to drown. And then at some point people started clapping, so Stick clapped too. They all got out of the pool, wet and shivering, and a man in a dark suit went along the line and hung a medal on a blue-and-white ribbon around each kid's neck. Stick saw Bea scanning the seats, looking for them – left, right, left. He waved, but she didn't see him.


They waited for Bea, standing in the foyer by a noticeboard pinned with adverts for yoga and sports massage and toddler groups.

'Will you come for lunch?' Jen asked, and before he could answer she said, 'She would love it, Kieran, if you came. She really would.'

And then Bea was there, her hair all wet and messed up,

wrapping her arms around his legs. And so he went, holding Bea's hand as they walked to the cafe. Wooden tables, fairy lights, pointless home-made craft stuff for sale in the corner. Crap music on the radio. Weird things on the menu: goat's cheese and tofu and couscous. He ordered a burger and a Coke, which arrived just as the radio went to its news bulletin. The woman behind the bar turned it up and the other people in the cafe stopped talking, tilted their heads to one side to listen, the way Shelia had when she was pretending to channel Sophie's spirit, or whatever it was she was supposed to do.

There was rioting in London. All night people had been running into shops and taking what they wanted. It was chaos, a woman kept saying, sounding panicked and excited at the same time.

'London?' Stick looked at Jen. Her cheeks were pink, like someone had drawn circles of paint onto them.

Mac had hated London, even though he'd never been. *Full of bankers and wankers*, he said. *Gets all the money and all the attention, and they still ponce about whinging.*

'I just feel sorry for that man's family,' Jen said.

'The black guy?'

Jen narrowed her eyes and nodded. 'Your son gets shot by the police, you're going to want some answers,' she said. 'But it's out of hand now, by the sounds of it.'

Stick tugged a bit of lettuce out of his burger and dropped it on the plate. He wanted some answers too. Maybe he should start a riot in Manchester – throw shit at the police, set fire to something, keep on doing it until someone fucking explained.

The radio had gone back to playing music – a guy crooning about a girl who loved someone else.

'I used to live in London,' Jen said. 'Not where all that's happening. I was in Clapham.'

Stick looked up in surprise and she laughed. 'I didn't come into existence when I married your dad, you know.'

Stick thought about the photo of Jen and his dad on the mantelpiece in their living room – his dad in a suit, Jen in a white dress with her head tipped back, laughing, confetti blurring around them. It sat in a crowd of other photos, of Bea and Rosie and one of him too, his hair longer than it was now, scowling at the camera. Stick had refused to go to the wedding. His mum had half-heartedly tried to make him, and then shrugged and took him to the Trafford Centre, bought him new trainers and a new tracksuit, let him order whatever he wanted in McDonald's.

'Why did you marry him anyway?' Stick said.

She laughed. She looked pretty when she laughed. 'He's kind,' she said. 'He's funny. He cares.' She brushed a bit of hair away from her eyes. 'We're all right, Kieran. Your dad and me, you don't need to worry about that.'

He wasn't worried about that. He was worried that Owen Lee was walking the streets of Manchester, laughing about getting away with it. He was worried about his mum. He was worried he'd forget what Mac looked like, what Mac's voice sounded like. He was worried he couldn't think of one single job he wanted to do and he'd never have any money or anywhere to live and J would realise he was a loser and leave him before they'd even had sex.

'What is it that you want, Kieran?' Jen said.

The tears surprised him. He didn't let them out, but he felt them pushing up towards his eyes and had to blink them away. She saw; he could tell by the way she looked at him. He was about to get up and walk out, but she put her hand on his forearm.

'It's a difficult question,' she said.

Stick took another mouthful of his burger. It seemed to get bigger the more he chewed. He breathed in through his nose – tried again. Chew, swallow, chew, swallow.

'What do you want for you?' Jen said. 'For your life.'

She'd ordered scrambled eggs and smoked salmon. It looked disgusting. Stick watched her cut a neat triangle of pink fish and place it on top of a square of toast and egg, then stab her fork through the whole thing.

He swallowed again, his mouth empty at last. 'Is that what all this is for?' he asked. 'You bring me here, buy me lunch and then start on about that double-glazing job? Is Dad about to turn up with a contract?'

Jen smiled and shook her head. 'I know you don't want the job.'

'So what are you on about?'

'I know what you don't want,' she said. 'I just wanted to know what you do want. I'm interested.'

'I don't want anything.'

'I don't believe that for a second.' She fussed about, arranging egg and salmon on another tiny square of toast. 'What do you like?' she asked.

Stick shrugged.

Jen put her knife and fork down. 'OK. What makes you excited?'

J. The way she looked at him when she took her bra off. He couldn't say that to Jen.

They were back talking about the riots on the radio. That was exciting. London was two hours on the train away from Manchester. Fires. People throwing bricks through windows and no one stopping them.

'I get it, Kieran, I do.'

'No offence, Jen, but you have no fucking idea.'

218

She glanced towards Rosie and Bea, who sat with colouring books, the pages a mess of felt-tip scribbles.

'No fucking idea,' Stick said, louder this time.

'OK, fine. Look. Close your eyes.'

Stick folded his arms over his chest.

She sighed. 'Ten years' time,' she said. 'You're twenty-eight. It's Monday morning. Your alarm goes.'

'Bippity beep. Bippity beep.' Stick met her gaze but she didn't flinch.

'Where are you?' she said.

'In bed.'

'Close your eyes. Where's the bed?'

'Is this hypnosis or something?'

'Where are you?'

'Because I've got enough of that with crazy Alan.'

'Close your eyes. Tell me where you are.'

Stick looked at the row of houses opposite the cafe. Net curtains in folds across a window. Ivy creeping up towards a roof. Where was he? A double bed. J next to him, her hair blue or pink or black or orange, spread out over the pillow. Downstairs, a little kitchen diner, a living room with big leather sofas. A dog – maybe a pug – curled up in a basket by the back door.

'Are you getting up to go to work?' Jen asked.

'I don't know. I don't fucking know.' He could feel the tears again. 'Can you leave it?' he snapped.

She sat back, looking a bit deflated. 'I'm just trying to help.'

He'd thought his dad had put her up to it, but suddenly he wasn't sure. Maybe she was just being nice.

Jen placed her knife and fork together across her empty plate. 'Perhaps you could try making a list,' she said.

He would go back to his nan's, get in bed, go to sleep. He

could imagine it, the duvet warm and soft against his chin. The water ticking in the pipes. The noise of traffic seeping in through the window.

'A list of things you like. Things you're good at,' Jen continued. 'It might give you some ideas.'

'I'm not good at anything.'

'That is not true.' She said it so forcefully he almost laughed. 'It isn't,' she said. 'Look at you and Bea.'

Bea glanced up. 'I'm a dolphin,' she said, and held out the medal that still hung around her neck.

Jen stroked Bea's hair. 'Some people haven't got the first idea how to talk to kids.' She paused. 'And your mum.'

'What about her?'

'I coloured in the princess.' Bea held her colouring book out towards Stick. The picture was of a thin-waisted girl with big hair and a long dress, a poodle sitting in her lap. Bea had scribbled over the whole thing in blue.

'Pin-cess,' Rosie said. Jen leaned over with a tissue and wiped Rosie's snotty nose.

'What do you mean, and my mum?' Stick said.

'I just meant, the OCD and—'

'How do you even know that?'

'And you deal with that great. You might do – I don't know – nursery work? Care work?'

Stick picked up the salt and poured a pile of it onto his plate. He glanced at Jen. She had blonde eyelashes, the same as Mac's used to be. He tried out the words in his head before he let them out. 'She said she'd go to the doctor's but I know she hasn't.'

There was a long pause. Jen was looking at him, but he wouldn't catch her eye. Rosie scribbled over a picture of a donkey, the pen scratching at the paper, round and round and round.

'It's something she's got to sort out herself,' Jen said. 'You can't do it for her, however much you want to.'

Stick pushed the salt into a line, then a square, then a line again. 'Do you think I'll end up like that?' he said.

Jen frowned.

'Checking plugs and locking doors and whatever?'

She was looking at him like he wasn't making any sense. 'It's not hereditary,' she said.

He meant would he end up like his mum because of Mac, because he couldn't get over him dying. Would he get stuck? He wanted to ask her how you got over someone dying without them just disappearing into nothing, like you'd never cared about them in the first place. Instead, he said, 'I like building.'

'Building?'

'Construction.'

Jen nodded, her lips pulling down a bit at the edges, and Stick felt himself flush red.

'What, it's too rough? It's for stupid people? You don't want your precious girls with a fucking bricklayer for a half-brother.' It was easier, being angry. 'That's what you think, isn't it?' he said.

Jen shook her head, but Stick kept talking; he couldn't stop himself. 'You and your snobby house and your snobby pizzas and Sunday lunches and holidays in fucking France, the lot of you looking down at me.'

Rosie started crying, her voice rising into a high-pitched wail. Jen reached over and patted her arm. 'It's OK, sweetheart, it's OK. What a beautiful donkey, Rosie. Aren't you a clever girl?'

Stick looked around the cafe. Everything was too close together: too many things on the tables – stacked glasses and water jugs and brown paper menus propped between the ketchup and the salt; too many things on the walls – wooden boxes filled with wooden letters, pictures made out of fragile-looking bits of paper; too many people.

'Actually, my brother's in construction,' Jen said, once Rosie had settled. 'I could talk to him.'

Stick drew a circle in the pile of salt.

'He has a few boys working for him. One of them just did a course, I think. On a day release thing. In Salford, or somewhere.'

Stick stared at his plate and shrugged.

Jen sucked her tongue against her teeth. 'It's up to you, Kieran. The offer's there. I can call him, put you in touch.' She paused, and then said in a gentler voice, 'You're a great lad, Kieran. You can do whatever you want to do, but the world isn't going to come towards you if you don't go towards the world.'

'Can I get a lift home?'

Jen started to say something else.

'My head hurts,' Stick said.

She pressed her lips together and looked at him for a long time, then stood up, saying, 'All right, fine. Let me pay.'

# 24

Stick sat in the passenger seat and tried to work out how to tell Jen he was sorry – that he knew she was just trying to help; that he knew he was being a twat but sometimes he couldn't seem to help it. He glanced in the rear mirror at the girls, like little astronauts strapped into their chairs. I like them, he wanted to tell Jen, I really do. I'm glad they're around. But he wasn't much good at saying things like that.

He didn't register she'd driven him to his mum's until they came to a stop outside the house. His mum was in the front garden picking dead leaves off the plant with the orange berries. It was too late to ask Jen to turn around and take him to his nan's.

'Thanks,' he said, opening the car door. 'For lunch and that.'

'No problem,' Jen said. 'Oh. Bea's card.' She leaned across to the glove compartment and pulled out a piece of paper folded in half. 'That's you.' She pointed at a tall figure drawn in red crayon with a massive black bandage around the head. 'And that says get better soon.' She pointed to a scrawl of yellow crayon at the bottom of the picture.

'Thanks, Bea.' Stick turned in his seat and smiled at the girls, but they were both fast asleep.

'We'll see you next weekend?' Jen asked.

Stick nodded. 'Sure.' He hesitated, then said in a mumble, 'You're all right, Jen.'

Jen laughed.

'I just mean—' He felt himself blushing.

She smiled. 'Thanks. Now take care of that head of yours, won't you?'

He got out, waved as Jen did a three-point turn.

His mum opened her arms when she saw him. 'Kieran! I thought— I didn't realise—' Her eyes followed Jen's car down the street. 'How are you, love?'

'My head feels like someone's hitting it with a hammer,' he said, and then looked at her expression and regretted it. 'I'm fine,' he said. 'They let me out.'

'The police called,' she said, and Stick was suddenly alert.

'They've recharged him?'

'About the car, love. I said you'd call them back,' she said. 'I've written the number down. It's in the kitchen, I think.'

Stick lifted his face up to the sky – flat grey clouds; the blink of an aeroplane's wing light. His head throbbed. His body hurt even more than yesterday. His eyes felt like someone had taken them out, rubbed them in sand and put them back in again.

'You're home then?' She sounded so hopeful he didn't know what to do except shrug. 'I'm at work two till eight,' she said. 'If I'd known I'd have tried to swap shifts. But I'll bring us back something nice for tea, shall I?'

'It was an accident, Mum.' He looked at her. 'Dad said you thought I'd tried to top myself.'

'Oh.' She picked off another dead leaf and rubbed it between her fingers so it crackled. 'Oh, well that's good then, isn't it?'

———

224

When she'd left for work, Stick went upstairs and lay face down on his bed. His mum had washed the sheets. They smelt of soap and summer. Make a list, Jen had said, like he was still at school. She'd been trying to help, though. She hadn't told him to take the double-glazing job.

Stick pulled himself up, rummaged about in his desk until he found a piece of paper and a pen. He sat on the bed with his back against the wall, laid the paper on his lap and wrote *what do I like?* at the top, his writing wonky, the paper creasing against his leg.

*Fried chicken*
*Mum's cheese on toast*
*Mum*
*J*
*Bea and Rosie*
*Nan*
*Smoking*

He drew a picture of a cigarette with smoke curling up from the end.

Couldn't get a job smoking.

He drew a picture of a window and then scribbled it out, the pen jabbing through the paper and onto his trousers.

He drew a picture of a house with two people and a dog standing at the front door. Then he turned the paper over and wrote, *what I hate.*

*Owen Lee*
*Dad*
*Mac (for dying)*
*that shit heap of a car*
*Manchester*
*Sophie being dead*
*writing lists*

He crossed out 'Dad' and 'Manchester', and then wrote

'Dad' again at the bottom of the page and looked at it. *He's kind, he's funny, he cares*, Jen had said. *At least he tries*, Mac had said, more than once. Stick made himself picture his dad – his balding head, too-red lips, his eyes like a dog's, eager to please. *He's kind, he's funny, he cares*. He'd tried to get Stick a job. A shit job, but a job all the same.

He crossed out 'Dad' for a second time and then turned on the TV and flicked through the channels. *Family Guy*. Something about frogs. A building on fire. A woman in a forest shouting at a man. An advert for Special K. Stick went back to the fire. A massive corner building burning against a dark sky – its skeleton revealed amongst the flames. The picture switched to a bus on fire; police vans on fire; cars on fire; a bike shop, its windows cracked and one of them broken clean out, bikes falling through onto the street.

Riots. They were spreading, the newsreader said. Racing through London as if they were a fire themselves, one bit igniting the next, and the next. It was a tragedy, someone else said. A disgrace. Unforgivable. The screen showed daytime shots: the burning cars turned ash-grey; the dark streets a mess of broken bricks and scattered glass; the big building – a carpet shop, they said – charred black and half falling down.

Stick turned his piece of paper over and added 'riots' to the first list, then folded the paper in half and put it in the desk drawer. He called J and asked her to come over, said he was going to cook for her and his mum. She was as full of the riots as he was, drunk on the idea of them. Maybe we should go to London, Stick said, see for ourselves, but she said no, they'd come to Manchester any day now, they just had to wait.

———

His mum got back just as Stick had let J in. J's hair was half blue, half blonde. She'd painted her lips dark red and he felt the lipstick tacky on his skin where she'd kissed his cheek.

'Mum.' Stick wiped his face and smiled at her confused expression. 'I've made pizza, and bought beer.'

'Oh, but I—' His mum held out a plastic bag. 'Well, but this is nice.' She looked at J.

'I'm J.' J stuck out her hand.

'Let me guess, J for Janet? Jennifer?' Stick's mum took hold of J's hand and then let it drop. 'Or is it something more – exotic?'

'Just J,' Stick said. 'Like in the alphabet.'

'Oh,' his mum said, patting at her hair. 'Well, it's nice to meet you, J.' And she turned to Stick. 'You made pizza?'

He hadn't exactly made pizza. He'd taken two cheese and tomato ones out of the freezer and covered them with stuff he found in the fridge. Slices of onion and garlic and red pepper. Strips of ham. More cheese.

'Ready in ten minutes,' he said.

His mum looked at him like she was trying to see inside his head.

'How was work?' he asked.

'Fine.' She frowned. 'Good.' And then she drew J into the living room, saying, 'Now you must tell me about yourself, J. Kieran never tells me a thing. Are you at college?'

This is J, my girlfriend, Stick mouthed to himself in the kitchen, taking three cans of Foster's out of the fridge. This is J, my girlfriend. He opened the oven and a waft of steam blew up in his face. The edges of the pizzas were dark brown and the cheese was bubbling. Stick eased them off the shelf

– one onto the chopping board, one onto a plate. He took the biggest knife out of the drawer.

'Dinner is served,' he announced, a pizza in each hand, the knife balanced on top, and the cans of beer cold between his arm and his side.

'Well, you're a good influence, clearly,' Stick's mum said to J.

'Your mum likes my hair,' J said.

'Isn't it fabulous?' his mum said, her voice loud and falsely bright. Stick wanted to tell her to stop trying so hard.

The pizza wasn't great – the crust overdone and the onion and garlic still raw, but J and his mum both ate plenty and said they liked it, and his mum had two cans of beer and then said she might as well open a bottle of wine and would J like a glass? And the two of them chatted about J's A levels and where she lived and what her parents did, and when his mum said, 'Oh, and these riots in London. I can't even bear to watch the news,' J nodded and murmured something that sounded like, 'Yes, it's terrible,' and didn't look at Stick even though he was staring at her. It was almost normal, Stick thought. It was almost like a normal family sitting down for a normal dinner.

His mum said she'd wash up and as soon as she'd left the room Stick leaned forwards and kissed J on the lips.

'Will you stay?' he asked.

J glanced towards the kitchen.

'It'll be fine. Will you? Please.' When she tried to say no, she couldn't, he kissed her again until she started laughing. 'Call your parents and say you're at a friend's,' he said. 'Please?'

———

When his mum came out of the kitchen, they were halfway up the stairs. Stick saw her jaw clench.

'Kieran?'

'We're just going up.' Stick nudged J, a gentle hand on her bum, and she carried on walking.

'Up?' She stared at him.

'Up,' he repeated, staring back.

She licked her lips and then coughed. 'I'm not—'

'We'll see you tomorrow,' Stick said. His voice didn't shake but he could feel the sweat across the palms of his hands.

His mum frowned. She opened her mouth and then closed it again. 'Well, thank you for dinner,' she said.

Stick nodded and followed J into his bedroom.

She'd turned the TV on and was staring at the screen – people throwing bricks at lines of police, ramming street furniture against shop windows, running into smashed-up shops and coming out with their arms full: clothes and food and flat-screen TVs.

'We could start it. I swear, Stick, we could go Piccadilly Gardens right now, and start it.' J sat at the end of Stick's bed and crossed her legs.

He wanted to kiss her. He wanted to take her clothes off and kiss her all over. He wanted to put his nose against her skin and breathe her in.

'Look!' J jiggled her knees up and down so the mattress shook. 'They can't do anything about it.'

Stick sat next to her and watched a line of police with plastic shields, spanning a street he didn't know. People were facing up to them, throwing bricks and bottles.

'Serves them right.' He scanned the faces of the rioters – most had scarves pulled over their noses and mouths but he could see that their eyes were lit up with excitement. 'They deserve a pasting,' he said.

J pulled off her socks and dropped them onto the floor. 'Were you really going to kill him?' she asked.

Stick grabbed her ankles and pivoted her around so she sat with her back to the TV. He put her feet across his lap.

'Don't look at my weird foot.'

Stick drew his finger between her second and third toe, where there should have been a gap. 'I like it,' he said.

J pulled a face. 'Were you?' she said. And then, 'Stick, quit it, you're tickling.'

'You've got really soft skin,' Stick said, running his finger from her big toe over the top of her foot, her ankle, up her calf until her jeans stopped him.

J laughed.

'You do,' Stick said. 'It's nice.'

Someone on the TV was talking – *there is no excuse for violence, there is no excuse for looting, there is no excuse for thuggery.*

Stick licked his lips. He had the start of an erection, but she wouldn't be able to tell. 'Are you a virgin?' he asked.

She pulled her feet away, hugging her knees up to her chest and turning back to the TV. 'No,' she said.

*. . . the police, putting themselves in harm's way . . .*

Stick swallowed. 'Sorry, I just wanted to—'

She didn't move.

'I said I'm sorry.'

*. . . we've heard people saying they felt in some way abandoned . . .*

Stick reached out and touched her shoulder and she turned back around.

'Are you?' she said.

Stick thought for a minute of the girl in the blue sequinned top, holding his hand, leading him out to the toilets. He shook his head.

'Are you lying?' J said.

'No.'

'So why are you blushing?'

*. . . we need to ensure we bring an end to this, that we bring an end to this soon . . .*

Stick rubbed his hand over his mouth. 'I've never spent a night with someone,' he said, making himself look at her. 'I've had a shag, but I've never, you know—' He rubbed at his mouth again. 'Done it properly.'

'Properly?' She grinned.

Stick shifted his weight on the bed. 'Slow. I mean slow.' He glanced up at her. 'Now you're blushing.' She looked pretty, her cheeks flushed. 'I'd like to,' he said. 'With you.'

A smile flitted across her face, but she didn't say anything.

'I'm not begging,' he said. 'It doesn't matter.' He shifted himself forwards so his feet reached the floor.

*. . . the investigation will be called Operation Withern . . .*

Her hand on his shoulder. She'd pulled herself onto her knees and was close next to him.

'I know,' he said. 'That other guy. I know.'

J shook her head and kissed him, lightly, on the mouth. She tasted of beer and pizza. When she moved away Stick leaned forwards and kissed her again, her silver stud pressing into his lip. Then he pulled back and they sat and looked at each other.

'Your mum's not going to come in?' J said.

Stick shook his head.

*. . . violent clashes with police in Enfield . . .*

J lifted the remote control from the windowsill and muted the TV. She tugged at Stick's arm and he turned towards her, pulling himself up onto the bed, his lips on hers. His cock hard. His heart pumping. She let him lower her onto her back, his knees either side of hers; her lips were smooth and wet against his. He thought he would burst. J reached her hands up and pulled him against her. He winced.

'You all right?' She let go.

'Bruised.' He laughed and pulled up his T-shirt.

'Fucking hell.'

Now she tipped him onto his back and took his T-shirt off, traced her finger over his bruises.

'Tickles.' He grinned.

'You're an idiot, you know that?' She bent her head over his chest and he felt her lips on his skin, kissing each bruise. He could feel everything unravelling, disappearing – the car and the hospital, Owen Lee, his mum, Mac lying on the grass, riots on the TV – until it was just him and J. The two of them pulling at each other's clothes and yanking at their own, just them and their skin against each other.

She was beautiful. Smooth and beautiful and perfect. He could feel her bones. He could feel her pulse under his fingers. He could feel her blood, moving. On the TV, film footage repeated itself over and over. A woman jumped from a blazing building into the raised arms of firemen below. A hooded boy shouted at the camera. Men ran towards an empty police car with bricks, ramming them into the windows and against the bodywork until the glass smashed and the metal scarred. A kid wearing a beanie ran out of a shop with a bottle of wine in one hand. But it was just them. Just him and J. And she was beautiful.


She wouldn't stay. 'I can't,' she said, tracing her finger along the purple-red bruise just below Stick's collarbone. 'You've not met my dad. I really can't.'

'It's raining.' A light *tap tap* against his bedroom window.

'I won't melt.'

'It's late.'

'It's not even ten.' She sat up and started getting dressed.

So he went downstairs with her. The TV was on in the living room, louder than usual, but his mum didn't come out.

'Don't go.' He could still feel J's hands tracing his body; her hair falling over her face as she bent over him.

'Bye.' J opened the front door.

'I'll walk you back.' Stick reached for Mac's trainers.

'I'm a big girl.' She smiled. 'Stay.' She glanced at the closed living-room door. 'I'll see you tomorrow?' Her eyes widened like she'd just remembered something. 'I reckon the riots'll be here then.'

'You're beautiful,' Stick said.

J raised a hand in farewell and half ran down the steps onto the street. Stick watched her go; watched her get smaller and further away and then turn a corner and disappear. He tried to ignore the twinge of panic in his stomach and the tears suddenly crowding behind his eyes.

# 25

The next day his dad called, and Stick made himself answer, bracing himself for a lecture about sex, or another fight about the job. He was sat up in bed, watching TV. The riots had started to spread all over London, even Clapham where Jen had said she'd lived. And then further: West Bromwich, Bristol, Birmingham, Nottingham, up to Liverpool, but not Manchester, despite J's prediction – J, who had called earlier to say her dad had grounded her but she was working on it.

'I just wanted to check you were OK,' his dad said.

He ached still, his body as stiff and sore as an old man's. 'I'm fine.'

'Good. Good.' His dad sounded like he was walking down a busy road – a police siren in the background; car engines; a lawnmower. 'Do you need any help with the car?'

He never wanted to see the car again. 'Nah, thanks. I've just got to call the police and sort it.'

'Well, say if I can do anything.'

Stick grunted an acknowledgement and then listened to his dad breathing on the other end of the line.

'So, what do you think about these riots then?' His dad said it like it had just come into his mind, like it was nothing big.

Stick rolled his eyes.

'Kieran?'

'They're riots.' The TV was showing the carpet shop on fire again.

His dad cleared his throat. 'If it starts here I don't want you getting involved.'

Stick imagined himself, his hood up, his T-shirt covering his mouth, throwing a brick at a window, his reflection cracking into pieces, and Mac standing beside him, grinning. 'Dad. I'm eighteen.'

'So you get arrested and you're in a proper prison, not some juvenile place.'

A cell. A tiny window too high to show anything except a square of sky. A door thicker than his arm.

'You've got a future, Kieran.'

Stick watched the fire rage on the TV. They were showing an aerial shot, the building falling to pieces and the flames getting stronger and stronger.

'Look, if anything happens, if you get in a situation, you call me, OK?'

'There are mums handing their kids over to the police, aren't there?'

His dad cleared his throat again. 'Just call me if you need to call me. Kieran?'

Stick pictured his dad walking through smashed-up streets, past fires, through police lines, his forehead creased into a frown, his hands in his pockets to make him look braver than he felt. 'I'll be fine. Thanks though.'

After he'd hung up, Stick stayed in bed watching TV. They kept playing the same footage on loop. The woman jumping out of the window; the kid with the bottle of wine; the boy in shades and a hood saying *who cares*, saying *fuck you*; the photo of the man who got shot. Stick had started to feel like he knew them, like they were characters in a soap opera. And the more he watched, the more something inside of him lifted. The more he thought it might be possible – to find Owen Lee and put a knife through his heart; to buy two coach tickets and sit next to J watching the world flash past; to find a flat, buy a dog, start being alive again.

Stick was still in bed when his mum came home. He had the TV on – a grey-haired man stood in front of a map of England, stains of red showing where the riots had spread to – but he was thinking about J: how she'd shunted herself down the bed, held the bottom of his cock and his balls lightly with both hands and then wrapped her mouth around him.

He got up, closed the bathroom door loudly and turned the shower on – finished himself off with the water splashing over his skin. It left him feeling edgy instead of relaxed.

Downstairs, his mum was sitting at the table with a cup of tea and a pile of computer printouts.

'I went to the doctors,' she said when she saw Stick, and pushed the papers towards him.

The top page was titled *Obsessive Compulsive Disorder*. Stick scanned further down: *anxiety; fear; reassurance-seeking behaviour; treatment*. He felt his stomach tighten.

'Dr Roberts said she'd put me on the list for –' she took the papers back and flicked through them – 'cognitive behavioural therapy.' She looked up at Stick. 'I said I'd fix things, didn't I?'

Her eyes were bright, her face excited, like a kid. Stick had a sudden memory of an art class at school: making something out of plaster of Paris – the white liquid cold when he poured it into the mould, then almost too hot to touch as it set. And he remembered throwing whatever it was at a wall – end of term, on the walk back from school. Hurling it hard, and the whole thing smashing against the brick, leaving a white chalky mark, like the scuff from a football.

'I thought maybe I'd give up smoking too,' she said, and then laughed. 'Why not, eh? They've got a special clinic for it, and a support group.'

He wanted her to stop talking.

'She was so nice, Dr Roberts,' his mum went on. 'Really listened. Took the time. I didn't think she'd be like that.' She looked at Stick. 'Aren't you pleased, Kieran?'

'Course I am.' He made himself smile. 'Course I am, Mum.' Babs slunk into the room and Stick bent to scoop her into his arms, felt her warm against his chest, her heart beating and her claws on his forearm. She pushed against him, straining towards the floor, and he let her go.

'And you know I was walking back and thinking that now you're eighteen and there's more council tax and less Housing, I'm going to have to start asking you to contribute. Not straight away, but we're going to need to make plans, love.'

He wanted to be in London – all those people on the streets nicking stuff, running, shouting, doing whatever they wanted. 'Dad called,' he said.

His mum raised her eyebrows.

'Telling me not to get involved in the riots.'

'But you wouldn't.'

Stick thought about the man in the hoody silhouetted against the flames.

His mum fussed with the printouts, arranging them into a neat pile. 'Would you?' she said.

Stick shoved his hands into his pockets. 'Course not.'

His mum picked up her cup of tea but didn't drink. 'I was thinking we could go and see her,' she said.

Stick frowned.

'Sophie. At the weekend maybe? We could take some flowers? For Mac too.' She looked up. 'You're doing so well, Kieran, dealing with Mac. I know how –' she put the cup down – 'difficult that is. I'm proud of you.'

Stick swallowed. He could feel tears lurking behind his eyes. He wanted to grab the pile of paper and chuck it across the room. He wanted to break something.

'I thought I'd take a leaf out of your book.' Her voice wavered a little. 'I thought it would be good to go. Don't you think?'

He wasn't doing well, he wanted to tell her. He didn't even know what doing well meant. 'Yeah,' he said instead. 'Sure. Why not?'

It started in Salford the next afternoon. Stick's phone bleeping with messages. The TV with a new lot of footage to repeat. His mum stood at the back door, silent and pale, smoking one cigarette after another, shaking her head and saying, 'Here? Not here,' and then turning to him and saying, 'You wouldn't, Kieran? You won't, will you?'

By evening, the city centre was kicking off and Stick couldn't stay in the house a minute longer. He kept calling J but no one answered, so he pulled on Mac's trainers and ran to her house. His mum didn't stop him going, just told him to not be an idiot, to keep safe, that she trusted him.

No one answered the door, so he crept round to J's window and tapped on the glass until she drew back the curtain, her finger pressed against her lips.

He wanted to fuck her. He wanted to take her clothes off and fuck her until she came, hard, with that little gasp like she'd been taken by surprise.

She opened the window.

'It's started,' Stick whispered. 'In town.'

'I know. I told Dad I needed to be there for college. Sociology,' she said. 'They'll make us write an essay about it. I told him if I'd been there I'd get a better mark.'

Stick laughed and she gestured for him to be quiet.

'He said he'd kill me with his bare hands if I went anywhere near it. But Mum's away and he has to go to work in, like, half an hour.' She turned to some noise in the house Stick couldn't hear. 'Go.' She waved him away. 'Quick.'

'I'll wait.'

'No. Go. I'll meet you outside Arndale. By the burger van. In, like, an hour. Go on, go!'

# 26

Stick ran into town, Mac's trainers hitting a rhythm on the pavement. Down Oldham Street to Piccadilly Gardens where shop alarms were wailing and the sound of smashing glass and shouting made his heart lift. Mac would have gotten involved in this. Fuck, Mac would have started it. He'd have thrown something through a shop window. He'd have been at the front of the crowd pretending to be Mel Gibson in *Braveheart*, his hands in the air, shouting.

Two boys were trying to lever the shutter away from a shop window. The metal rattled and groaned, but wasn't quite ready to break. Further towards Market Street, a crowd surged around Primark's doors – people running inside and coming out with their arms full, coat hangers clattering to the ground.

There were no buses, no cars, no trams. The traffic noise replaced by shouts, whistles, running feet, breaking glass, burglar alarms. The smell of car fumes and coffee and Greggs' pasties replaced with cigarette smoke and weed, and the sharp, choking stink of burning plastic that reminded him of the toy rabbit they'd burnt down by the canal – Mac smashing its eyes into tiny sharp pieces.

In front of him, two men were aiming kicks at a newsagent's. A third had a fire extinguisher and was hitting it against the window. The glass was strong and bounced the men back at themselves with a dull thud. Then, as Stick got closer, the edge of the extinguisher made an impression, like stamping hard onto thick ice – a puncture, cracks fanning out around it like a spider's web. Stick stared as the man with the extinguisher made another hit, then another, each time grunting like an animal, and the other two, still kicking, aiming now at the cracks, almost but never quite crashing into each other. The men kept on punching and kicking and, just before the window gave way, Stick thought of Mac lying on the ground and that bastard stabbing him, the knife – which they'd never found – coming down again and again and again into Mac's body. *One, two, three, four, five.*

The glass crumbled, leaving a hole big enough to walk through, head high. The three men ducked into the shop and more followed them, coming out with a bottle of wine, a bag of crisps, packs of beer. One man had a tin of shaving foam; he shook it up and started spraying, yelling like crazy, white foam spurting over the pavement, the broken glass, the tram lines. Stick thought of his mum, stood at the back door, smoking, but still he felt a jolt of excitement. He could walk in and take whatever he wanted. How was that even possible?

He wanted Mac there. He wanted J there. The three of them, J in the middle, their arms stretched out like the paper dolls Sophie used to make. Mac would have loved it. He'd have lived off it for years. Do you remember? he'd say. That day? That Tuesday? When everything they said you couldn't do you realised you could?

By the time he stepped through the window into the shop, it was a mess – as though a lunatic had come in, swept everything off the shelves and then jumped up and down on it; opened the fridges and pulled out every can, every bottle, every pint of milk and plastic-wrapped samosa; opened the freezer and thrown all the ice-creams up in the air, high enough so they smashed and split when they hit the floor. He wanted to get something for J but he didn't know what. His feet crunched over the mess as he stalked the aisles. In the corner by the till sat a yellow bucket with a bunch of red roses inside, still perfect. Stick lifted them out and tucked them under his arm.

He reached Primark at the same time as the police, a group of them with dark uniforms, shields like giant contact lenses, helmets with plastic visors. They started hitting at people with batons. One dragged a woman to the ground, her cheek pressed against the pavement, her hands twisted up behind her. They'd do that to J. They'd do that to him. Except there were too many people, and the people turned, started chucking bottles and stones, handbags and shoes and coat hangers at the police. The thump and smash of it against the riot shields, and people still running into the shop, coming out laden with stuff.

Stick stood and watched as the police backed away from the crowd.

'You couldn't even keep a fucking murderer locked up,' he shouted into the noise of the street. 'You couldn't even get your shit together enough to do that. So fuck you.'

It felt good, standing in the centre of Manchester, shouting.

'Fuck you!' Someone took up his words, then someone else, until there was a group of them, chanting at the police: 'Fuck you, fuck you, fuck you,' until Stick felt like his skin had turned into sherbet, fizzing and alive.

Around the corner, Jessops was smashed up, the shutters peeled back and the shelves stripped bare. The ground outside HMV was littered with CDs and broken plastic cases.

Stick walked down Market Street, past the elevators up to the Arndale Food Hall. Past the crowd of people by the locked shopping centre doors. Down to Topman, where a handful of police officers in riot gear stood, the visors raised on their helmets like they were taking a break from welding. He could feel them watching him. *Fuck you*, he said in his head. *Fuck you*. He hugged the roses against his chest, turned and walked back the way he'd come.

And there, stepping out from under the trashed security shutter of Schuh, was Owen Lee.

It couldn't be. But it was. Owen Lee. Jeans. White trainers. A blue top with the hood pulled up. Two shoeboxes wedged under his arm. The face from the newspaper. The face from the screen. He was taller than Stick had thought – his shoulders broad and meaty.

Stick opened his mouth, then closed it again. He thought about the knife in the car's glove compartment, its blade sharp enough to break skin. From their right came the sound of breaking glass; the angry wail of a shop alarm like a child screaming; someone whistling, sharp and clear.

Owen Lee was looking left to right like he was about to cross a busy road. His gaze skimmed over Stick as if he was no one in particular. He started walking, and Stick followed him, curving his left hand around the heavy, polished bloodstone in his pocket.

He tried to believe Mac was there too, close by his side, saying, *Go on, do it. Give the bastard a taste of his own medicine.*

He felt completely calm. Manchester raged around him, but none of it seemed important any more – the shouting, the smashing, the catcalls and the laughter. It was as though he'd put ear defenders on: the world muffled and his own heartbeat sounding in his ears. It was just him and Owen Lee.

Owen Lee. Who stopped by the doors to the Arndale

Centre, lifted the broken glass like a curtain, and slipped inside.

Stick went after him into the quiet, white space. All the shutters were down. All the lights were off. It was empty, save for them. Stick dropped the roses onto the nearest bench. He would say something first, he thought, Mac's trainers squeaking against the floor tiles as he walked. *This is for Mac. You can't get away with doing that to my best mate – to me.*

There was a flurry of noise ahead and a crowd of men came around the corner, running.

'Pigs,' one of them shouted.

Owen Lee turned and ran towards Stick. 'Get out,' he yelled, as he approached. 'Feds.'

Stick stayed quite still. When Owen Lee dodged to one side to avoid him, Stick also dodged and the two of them collided.

'Get out the fucking way,' Owen Lee hissed.

Stick was close enough to see tiny beads of sweat on his top lip, close enough to smell him. He took the bloodstone out of his pocket. *It gives courage to overcome obstacles and wisdom to decide how to do so.*

Owen Lee shoved him in the chest – the edges of the shoeboxes hard against Stick's bruises – but Stick got hold of his sleeve and didn't let go.

'What the fuck is wrong with you?' Owen Lee shouted. He sounded frightened.

Stick realised he could do anything. Owen Lee was taller and broader but Stick was stronger. He could lift him up above his head and throw him as far as he chose. He could headbutt him until his skull cracked. He could smash the bloodstone into his face until it wasn't a face any more.

The other men swerved either side of them, like a river splitting around a rock. They were facing the doors now,

Owen Lee struggling to get away. Stick looked past him and saw a flicker of orange flame reflected in the shattered glass. He took a breath and thought of the anger-management woman, sitting at the front of the classroom, a lifetime ago – you can make a choice – and then he looked at Owen Lee, wriggling like a caught fish, dragging Stick towards Market Street. J would be there by now, looking for him. And Mac was dead – nothing was going to change that.

He let go.

Owen Lee catapulted forwards and ran to join the scrum at the doors. Mac would be dancing through the streets if he was here – his arms above his head, fists punching the air, whooping and yelling. He'd nick bags of sweets and cans of beer and then give them away. He'd help out people who'd fallen over, or cut themselves on broken glass. He'd be having a ball. Stick felt his friend's absence like he'd been punched just below the ribcage.

The police were coming. Stick heard the tramp of their boots and as he turned to look it struck him that they must be hot – maybe even scared – underneath all that protective gear. He grabbed the roses off the bench and slipped out onto the street before they reached him.

Miss Selfridge was on fire. Flames surged out of the shop window, their edges gushing black smoke up over the bricks into the cool early-evening sky. Groups of people stood and watched, the blaze repeated over and over again on tiny phone screens held up to catch the action. And there, in amongst the crowd, was J, standing by the burger van like she'd said, strands of blue hair escaping from the edges of her hood.

He watched her watching the shop burn. *You're beautiful*, he wanted to tell her. *I want to fuck you. I want to run away with you. I want to marry you.* She'd laugh and punch him on the arm, and say *give over, get out of here.* Or maybe she'd say *yes, me too.*

J looked up, as though she could feel his eyes on her. She saw him and grinned, waved. When he reached her, he slipped an arm around her waist and she turned towards him, lifted her face and kissed him hard, the roses squashed between them, her skin hot from the fire.

# Acknowledgements

For me, research is a process of conversation and observation, all of which gets filtered through multiple drafts until it becomes something perhaps unrecognisable but still rooted in a word, a gesture, a story told. Many people shared their expertise, experiences and opinions with me throughout the writing of *Before the Fire* and I am grateful to them all: Martin Bottomley, Tony Heslop, Karen Ryan, Jean Betteridge, Thomas Nicholson, Paul Hunt, Sam Baars, Jill Johnson, Eilish Blunn-Galagher, Cath Potter, Razia Shah, Katie Parr and students at St Augustine's: Moyzz, Kevin, Maria, Malika, Naomi, Mariam, Jasmine, Joel, Bradley, Fatimata, Samira and Tayyibah; Moona Khan, Sarah Whittington and students at Manchester Communication Academy: Riler, Kyle, Remy, Mo, Tyler, Thabi, Luke, Mohammed, Habib and Keifer; Rose McCarton and the over-fifties group at the TLM Centre.

Writing *Before the Fire* also coincided with a writing residency hosted by Age Concern Lancashire and CSV Learning North West, working with young people and people living with dementia. I'm especially grateful to Mechila, Daniel, Shakira, Liam, Aidan, Shelia and Rob Warbrick for their time, energy, honesty and patience.

The characters described in the novel are entirely fictional, but conversations with all of the above were invaluable in helping me imagine them and their world.

In 2012, I wrote my MSc Urban Studies dissertation on narratives of the riots of 2011, an experience which again permeated the writing of *Before the Fire*. Thank you to Jane Rendell, Steve Pile, David Roberts, Rebecca Lenkiewicz, Sophie Woolley and Luke Wright for their questions, answers, suggestions and support.

Thank you to Château de Lavigny and the Ledig-Rowohlt Foundation for a blissful month of writing in summer 2014, and to Sharon Morris for sharing her Pembrokeshire cottage and creating an equally productive retreat.

I have a fantastic group of fellow writers whose feedback and support is massively appreciated. Particular thanks to Emma Claire Sweeney, Emily Midorikawa, Paul McVeigh, Yemisi Blake, Sarah-Clare Conlon, Sian Cummins, David Gaffney, Benjamin Judge and Adrian Slatcher.

I also have a brilliant pair of readers in Andrew Kidd and Francesca Main. Particular thanks to Francesca for being the most incisive, dedicated, generous editor a writer could hope to have.

And thank you, as ever, to my family for always being there and always believing, and to Matt, for everything – this one's for you.